WHAT OUR EYES
HAVE WITNESSED

Text copyright © 2011 Daniel Fusch
Stant Litore is a pen name for Daniel Fusch.
Frontispiece by Danielle Tunstall.
Model: Martyn Dalzell
All rights reserved.
Printed in the United States of America.

Published by 47North
P.O. Box 400818
Las Vegas, NV 89140

ISBN-13: 9781612183930
ISBN-10: 161218393X

WHAT OUR EYES HAVE WITNESSED

BASED LOOSELY ON THE EVENTS OF
THE MARTYRIUM POLYCARPI
SECOND CENTURY AD

THE ZOMBIE BIBLE

BY

STANT LITORE

47N⬤RTH

To my wife, Jessica, for her love and her laughter
and
To my daughters, River and Inara—
may we strive to our last breath
to leave you a better world

Polycarp's gaze

CONTENTS

HISTORIAN'S NOTE

W H A T Y O U *are reading is one installment of* The Zombie Bible, *a series of narratives based on certain well-known records of humanity's enduring struggle with the undead. The original records are a mixture of poetic texts, lyrics to ancient songs set to drum and lyre, works of prophecy, legal testimonies, and chronicles both historical and hagiographical. Originally inscribed in Hebrew, Greek, Aramaic, and Latin on substances as varied as papyrus scrolls, chiseled rock, animal skins, and thin parchment, these records speak eloquently to us of one of history's few constants:*

Hunger.

The persistence of hunger as a defining factor in the human condition has never been more clear to us than today, as we face the resurgence of the old pestilence in several parts of our globe. In those regions of the world already broken by earthquakes and famine, where men and women no less noble or intelligent than you and I (though considerably more impoverished) each day face the menacing threat of the walking dead, the greater horror is the brutal reality that the dead represent: the reality that people devour people, and that when our dead rise, they look like us.

If we can learn anything from retelling the stories of our spiritual ancestors—whether Polycarp the martyr, David the lover, Devora the prophetess, Samson the warrior, Simon the fisherman, or any of a hundred others—we can perhaps learn again how to face a rapidly decomposing world with a wild and conquering hope, an impossible hope.

I do not know if hope can be stronger than hunger. But I know that they believed it so.

Few episodes in European history have left such a lingering impact on Western consciousness as the outbreak of the living dead in ancient Rome and the subsequent persecutions of the early Church and its sister sects. It's important to know that these outbreaks didn't occur until late in Rome's history. While it lasted, the Roman Republic had seen only a few isolated encounters with the undead— the loss of an embassy in Pontus, the discovery of an infected island in the Middle Sea during Pompey's campaign against the corsairs, and that terrible winter that left one of Julius Caesar's forts in Gaul surrounded by a forest filled with moaning and ravenous dead.

It wasn't until the time of the Emperors that an outbreak occurred within the Eternal City itself. At first, a few reports of cannibalism in the riverside ghetto known as the Subura were largely ignored or dismissed as the primitivism of the immigrants who in that century were already flooding into Rome in great numbers from the East. But in Rome under Nero, conditions in the swollen belly of the Subura became so crowded and so unpoliced that the pestilence grew to an epidemic that threatened to consume Rome itself. Nero in his madness and panic torched the city, then blamed both the plague and the fire on an obscure Eastern cult that had taken hold in the Subura. The cult, who called themselves Brothers and Sisters of the Fish, had seen enormous gains in membership during the year of the plague, as their apostles offered both a promised cure for the walking death and a vision of a more egalitarian city in which no crowded and hungering Subura would exist.

The fire ended the outbreak, but Nero's persecutions afterward did more to secure him a place in history than either the dead or their elimination. Tacitus's Histories record the lurid details of what occurred in a tone so objective and documentary that its power to shock the reader is magnified. Pointing to the cultists' communion rite, which on the surface appeared to resemble acts of cannibalism, and to their talk of the "Gift" of a cure that involved touching and absolving the restless dead, Nero apparently adopted an extreme "punishment shall fit the crime" approach to extinguishing their gathering. The few walking corpses that had been rounded up and chained were loosed in Roman arenas on hundreds of captive Christians, and Roman crowds cheered to see those who had (presumably) brought the plague to Rome devoured by it.

Mindful of how fire had cleansed the city, Nero made living torches of the cult's leaders, both men and women, burning them on trees in the Emperor's gardens. Senators and patricians of Rome walked through the gardens while the captives burned around them; they talked of the latest scandals, or affairs of state, or how to replace members of the Senate and the People that had perished in the epidemic. They did not glance for more than a moment at the human torches that lit the garden paths, nor listen too closely to the muffled screams from their gagged mouths. In this way, Rome balanced its accounts and banished from its streets both the memory of the plague and (they believed) the presence of those they blamed for it.

Modern readers are often astounded by the crumbling of Rome; everything we know about the Roman military (its discipline, its encouragement of innovation and creative problem-solving, and its adherence to a rigid code of duty and patriotism) appears well suited to the task of quarantining and eliminating an epidemic of the undead. Yet everything about Roman culture and religion conspired to leave the Roman civilization helpless against the actual occurrence of that plague within their own city. Three cultural norms made this the case: sanitation, caste, and ancestor worship.

First, the Romans placed an unprecedented importance on sanitation; as the river was badly polluted, nine vast aqueducts carried clean water to the hillside homes of the wealthy and to public fountains throughout the city. Additionally, the more affluent classes spent several hours a day bathing and oiling their bodies. The Romans invented the world's most advanced sewage system up until that time. The wealthy housed their dead in marble mausoleums, houses of dignity and silence; the poor housed theirs in catacombs beneath the city—in both cases, out of sight. This concern with cleanliness translated too easily into an aversion to contact with the lower classes.

That brings us to caste. In the days of the Republic, an enterprising man could raise caste on the basis of merit and money. By the time of the Emperors, the caste system had become much more rigid. The ghetto dwellers in the Subura, in particular, were ignored unless they began to riot during a grain shortage—a circumstance that Rome's upper castes feared more than any other horror. Pestilence along the riverside tenements and insulae—unless it spread to the wealthy villas on the Palatine Hill—represented only the loss of so many hungry mouths. This meant both that the majority of residents in the Eternal City lived out their lives in almost unspeakable poverty and hopelessness, and that the Roman government paid little if any attention to outbreaks. The Roman military, barred by law and ancient custom from crossing within the boundaries of the city, had its eyes on the distant borders, not on the slums at home.

Third, ancestor worship. The Romans looked to their entombed fathers for religious guidance and for intercession with the gods. When high-caste Romans found their fathers, brothers, wives, husbands, and slaves rising from their deathbeds and hungering after their flesh, this crisis was a negation of everything they lived by, everything they'd known to be true. The realization that their honored dead could not be called upon to aid them in their crisis—that the dead were the crisis—shattered them.

When the dead walked the streets, Romans shut their doors—but the type of refuge one took depended on caste. The patricians on the Palatine Hill lived in vast, one-story villas with no outward-facing windows; all windows looked inward, on a shrine about the hearth and on a garden atrium spacious enough to walk about and take pleasure in. Before the rising of the dead, this lack of outer windows served to prevent the inconvenience of looking at one's neighbor; a high-caste villa (inhabited by a single family) was its own unit, inviolable and inviting no interference in its own governance.

The multistoried and crowded apartment complex one encountered in the slums, known as the insula, was a very different type of shelter. While there were no outward windows on the first story (originally a precaution against thieves), the upper stories had windows looking both inward on the narrow atrium and outward on the streets and the other buildings that loomed near. In the insula, it was impossible to ignore one's neighbors. You could hear them through the wall. You could smell them. You could hear the splash as the next-door tenant tossed his offal into the street. If you stepped to your window, you could see the daily traffic of the Subura, and once the plague began, you could see the dead hunting.

This fierce proximity likely contributed to the persistence of the forbidden religion, despite the persecutions of Nero. The early Christians insisted that all human beings smelled the same, hungered the same, suffered the same; their message of the essential value of every Brother and Sister of the Fish, regardless of caste or sex, was one that resonated with the riverside tenants and eventually even with some youths in the high-caste residences on the hills. The stories they told also offered a fresh way to understand the loathsome rising of the dead, in their emphasis on a break from a tragic past (whether a communal past or an individual one), absolution rather than personal responsibility for atonement, and the promise of an eventual restoration and recovery of everything that had been or would be lost.

It is perhaps one of history's great ironies that the Church of later centuries fell so often into the same cultural dead ends that the early apostles abhorred, permitting reverence for the dead to take precedence over compassion for the living. My own hope is that this narrative, an account of the acts of Polycarp, might hold for us an admonition and pause for thought, even here in the towns and cities of our own time.

Our story opens several generations after the reign of Nero. Though barely recognized as such on the Palatine Hill, Rome's second outbreak was already well underway.

THE DAY BEFORE THE IDES OF AUGUSTUS

CAIUS CROUCHED and lifted a bit of the creature's gown between his thumb and fingertip, then used the fabric to wipe away the gray, viscous matter from his dagger. The corpse was *distorted*, a nightmare version of a woman. Perhaps a woman as demons of the underworld might imagine her, if they had never seen one. Its face drained of all pigment except where it had been gnawed and chewed, between the woman's lip and her right ear; half her upper lip had been bitten away, exposing the long roots of her teeth. A mangled cavity where the woman's nose had been, and pale eyes that were like the eyes of dead fish. A few moments before this thing had torn through the door of Caius's official station, hands lifted to grasp at him, its mouth emitting a low cry of hunger that Caius could still hear, loud in his ears, even now that this thing lay still on the floor.

For a while Caius stayed crouching, his heart racing, waiting for that cry to fade from his mind. He found it difficult to breathe; the walls of his little office were very close. Struggling for calm, he took note of details about the corpse. One arm was broken and twisted at a terrible angle. Much of its left leg was chewed, and across its lower belly, the white garment it still wore was torn. The flesh beneath it was ripped open too. When this thing had been a woman, when she'd died, something had been *eating* her. Numb, he drew his eyes from the thing's wounds, scanned the rest of its body. Hair done up in what must have been an elegant coiffure. Blood matted in it now. Traces of cream on the thing's one remaining cheek, some expensive cosmetic. The smaller two fingers on its right hand were missing. On its left, a silver ring graced the third finger. That held his attention a moment; he swallowed. The ring was familiar, and though he tried, he couldn't recall where he'd seen it before.

He drew a slow breath, pressed the back of his hand to his lips, tried to recover. One thing was clear. The corpse that'd smashed into his office wore a white gown of the finest fabric, though much of it was now in tatters. A patrician's gown. When this creature had been a woman, screaming as other lurching dead fed on her, she'd been a *patrician* woman, a daughter of Rome's highest families.

"Where did you come from?" Caius whispered. Sweat on his palms.

"I'll try to find out, dominus," a thin voice said behind him.

With care, Caius set aside on the floor the knife he'd driven into the thing's head. Gradually, the world around him began to exist: the guttering of the oil lamp, the breeze through the broken door lifting tiny bumps on his skin; the warmth of his dagger's hilt in his hand, slick with his sweat; the sweet, nauseous reek of decay; the too-fast breathing of his aide who stood behind him. Uneasy, he lifted his eyes toward the shattered cypress wood of the door, catching a glimpse through the broken wood of the sunlit public square beyond and his lictors moving to guard the exits into the nearby streets. His lictors were not really guards—just a ceremonial entourage accorded to the city's highest-ranking official. No doubt taking up station around the square made them feel useful. The actual guardsmen stood somewhere outside near the prisoners' sheds; he'd hired those with coin.

There was no one else in the square; at the cry of the dead, Romans did not come to look—they shut their doors.

The corpse beside him had filled the office with its stench. "Burn it," Caius growled without looking from the door. "And bring me the old man."

He heard his aide retreat farther into the building. With an almost silent groan, Caius got to his feet, retreated behind his desk, and stood there, splaying his hands on the wooden surface and leaning forward. The grain of the desk was fine cedar from Gaul. The luxury of it brought him little comfort. Nothing he owned brought comfort or solace anymore. This desk, the military medals on the wall behind him, the sword that rusted in its sheath in his study at home—they were only tokens of failure. He had stopped looking at them.

Caius measured his days now solely by the slow walk from his high villa down to the baths, a few streets below on the slope. There he sat in long silences while dutiful slaves scrubbed his back and other men, young and old, chattered at the other end of the shallow pool about politics or scandals or heroic ambitions, or other things that were dry and constant as dust. They had learned not to interrupt his silences. Caius would let the water lap at his thighs and breathe in the steam, then stand while the slaves clothed him in a toga immaculate and perfect in its summons to duty. After that, the walk back up the hill to the temple of revered Justitia, defender of the wronged—a walled, marble complex of vast size on the opposite slope of the Palatine from his villa, with his small official station an annex just outside the wall, like a barnacle on a ship's hull, and beside it a row of wooden sheds for the temporary holding of the accused. He walked with firm, quick steps and without any slouch to his shoulders, though his insides were hollow and empty. The small clump of official lictors carrying their bound rods of office trailed behind him, signaling to any who looked up as they passed that here walked one of the senior magistrates of Rome, in whom was invested the hopes and the keeping of the Eternal City.

The walk always ended here, at his office.

Caius didn't watch the two slaves who entered the room from the inner door, though he listened to the slide of the corpse across the floor. "Scrub that floor," he called without glancing up, and heard them stop by the door. "I want no trace of that thing left, not a drop of blood, not a flake of skin, not a strand of hair. You hear?"

"Yes, dominus," one of them murmured, and when Caius remained silent, the slide of the body resumed. Caius heard the crack of the door being kicked the rest of the way open, a wooden rain of splinters. That walking, hungering corpse had made kindling of his door. Always before, when someone had come to that door, they had come not as a visitor nor a passerby nor a client but as the accused, as shattered Romans driven by hunger to sometimes extravagant crimes. Often men had been forced through that door, trembling. Caius had seen their heads jerk when they heard it click shut behind them.

Until today. This ravenous corpse had burst through like an accusation itself. And what strength these dead had, to break a door! The dead could use *all* their strength, uncaring; they would break themselves in breaking through a door to get at the living, in the desperation of their hunger. This one had broken its arm doing it.

The accursed thing had worn a patrician's gown and a ring of considerable price. This hadn't been some wretch come crawling uphill from that rats' nest of the Subura—that throng of riverside tenements and crowded insulae that smothered the banks of the Tiber. That river ran brown, having taken within itself all the sewage and offal of the Eternal City. The midstreet ditches carried refuse downhill from the quiet villas and gardens of Rome's upper castes, and in the entrails of the Subura, men and women who lived like animals chucked their own vomit and dung in after it. Caius's lips thinned. All filth, both Rome's offal and Rome's human dregs, drained down into the Subura—where, a year ago, those dregs had overwhelmed and drowned his son. His only son. Now all that filth was backing up; the diseased dead were stumbling up the long slopes. A few packs of dead stalked even the Palatine Hill, and Caius's hired guardsmen were kept busy thinning their numbers. Men said in the streets that the statue of Roma in the Forum Romani had been heard crying out Rome's secret name in the dark watch before dawn—the name that once uttered must bring about Rome's fall.

But that loathsome corpse that had shattered his door—that was no thief or whore from the Subura. It was not even a merchant's wife who had lurched free of her tomb after being bitten by a thief. This was one from the *old* families. What, by the *gods,* was it doing here? He leaned harder on his hands, sucking in breath and trying to think past the roil of emotion in his chest. The walls *were* very close. One fact was a cold, clear light in his mind: he had the old man, the Greek, who led those who disturbed the dead. He glanced up, noted the trail of slime left behind by the slide of that corpse. As with the dead, so with the rotten among the living: cut into the head and the body dies.

"Dominus." It was his aide, speaking from the inner door. Caius raised his head and looked past his aide to see the old man standing in the doorway. A man preternaturally tall, his head bald and his wrists manacled before him.

"Polycarp," Caius said curtly, an identification not a greeting. He gestured to the space of floor in front of the desk. A smear of viscous fluid led from that space to the hole that had been the outer door. The aide remained by the inner door, and the old man came forward and stood before the desk. His eyes were calm, though they held weariness like the stress of an old house in a high wind. He stood straight, exuding confidence, though the creases about his eyes told of physical pain—possibly his joints, judging from how gingerly he held his manacled hands and how slowly he had moved. It was not the slowness of reluctance but the slowness of one in pain who takes great care with where he places his body, which muscles he chooses to move and when.

"Good day." The old man's voice rasped a little with age, but there was strength in it.

"You know who I am?" Caius fixed his eyes on the man.

Polycarp looked back without blinking. Or answering.

"I am Caius Lucius Justus, the praetor urbanus. You are arraigned for sedition and treason, Polycarp. My guardsmen took hold of you because they were informed that you lead the new atheists."

"We are not godless," Polycarp murmured. "We simply devote ourselves to a different God."

Caius waited a moment, getting his emotions under control. "I will not insult you by asking you to explain that *we*." His voice had grown icy. "I know you have followers throughout Rome, probably many. Nevertheless, I have you, and others from your insula. It is enough. I mean to put a swift end to this infection in the belly of our City."

Polycarp glanced over his shoulder at the brown smear across the marble tiles. "It seems you have other infections to worry about," he offered dryly.

Caius flexed one hand, feeling the grain of the wood beneath his palm, resisting the urge to beat the desktop with his hand, driving his anger into the wood. Then he stiffened. Out of nowhere, the thought hit him of where he had seen that ring before. That little silver ring on the dead hand. It was a betrothal ring, bearing no device or gem—an ostentation of the Aemilii, who considered themselves too famed to need any device and thought their family name an adornment richer than any other they might offer. That dead, half-eaten girl had been Flavius's daughter, who would have wed Drusus Aemilius in another year. Caius couldn't recall whether he'd ever met her, but he knew her father, and he knew that ring. His hand shook slightly. Flavius's daughter. Gods. Not just any patrician girl. The daughter of a senator, and not a quiet backbencher at that—one of the first men in the city.

"This thing is devouring Rome," he muttered. Across from him, Polycarp was watching him as though to peer into his heart. Something in Caius's chest constricted and hardened into a tight, enraged knot. "This is your doing." He gave Polycarp a cold, assessing look. "Even youths on the Hill neglect the rites and the obligations to our honored fathers. Because of your teachings, too many youths no longer bring offerings of fruit or bread or wine to the shrines of our fathers, who hunger now and cannot rest. And whom they devour—" He blanched. "Those cannot rest either," he muttered after a moment.

A crawl of silence. That terrible stain on the floor.

Once, the festivals for the honored fathers had been lush, extravagant affairs—*magnificent* affairs. Now each season, fewer attended, fewer brought gifts to feed the ancestors and quench their thirst. Polycarp's superstition was taking too great a hold on the city. Caius shuddered at the thought of so many hungry, neglected dead. Now they were rising and feeding on the living—on the very people who left them ravenous.

Polycarp was watching him with an intensity in his gaze that Caius found unsettling. He struggled to hold his temper, distracted himself by shuffling through the sheaf of parchment on his desk—notes from his informants and reports from various minor officials on this movement that had taken hold in so many border towns and now in Rome itself. "Polycarp the Greek," he said, his tone clipped. "You were in Smyrna for a while among the Christians there. Then you came here, to Rome, where in the past we have put your leaders to death. Why?"

"I am most needed here."

"I might not agree with that," Caius muttered. "But certainly the filth of the Subura has proven fertile ground for you."

"Yes," Polycarp said softly. "I know you think that. Probably you imagine me to be some parasite fastened to Rome's belly. But you've found the gathering here on the hill, and it frightens you. My calling has been to feed all of Rome, Caius, not only the Subura."

Caius sucked in a breath, his hand pausing over the papers. "What do you mean by that?" His hand trembled slightly, almost too slightly to be seen; yet Polycarp's gaze flicked to his hand and then back to the praetor's face.

"We share bread," Polycarp said. "An act of remembrance and purpose in this city where both the living and the dead hunger. We have shared bread with slaves and with their masters in the Subura. We have shared it with merchants of the lower slopes. And we have shared bread with sons of the Palatine Hill."

Caius's eyes burned with the thought of his own son. His hand kept shaking.

"You intend to put me to death," Polycarp continued. "This seems certain to me. But it will do you no good, Caius, and even if you succeeded in suppressing the teaching and the sharing of bread, it would only do Rome harm. But you will not succeed, for it will not end with me. You have the wrong man." Polycarp smiled wearily.

The praetor bristled at the man's bravado, his arrogance, but kept his emotions under tight control. "Who is the man I need to execute, then?"

"He is not here. Though he is, I trust, in all places."

"Speak plainly, you abominable Greek," Caius snarled.

Polycarp gazed at him a moment and his smile faded. There were lines about his eyes, but they were lines of fatigue, not fear. "Your mind is very Roman, Caius, and very literal," he said after a moment. "Perhaps you think the only way to deal with the dead or the living is with a sword cut, as though all ailments are of the body only. But however many heads you cut, the dead keep rising—because you have not understood why they hunger, why they find it necessary to rise and eat. You make the same mistake with the living who are discontented in this city. There are other ways, Caius, to give the living and the dead rest—"

"So I've heard," Caius cut in. "You *touch* the dead." He glanced at the grain of the wood beneath his hands, struggled for calm, composure, *dignitas*. "Some magic from the East, the informant tells me. The most debased kind of superstition."

"I might call *yours* debased, praetor urbanus. You try to feed the dead with wine and bread and fruit, carrying bowls of it to your mausoleum, while your brothers and sisters in the Subura live famished and ravenous lives without bread or wine or fruit or hope. In your literal-mindedness, you give the dead the food they don't need and keep the living starving for the food they do need. You are the highest officer of Roman justice. I ask you, Caius Lucius Justus: what justice is this?"

"Your words twist everything," Caius said. "But I know everything you have done in Rome, Polycarp. I have questioned Julia and others my guardsmen took from your insula. I know about your sharing of bread. I know about the rites where your followers pass around a cup of warm blood and a handful of flesh. I know how you meet in the tombs and Catacombs, disturbing the dead in your obscene belief that you can satisfy the wrath of our ancestors with no more than a wish and a hope and a mumbling of platitudes brought here out of the East." He took a shuddering breath. "And you have the gall to tell me you are not troubling our dead, that you are not spreading this desecration in Rome."

"I am not spreading this desecration in Rome," Polycarp said softly.

"Don't mock me."

"What do you wish me to say?" Now there was an edge of anger in the old man's voice, and his eyes burned. "The dead hunger and walk. You need someone to blame, and it's clear you've brought me here to make an example of me. Yet I am a Roman citizen—"

"Then you will be tried as one!" Caius roared, his face livid. "Tomorrow! I have witnesses against you, Polycarp. We will satisfy Justitia, whose temple this station serves, and then you will burn!"

"Why even a trial?" Polycarp asked. "I am condemned already; your words confirm it. Why not burn me today?"

"Don't tempt me."

That smile, that self-affirmed smile, returned to Polycarp's lips. That smile that said, You do not shake me. I know who I am, and you cannot bend me.

"You wish to silence me," Polycarp said, "so you will give me a jury of ears to hear me."

Caius leaned forward, enunciating each word. "Some on that jury will have lost someone to the dead. They are furious. They want someone to suffer for what has been done in Rome. So do I. You will burn, Polycarp. I promise you that."

Polycarp's eyes darkened. After a moment he said, "The shed I'm kept in is dark and quiet, and a good place for prayer. I am growing fond of it. May I go?"

His voice was so calm and clear. He did not sound as though he were asking for permission. He sounded more like he was *dismissing* the praetor.

Caius bit back the words he wished to speak, words that would diminish him and the dignity of his office. After a moment he gestured for his aide, who quickly took hold of Polycarp and led him out of the room, taking him down the hall toward the other door that led out to the sheds. Polycarp left without a glance over his shoulder at the praetor. Alone again, Caius drew in a deep breath, then slammed his hand on the desk.

That detestable Greek and his followers—the dregs of Rome—had taken Caius's son from him. Had destroyed him. Had destroyed his house. Caius heard the sound of a door opening and shutting elsewhere in the building: Polycarp being put away. *Burn* him.

His gaze lifted to the shattered door; his slaves were there, waiting permission to enter. One held a cloth, the other a pail of water. Caius's gaze settled on the brown smear across his floor, and he ignored the slaves.

Flavius's *daughter*. Gods.

He was alone here, alone with those medals on the wall, mute reminders that whatever his fortune in past battles on far borders, he had lacked the strength to protect or preserve his own. Even here within the walls of his own city. In his way he had failed Rome as surely as the old Greek had; the heat in his breast flickered out as quickly as it had come, leaving only cold hollowness in its place. It was often so. He would stand in his toga behind his cedar desk and prepare judgments, yet inside that toga and inside his skin, he was only the husk of a man. He was alone. No living members of his family. If not for dignity and duty, he would have thrown himself on his sword months past.

It was a powerful thing, that Roman dignity. It must be observed not only in word and deed but in the posture of his body, in the stillness of his hands when he spoke, in the fashion of the draping of his toga after the baths, in his gait, in the austerity of his face.

His forehead ached; he opened his eyes, realized he was leaning over his desk like a woman grieving. Angrily he lifted his head, stood like a man. He stood there, breathing, just breathing.

A tap at the door, and his aide's voice. "She came right from her villa, dominus."

"What?"

"The dead girl. She must have come from her own home. The guardsmen saw her stumbling down the street from the uphill villas."

Caius turned on the aide. "Why didn't they bloody stop her, then?" He gestured furiously at the splintered door, then strode to it, his aide following. He shoved the broken door out of his way and stepped into the sun.

The sky was blinding after the close dimness of the station office; he stood and let his eyes adjust. A guardsman, armed with a stout pole, leaned against one of the sheds along the wall of the temple compound, ten strides away—the sheds where the prisoners were kept. The man looked pale. Caius gave him a cold look. Why hadn't his guardsmen stopped the corpse of the patrician girl? The sight of her stumbling toward them, reeking like a thing on the wrong side of the grave and hissing at them, had terrified them. That was why. Nearer at hand, Caius's entourage of lictors waited faithfully, togate men carrying bundles of rods bound with cords, emblems that he whom they walked behind carried power to discipline and correct the Roman people.

Caius glanced down at the grit and dust of the station's doorstep. Perhaps there had been footprints there, mute records of the coming of the dead; now there was only a long, smudged swath through the dust where the body had been dragged back out. He grimaced and squinted uphill against the sun. Flavius's villa was ten streets above them on an offshoot of the Via Sacra and was significantly larger than any villa around it; it was right near the hilltop, below the Palatine House where the Emperor would reside during the colder months. The Flavii were an old and wealthy family, much older than the Emperor's.

Everything was still on the hilltop. In the afternoon heat, none of the living were stirring; no slaves were in the streets and would not be, perhaps, for another hour. Caius imagined the dead girl lurching along in the street, making her way on shuffling feet to his door, her arms lifted in accusation. She had come to *his* door. The door of the man who bore responsibility for the city and for the safety and public dignity of the city's patrician class. He cursed softly and shaded his eyes.

"Are you going to ask the Senate to convene?" his aide asked.

"Why?" Caius murmured. "So they can sit around and argue while this gets worse? The Senate can go to oblivion before I let them waste my time." He looked out over the city, listening. There—he could hear it now. Moaning, carried to him on the wind: the cries of the dead. Somewhere in the city. He glanced uphill toward the villas of Rome's high families and clasped his hands behind him to keep them from shaking. That had been *Flavius's* daughter. The dead were not just a few lurching shapes in the lower gardens of the Palatine; they were bursting into villas now, or perhaps seizing and ingesting good citizens from the street. He didn't know. But they were here. They were breaking through his door. And he was left alone to deal with them; the Imperial Family, and the Praetorian Guard with them, had left the city at the start of the summer. No doubt they were in one of their expensive country villas, where opulent pleasure gardens to arouse the envy even of the princes of Susa were enclosed within walls within walls within walls. The Imperial Family had walled out the dead and all the living who were of lower classes than themselves—indeed, all of the City of Rome. That left Caius and any guardsmen he could hire out of the shrinking public funds to keep order in the city. He could write to the Emperor, of course, but the wine-sotted fool would only accuse him of exaggeration.

Caius's face darkened. He should have had that cesspool, the Subura, burned to the ground last winter, when the pestilence first began to cause real trouble. But he had not understood the extent of the threat. How could he? Rome Mighty and Eternal had survived everything: riots, grain shortages, screaming Celts leaping over the walls, axes in hand. No doubt it could survive this too. Anyway, the use of fire to stop pestilence was no small thing. In a city as crowded as Rome, fires could be ill afforded because it might prove impossible to put them out.

Coldly he took stock. He had guardsmen. He had Polycarp in custody. And a few others of his kind, minnows he'd netted with the whales. The wench he'd interviewed earlier that day, the former slave, Dora Syriacae, with the proud look in her eyes and her bearing; his heart troubled him at the memory of her words. And the youth, that *boy*, a patrician boy, one of the Caelii, hardly older than his son had been. *Another* patrician sneaking into the Subura to worship with the desecrators. But tomorrow, a trial, and Rome would be cleansed by fire of that foreign vine in their city whose growth so entangled their youth and starved their dead fathers.

"One hundred eighteen," he murmured.

"Dominus?" His aide sounded uncertain. Well, this day would rattle anyone.

"One hundred eighteen," he repeated. "Guardsmen."

"One hundred twelve, dominus."

"One hundred twelve," he repeated.

"Yes, dominus. A century and twelve. Six didn't return from the Subura last night, when they took Polycarp."

"Why wasn't I told?"

His aide paled. "I only received the report an hour ago, dominus. They ran into some dead in the alleys, and I take it the encounter was harrowing. The captain got himself drunk and didn't come in this morning."

"I'm not paying him to drink," Caius muttered. He should see the man, reprimand him, but he hadn't the energy. "Dismiss him. Find his lieutenant and have every man posted on this hill. They are to patrol these streets."

"*These* streets, dominus? The streets of the upper Palatine?"

"That's what I said. I don't want any more shattered doors." He glanced at his own door, what was left of it. "Have that one replaced. Reinforce it with iron. No, have Decius do it. You get to the villa of the Flavii. Find out if they know what has happened and if all is well there. Then find me and report."

"Yes, dominus."

"Dismissed."

His aide hurried up the street, and Caius stood in the sun, resisting an urge to rub at his temples. No use calling the Senate together. The only real power in Rome now was his—the keys to what remained of the state treasury, the authority to hire armed men, to convene treason courts, and to order executions. As for the Emperor…Caius grimaced and counted the days. Tomorrow was the Ides. On the Kalends, fifteen days ahead, the Emperor would be starting back to Rome. He would have to write to warn him against returning before the pestilence was better contained.

Pestilence.

He suppressed a snarl. This was not malaria or blue fever. This was unquiet among the dead, an omen of Rome's fall, a rebuke to Rome's living for neglecting their ancestors. He stared at that splintered door and whispered a prayer to Janus, the two-headed keeper of doors both visible and invisible. Caius's hands shook even as he clasped them more tightly. With a shudder, Caius thought of the cracking of Rome's invisible doors: the doors between the patrician hills and the plebeian sewage of the Subura; the doors between life and death; the doors between the open Forum of the present and the cluttered, private chambers of the past. Could nothing be held closed? Would there be no order and health in Rome's house?

One locked door, in particular, stood in his mind, with fresh horror after his day's encounter with the gowned dead. His son's door. He wanted to see his son. Nodding curtly to his lictors, he began to take measured steps out into the street, walking with anxiety and dread back to his own villa and the door to his son's room. The lictors filed behind him, duty-bound to escort him to the doorstep of his home.

All about the bed in his son's room hung the masks of his ancestors, their masks for public occasions, dried now, some of them cracked, some of them faded in color and as hideous themselves as the faces of the dead; but they were his ancestors. Only the *di parentes* of his family could watch over his son.

The thing on the bed snapped its teeth in the air and twisted and bucked, writhing, its face contorted with terrible hunger and rage, its eyes blind, like small, scratched gray coins. Caius sagged back against the door and watched, just watched. Beyond that door and all about him, this villa high on the Palatine Hill was silent; the slaves tiptoed when their master was with his son.

Caius recalled the first time he'd seen his son like this, back at the end of the winter when the dead first appeared in the Subura. Caius hadn't known the dead were rising at the time, hadn't believed the reports he'd heard. He'd only known there was violence, a riot, on one street in the slum. In most seasons the Subura was best ignored, but a *riot* could not be tolerated. Riots left unchecked became very dangerous. Caius had sent guardsmen in.

When the guardsmen came back—their numbers diminished—they had brought with them, chained and gagged with bloodied cloth, the praetor's son.

Seeing him, Caius had crumpled to his knees—he, a Roman, on his *knees*!—and it seemed hours before he could move or speak. His lictors stood silently by, shifting their feet, nervous at the nearness of the chained, animate corpse. The captain of the guardsmen who had brought him stood by as well. Waiting. They seemed to understand that the regular rules and expectations of *dignitas* did not apply here, under these conditions. Dignity operated by entirely new and different rules, when Rome's highest public official saw his son so devoured by the dead and so changed.

At last Caius had beckoned one of the guardsmen near with his hand, asked the questions he had to ask. Briefly, giving his report in quick, clipped phrases, the hired man described what he had seen on that street.

"How did it happen to *him*?" Caius interrupted, his voice hoarse and choked.

"We found him at an insula. The Christian women they call 'holy widows' were there, and there were dead coming at them out of the alley. Eight of them, growling and hissing like beasts. Your son was with four or five men holding the door of the insula against them, unarmed. The dead broke through. My own cohort was close behind, and we encircled the entire district, five or six insulae. Several riverside tenements. I lost three men getting your son out of there. The women were—screaming. Inside the building." Sweat broke out on the man's brow. "After what we witnessed in there, praetor—we burned everything. All of it. A few dead came lurching toward us out of the fire—they were still walking, still moaning, even as they burned. We made sure to destroy all of them, all the bodies." The guardsman swallowed. "Your son. Those bites on his arms. He died of fever even while we were burning the street. We'd seen what would happen. We—we expected it, praetor. He was dead. Not breathing. Yet he opened his eyes as we carried him uphill, chained, on a litter. He opened his eyes. And he was like this." He gestured at the gagged, growling corpse.

It had been too much to take in; the effort of it had shattered him. He had clung to the few facts he could grasp: the rising of the bitten dead, his son's destruction, and his son's inexplicable presence in an insula in the Subura, defending the lives of some meaningless community of women. "I didn't know he was part of that—that cult." His shoulders shook; in a moment he would be sobbing.

"Get out of here," he whispered. "Let me be alone with my son."

———

Now, watched over by all the great men of his ancestry, Caius's son fought his chains on the bed. Looking on, Caius refused to weep. A magistrate of Rome should weep for Rome only and not for kin or companions lost.

Yet he was also a father.

He'd had his slaves nail the bed to the floor after the third time the corpse overturned it, wrenching hard enough that the bed flipped and came down on top of it. Such things only happened when someone was present with his son in the room. When his son was alone and the door was shut, as far as Caius could tell, his son lay silently on the bed, limp in his chains—until he heard someone move about or speak near the door, in which case he would thrash into wild motion again.

At first Caius had ordered his house slaves to feed his son and bring him drink, though he'd had to threaten his slaves with beatings, then with crucifixion, to make them approach the corpse. The first man with the courage to do it had lost two fingers to the snapping teeth when he tried to feed biscuits into the corpse's mouth. Knowing the pestilence would take him, Caius had his throat slit and had commanded the body burned.

Then he had one of the house's female slaves try; the slave women were less costly to replace. But the same thing happened; when she poured water into the corpse's throat, it was spewed back at her. With a hissing scream the creature lurched, almost upending the bed, and fastened its teeth deep into the woman's arm.

Her screams had been terrible to hear.

Only by cutting away a large chunk of her arm were the other house slaves able to get her loose from the ravenous, growling thing in the bed.

After giving orders for what was to be done with her, Caius had stormed from his chamber and raged into the atrium under the open sky. Standing there in the garden at the heart of his villa, he'd turned in circles, screaming at the windows of the rooms of his house: "What is *wrong* with you insects? Can't you even feed one boy! One bleeding boy! *What is wrong with you?*"

For an hour he'd shouted obscenities, the veins standing out in his neck. At last he collapsed and lay on his belly in the garden, weeping into the dirt. He stayed there all night. The earth felt cool against his cheek; in the end it was a comfort, something real, something he could trust.

The next day, he did not have anyone attempt to bring his son food or water.

Now Caius leaned against the door of his son's room, his chest tight. Though he had no cup in his hands to make a libation, and though he was not standing beside any fresh sacrifice in a temple, he prayed. He prayed first to his ancestors, staring fixedly at their masks of clay or woven grass where they hung high on their wall above the bed. He spoke with them for a long time, explaining the crisis and pleading with them. Then he prayed to the unseen *lares* of his house—the old, old gods of home and hearth, who have no names.

All the while, his son roared and snarled and spat, and tore at the tattered mattress with his nails. After praying, Caius stared down at his son, everything inside him gone empty and cold. He should end it. He knew that. He should have his son's body burned. But that was no way to give a Roman citizen rest. And this was *his boy*. He'd had only one son. Only one. His wife Scipia had died in childbirth; when the midwives had sent for Caius, he had come quickly, but not quickly enough. After hastily accepting the newborn son as his own and then handing the child to one of the women, Caius had stood silently by Scipia's bed, gazing down at the stillness in her eyes. For all that night, he gave no thought to his son (for whom the midwives quickly found a wet nurse), nor to the family hearth, nor to any of his responsibilities as *paterfamilias* of his house. He simply gazed down at his wife as her body cooled and hardened.

When he'd risen stiffly at last, in the chill hours, and went, half-aware, to tend the hearth, he had found it as cold as she. He'd reeled back in horror; the cold hearth was a sacrilege. A Roman patrician must never let the fire in his home go out; he, and he only, no slave or servant, must tend it, honoring *his* fathers who'd passed the fire down to him. In that one night, Caius had failed both his wife and the *di parentes*, his ancestors.

That was really when everything had gone wrong. The world had tipped on its side, and he had been sliding off ever since, his fingertips scrabbling for purchase. Since that day, everyone else he cared about *had* slid away. Only he was left, the last player clinging to a tilted stage.

When the boy's time came to greet the gods in person, Livius his son should have awaited them in a great stone mausoleum, high on the hills of Rome, with inscriptions of honor carved into the cool marble on which he lay. Now Livius reeked of decay rather than burial spices, and leapt in his bonds. And when Caius himself died, no son would tend the hearth for him or perform the rites to remember him and honor him. Caius Lucius would become a wandering shade, restless, hungry, homeless. An eater in the dark.

Shutting the horror of it away into some dim compartment far from his heart, Caius set his hand upon the door.

"*Vale*, Livius." *Be well.* The greeting seemed a terrible joke, yet Caius could never leave the room without speaking some word of parting. This was his boy.

He left, shutting the door quietly behind him. The growling of the thing could be heard too clearly, even through the barrier of stout cypress wood. Refusing to hear it, Caius strode down the hall and out into the atrium, crossing the garden toward his study. He walked blindly, by habit, his eyes noting neither the eyes of the slaves watching him carefully from the windows about the atrium, nor the last summer blossoms on the cherry tree, nor the vines that had twined about a neglected marble Cupid (not because of a neglectful gardener, but because the gardener had fled the villa the same day Livius was brought home to his bed; since that day Caius had attended little to the affairs of his house and had not bothered to replace him).

When he reached the study, Caius seated himself in his chair, keeping his back very straight. There was no need for public *dignitas* here, no need for posture—not even his slaves were permitted to enter the study—but *dignitas* was the one raiment left to him;

otherwise he was stripped and bared to the icy rain of a malicious world, one that had already cut from him his wife and his son, a world where the ancestors no longer interceded or cared. So even in the extremity of his grief, he sat like a Roman.

There came a knock at his door.

Caius took slow, slow breaths until he felt capable of answering. "You may open the door," he said.

The door swung open. The slave there—one of the females—knelt swiftly at the threshold, without entering.

Caius glanced at her briefly, indifferently. "What is it?"

"Your aide is at the door with a message, dominus."

Caius looked more closely at her. Her face was white, and the hands she held clasped in her lap were trembling. She kept her eyes lowered dutifully. Whatever the aide had said had scared her. A hard stone of dread settled in Caius's belly. "Well? What is the message?"

"He said to tell you he'd been to Flavius's villa, dominus. There was no answer at the door, but he heard moaning within. He—he heard—the dead, dominus. Inside. He went to the nearest villa, where Cassius Tertius and Portia live, dominus. Domina Portia told him that Flavius is away on business, touring Transalpine Gaul. His wife and daughter had the keeping of the villa. She said the moaning had started the night before, and they'd been too scared to go to Flavius's door."

Caius cursed. "Is my man still at the door?"

"Yes, dominus."

"Tell him to send guardsmen to the villa and to make sure the men don't speak of it to anyone. The hill is anxious enough after the past few days. We don't need a panic."

"Yes, dominus."

"And you tell the other slaves this. If anyone in *my* villa speaks of what they've heard, I'll have every woman in this villa *flayed*. And the left ear cut from the head of every man. Am I clear?"

"Yes, dominus." She was shaking.

"Leave."

"Yes, dominus!" She sprang to her feet and shut the door. Caius could hear her quick footsteps running down the hall.

Then silence.

Gods.

He sat in the silence, thinking of that enclosed villa farther up the slope. And thinking of the body of Flavius's wife, shuffling about its dim rooms. Were her slaves diseased and hungering as well—or had they fled? How had the daughter gotten out into the streets, and not the mother?

He shook his head, reached for his stylus and parchment and for a little bottle of ink. He uncorked the bottle, dipped the stylus, paused. He sat there awhile, the stylus held poised over the bottle, a great drop of blue ink clinging to its tip.

What was he to write?

What *could* he write?

Flavius was another man who had lost a wife and a child, even as Caius had, though he did not yet know of his loss. What was there to say?

Blinking the weariness from his eyes, Caius began to ink words into the parchment, in hard Latin capitals. *To Flaccus Flavius Germanicus, in Transalpine Gaul*, he wrote. *Caius Lucius Justus, praetor urbanus, Rome. Vale.* He dipped the stylus again, then began to write with a furious haste, barely making the letters legible. This infuriated him—a letter, as everything else, needed discipline and poise—but he did not slow his speed. He must write this quickly or not at all.

I must express my dismay in informing you that a tragedy has befallen your family in Rome. The nature of it is of such horror that I can only write of it because I am able to reassure myself that you will receive it with that same dignity with which you once received word of the tenth cohort's defeat along the Rhine when we campaigned together in Germania, so many years ago. I know that in you the blood of the ancients is strong and that you are well able to receive news of terrible misfortune. I must inform you, Flaccus Flavius, that your wife and daughter are deceased. They became afflicted with that unmentionable plague that appeared in Rome during the last winter. I know that it will bring you some comfort to learn that I have made arrangements to ensure that their suffering will be brief. The ashes will be held in a silver urn under the care of the Vestal Virgins and under the watchful eyes of the gods until your return to the Eternal City.

A dutiful and patrician wife, and a daughter of grace, beauty, and intelligence, betrothed to a fine house: Rome is lessened by their loss, and all Rome continues to hold the ancient, eminent family of the Flavii in the highest respect and reverence.

Si vales, valeo, amico meo.

He set the parchment aside to let the ink dry. Then he wrote, less hastily, a missive to the Emperor in his pleasure gardens.

There are wakeful dead within the city and they are many. Your Divinity would be best advised by his appointed magistrates and by the people of Rome to prolong the time of Your pleasure and rest. Though we know Your sense of duty to the Roman people is matched only by the wisdom of Your governance, the preservation of Your life is of great priority; I will make Rome safe for Your return if You but delay that return to the next Ides.

Finishing the message and placing it aside with the other letter, his face grim, Caius reached for another page.

There was one more thing that needed doing. He had known it, perhaps, from the moment that patrician girl had burst through his door. Dipping the stylus again, he began to pen the order, the last order he intended to give as praetor urbanus. He could pass the small parchment to his lictors after Polycarp's trial.

By this order, he would atone for his failure and for that of his family. He would atone for not having raised Livius a good Roman worthy of his fathers and for not having been there when he died. He would atone even for Flavius's absence when *his* daughter died, and for the shortcomings of all the fathers of Rome who had not kept the city clean and secure. He would not allow the next generation of Romans to let the hearth fires go out, misled by Polycarp's cult until all the patrician dead returned, even as the Subura's impoverished dead had returned already to wander empty Rome, neglected and ravenous. Caius would do more than simply put Polycarp to death. He would do Rome one great service: he would end the plague, regardless of the cost, regardless of any death toll needed to achieve it. His hand trembled as he inked the first words of the order.

AN ETHICS OF HUNGER:
EARLIER THAT WEEK IN THE SUBURA

ROME, EVEN then, was an old city—ancient and vast. Its great bulk sprawled over the slopes of seven hills, with the river Tiber winding between them, its banks choked by the crumbling insulae of the Subura. Each morning, the Subura's residents woke to the reek of diseased fish pulled from the river and human urine and goose shit, and to the honking of geese on the water—there were always many geese near the river. The birds were sacred; six centuries ago when the Celts had invaded, axes in hand, the warriors had startled a flock of geese on the Tiber. The birds had risen into the air with their loud voices, waking the people in time to defend themselves. Today the geese often clogged some narrow street, but when this happened, people stood by and waited for the geese to clear the way. To harm or show disrespect to a goose was one of Rome's oldest taboos. It was also treason, though the praetor's hired guardsmen rarely bothered with arrests in the Subura.

Lately—since this last winter—it was a comfort to see the birds. Where the foot traffic of the Subura was halted by slow-moving, placid geese, one at least knew there were no walking dead on that street.

So in the mornings, the people of the Subura woke to geese. Then the men hurried to market to buy the day's produce or sent out slaves if they owned any, then hurried themselves to whatever shop they'd found work at. The free women cleaned house or knitted fresh patches onto clothing that was already a patchwork of faded fabrics. The slave women were kicked from their masters' beds and sent to prepare baths. And while the streets were still shadowed—the sun blocked out by the looming buildings—lines of slumped-shouldered, weary women, both slave and free, could be seen trudging toward the nearest public fountain with lidded jars on their shoulders.

Regina walked with them, empty water jar on one shoulder, her other arm around an old woman whose steps stumbled more often than not. Like a few of the others in the street, both she and old Flora wore on their heads wide-brimmed hats, gifts from Father Polycarp and a precaution against the emptying of chamber pots from sixth-story insula windows. Urine brought a fair price from the fullers who used it in the cleaning of togas, but to some, hauling pots down from a fifth- or sixth-story apartment and then up the steep, cracked streets to the fullers' shops on the uphill edge of the Subura seemed not worth the trouble. Regina was used to the occasional splashes into the street; they were the least of the Subura's indignities. Yet she was grateful for the hat.

Flora didn't talk much; the walk to the fountain exhausted her. She made that walk every other morning, and on each of those mornings Regina slipped out of Father Polycarp's insula, pausing a moment at the doorstep until she heard Marcus slam the bolt shut behind her. Marcus Antonius was a young patrician recently taken in by Polycarp; over the past few months, he'd taken to helping out with odd jobs around the insula.

While Marcus shut and secured the door, Regina tugged the wide hat securely over her hair and looked out at the morning grimness of the alley (sometimes there'd be a smear of blood on the wall across the alley, or a silent body, or a not-silent body, and she would eye it carefully). Then she hurried down the Via Noctis to that other insula—one considerably larger but in far worse repair than Polycarp's—where Flora lived with her grandson. As Flora's grandson brought in some food by working from before dawn to after dusk as an assistant to the fullers, but had neither the coin to purchase a slave nor the meal to maintain one, it fell to old Flora to clean the apartment, prepare the morning and evening meals, and trudge down to the fountain and back. Regina had seen the grandson at the meetings in the Catacombs; he was one of theirs. So each of those mornings, Regina came to the door of Flora's insula and asked for her; and when Flora came down, Regina took the great water jar from the grandmother's trembling hands and lifted it to her own shoulder. Sometimes Flora kissed her cheek or smiled at her, with eyes that were beautiful and old; sometimes she simply trudged along beside her, grumbling quietly under her breath.

Fetching water was dangerous for the Subura's women. The brotherhoods that guarded the fountains at the crossroads might bother or molest them. Or there might be too many women at the fountain, and taking too long to return, those who'd waited near the end of the line might bring the water in only to receive a beating for it. Worse still, the women had to cast uneasy glances down each alley they passed. If Regina saw a dark shape moving slowly in the alley, she pulled Flora past as quickly as she could and hastened on with her head low, her heart pounding. The figure she'd seen might have been only a street thief or a beggar rising from his night's bed in the alley's refuse. Or it might have been one of the dead.

There had been quite a few in the spring, but most weeks in the early summer there had been only one or two. The last month had been bad; quite a few mornings, wary residents had emerged from their insulae to see dead feeding in the street, sometimes not just one but two or even three. And there had been the matter of the potter's shop on the second floor of the fourth insula on the Via Borealis. The potter had lived there with his two sisters and had just taken in his brother's family of six, who had been evicted. They now squeezed together into the potter's bedchamber, while the potter and his sisters slept on the floor by the wheel and the clay bowls. One of the brother's small boys was suffering from a fever that night.

This month, the potter's rent had been late, and the land-owner had finally unlocked the door, intending to go in and have a word with the potter about it. But when he opened the door, nine hissing dead spilled out. The other residents had slammed shut their doors, and after eating the landlord, the dead had wandered moaning in the atrium for a few hours. An infant in one of the first-floor apartments started to scream toward midday; the dead clustered at the door and pummeled on it until they finally broke through and devoured the family within.

Before dark, one of the crossroads brotherhoods appeared at the outer door of the insula, en masse, eight armed men—members of one of the small fraternities that considered themselves keepers of the winding streets, servants of the old gods of the Roman crossroads, and the Subura's honored caste, even though the rest of the Subura considered them thugs. Since the late winter when the dead had begun to walk, the crossroads brothers had taken to hunting in the streets near the insulae that paid them, slaying the dead they found. They traveled in pairs, or three or four together, and so far had kept the numbers of dead thinned.

The landlord's widow had hired them for an exorbitant fee, one that would almost certainly bankrupt the insula. Upon arriving, the men threatened to kill her if she couldn't pay inside of two months; in tears, she promised that she would sell the building and get them the coin. Then the brothers went in.

Only four walked back out.

That had been last week.

Word of *that* had spread through the Subura, and at least one landowner had taken to making nightly rounds, knocking on each tenant's door before dark and waiting for the tenant to call out that all was well. Most landowners, however, did not do this, though they shuddered at the tale. The last few days, when Regina had gone to the fountains or to the market, she'd taken to glancing up at the dark windows in the high buildings, fearful that she might see a gray, torn face peering back.

When someone was bitten, most of the time they concealed it, went home, locked their doors. Fever and death followed a few hours later or during the night. If others were locked in with them—their family or others who were either sharing rent or squatting along with them—they might be wakened later by grasping hands and devoured. If the person lived alone, they woke mindless, hungry, shambling about the room, locked in until kin came to look for them, or the insula's owner came for rent, or some thief picked the lock on the door, or until they broke through the door themselves. There might be many such rooms in the Subura now, people locked in with their own hunger, awaiting release.

This particular morning, Regina and the other women were filing down a narrow street that plunged downhill between the clammy stone walls of the insulae toward the fountains. They were near the river and could hear the voice of the brown water. The stones beneath their feet were moist and stank; in a few shadows beneath the walls where the sun never quite reached, handfuls of obstinate mushrooms had squirmed up through gaps in the stones, though not the kind of mushrooms one could eat. Here, the women stopped.

They were not waiting for geese.

A few of them turned the moment they saw what was in the street, and ran. Some of these dropped their jars, shattering them; others clung to theirs. Those who didn't run stood very still, frozen in their horror, their eyes all fixed on the same object. A corpse lay in the street on its belly, emaciated, its ribs showing through torn flesh; the arm it reached toward them was terribly shrunken, as though it had not eaten for weeks prior to its death. Its sunken, filmy eyes stared at them without recognition, and it hissed and snarled from a mouth only half-filled with teeth. It tried to drag itself toward them with its other hand, clawing at the dusty stones, but its legs were broken. Its jaws snapped at the air; then it moaned. The sound of its cry passed through the women like a shudder. Somewhere within earshot on some other street, there was the *clack* of a door slamming shut.

The thing's fingertips curled around a broken paving stone, and it dragged itself another inch nearer. Regina's heart was in her throat. She and the others stared at the hungry dead, still not moving. A girl who couldn't have been more than fifteen lifted her water jar high over her head, her face white, as though she meant to bash it over the corpse's head once it came closer. Regina kept her eyes on the corpse—wishing desperately that Polycarp were here, to bring his Gift to the dead and leave it unmoving, limp on the stones.

Then she heard quick, sandaled footsteps farther down the street, coming from the direction of the fountain, and she tore her gaze from the dead thing. From around the other curve of the street, behind the crawling corpse, two men appeared. They were dressed in dark tunics, but they wore black armbands beneath the shoulder and walked with a cold, certain gait that would have told anyone in the Subura who they were, even without the armbands. One carried an oak cudgel that had probably served previously as the leg of a table. The other carried a long knife, its blade nearly long enough to qualify it for the Roman *gladius*, or short sword—except that it was curved, and the etching of a stylized horse into the blade declared it was Numidian in origin. Perhaps some horse lord of the windblown steppes above the Sahara had once carried it strapped to his shin. It was a lethal-looking object, and illegal.

These two men strode up the street; the corpse hadn't noticed them—it was still trying to pull itself, bit by bit, toward the water carriers. The men didn't hurry. Any other morning, Regina would have watched them with wariness or fear; now, her fear was focused on the dead, and she watched the men approach with only a kind of terrible fascination.

As they neared the thing in the street, the two men exchanged a look. The one with the cudgel nodded; the other stepped forward. The creature still groped its way toward the gathered women, its teeth parting in a long, hissing snarl. Bending, the man took hold of its hair and drove the Numidian knife hard into the back of its skull. The thing convulsed, jerking, then lay still on its belly, its cheek against the stones. Its face concealed in its ragged hair. A movement like a sigh swept through the water carriers.

No blood seeped from the wound. Regina's arm tightened around Flora's shoulder. She lifted her eyes from the corpse, fixed her gaze on the men in the street.

The man holding the knife was breathing hard, and he remained bent over the corpse, the blade still sheathed in its skull. His chest moved as he drew in great breaths. He had done the thing quickly and with an efficiency that spoke of an easiness with killing. Still, even the space of time since the dead first began lurching along the riverbanks this last winter hadn't been enough for a man to let go entirely of the ancient taboo against defiling one of the bodies of Rome's dead. The other man hefted the cudgel onto his shoulder and clasped the knife wielder's arm, squeezing briefly. The tender gesture seemed an anomalous thing in that street, where those two scarred and armed men leaned over a heap of decrepit and slaughtered flesh.

The men were brothers, not by blood but by society. Theirs was the nearest of the crossroads brotherhoods, whose members included an assortment of veterans whose pay hadn't quite emerged from tightly locked state coffers (or had been squandered on drink), manumitted slaves who'd once served as bodyguards, and former professional assassins who'd been discredited and could find little work. They had in common wounded lives and a hunger for coin, and they extorted high fees from the insula owners in return for "protection."

The man with the knife tried to wrench the blade from the creature's skull but found the blade lodged deep; with a grimace, he shoved his boot against its back, then jerked the blade free. A few of the women hid their eyes; most didn't. The corpse rolled slightly, half exposing its face beneath a veil of filthy hair. At the sight of that face, the brother with the knife made no sound, but his hand that held the knife began to shake. After a moment he spoke in a low voice to the other crossroads brother, who answered back in an arguing tone. They debated quietly for a moment. Then the brother with the cudgel cursed and turned to the women, that crowd of both free and slave, with their wide hats and their water jars. "Follow me, see? I'll get you to the fountain. Move. Now."

He gestured furiously with his cudgel, then strode back down the street. The women began to follow; Regina helped Flora move along the edge of the street, with an insula's wall at their backs.

The silence that had fallen over them had broken; they were all whispering now.

"We're going to be dead soon." Flora looked up at Regina with watery eyes.

Her heart raced. "No, we're not."

The old grandmother clutched Regina's arm with a grip that startled her and rasped her words as Regina helped her along; the younger woman couldn't take her eyes off the dead thing on the stones.

"When I was a girl," Flora wheezed, "our insula had a pear tree. Great juicy pears. Juice'd run down my fingers. One time a boy kissed it off them. Gone now. Boy, pears, everything. Chopped down. No fruit, hardly no bread. And some of us as hungry as—as *that*." With her other hand, she stabbed a thin finger at the corpse. "Won't be long now."

"Come live at our insula," Regina urged, not for the first time. "We have bread there."

"I know. Grandson's gone before, brought it back. Kind, your father. Like an old cypress he is, branches spread over you, giving his shade. Up on the hill, the people with gardens have their praetor, and you down here have your father. But you can't fit all of us in his insula, dear."

"Someday we will," Regina whispered, her tone passionate, though the whites of her eyes showed as she watched the still figure in the street and the guardsman standing over it. They were past it now; she was looking over her shoulder. In a moment they would file around the curve in the street, and it would be out of sight. Yet she didn't feel safe. She wanted to be back in the insula; the longing in her was fierce for a wall around her, a high wall and solid, and one of her choosing. It took all her will to turn her eyes forward and help Flora on over the broken and treacherous stones.

———

It took a few moments for all the women to file past the corpse and follow the crossroads brother around the curve of the street. They flattened themselves against the wall of one of the two facing insulae, giving the fallen body a wide berth—all except for one woman, plump and gray haired, who walked up to the corpse, gave a contemptuous snort, and stepped deliberately over it before walking right down the middle of the street.

Eventually the street was empty. There was only the lone crossroads brother, still standing over the corpse, knife in hand, an anguished look on his face. He crouched on his heels and reached for the thing's hair. Hesitated a moment, then drew back his hand. Then, sucking air in between his teeth, he gathered up the thing's filthy hair in his fingers and lifted it free of the face.

He looked stricken. Long moments passed as he gazed at the face of the dead. He covered his mouth and chin with his hand; his eyes were moist. Perhaps it had been someone of his blood, a sister or a cousin. Perhaps a past lover, a warm, living woman he'd once held in his arms and kissed, who had whispered secrets into his ear and listened to his. Perhaps it was only someone he'd known as a youth, some girl he'd played ball with in the atrium on hot afternoons and whose dead, rotted face recalled long-neglected memories that hit him now with the violence of fire or flood, reminding him of things lost and things not quite gained, and of the sewage of time that carried everything downstream and away.

He let the hair fall, concealing the face, then he clasped his hands tightly and stayed crouched there. The tears in his eyes didn't spill. He just sat looking at the dead woman, weighted to the ground by the horror of it. He didn't notice the honking of geese or the murmur of the Subura about him or the slow, dragging footsteps of one of the dead lurching into the street behind him out of a dark alley. It approached stiffly, its head bent to one side on a broken neck, its hands half-lifted, ready to grasp. The thing moaned, low and desperate, as it reached the crossroads brother, and the man turned then, with wide eyes. In the moment it took him to pull himself out of the past and lift the Numidian knife, the thing had bent over him, grasping his shoulder in one hand and his hair in the other; even as he brought the knife up with a yell, its teeth tore into his neck.

Noon came to the Subura, and with it the sweltering heat of narrow spaces packed with too many living bodies. Men rested and napped briefly. They drank watered wine if they could. Within each walled insula, any children that lived there moved about in the atrium, laughing and shrieking if they'd been fed, or sitting beneath stunted shrubs and daydreaming if they hadn't, or weeping if they'd been beaten or had witnessed their mothers being beaten. There were quite a few insulae where laughter could be heard at midday, but there were also insulae that brooded silently in the heat.

In an upper-story room at one of these apartment structures, the laughter of two girls in the atrium below could be heard through the window, but those sounds of joy brought into the room only a bite of bitterness, like winter air seeping through a crack in the wall that has never been properly sealed, a draft that shivers its way through skin and bone. On a pallet in the room, a man lay with his eyes open and his hands clasped too tightly for him to be resting. The traces of flour on his hands and arms declared him a baker, though he was unusually lean for one. He had burned off any fat he might have had with worrying, which he did so deeply and so often that his body interpreted his anxiety as a particularly strenuous kind of exercise and responded accordingly.

Beside him, a plump, energetic woman was stuffing clothes into a haversack with a vigor most people reserve for shoving sandbags into a wall against a flood. She was even breathing hard.

"How can you be sure the praetor will keep his word?" the baker asked his wife.

"He's a patrician, isn't he?"

She crammed a rolled-up tunic into the bulging sack, then struggled to tie it shut. "Toss me that coat, husband." She nodded to the peg by the window. "We'll need to hide this 'til tomorrow."

With a small groan, he got to his feet and took the coat from its peg, then tossed it listlessly toward his wife; it hit her shoulders, and she sighed and bent to catch it as it slid to the floor. Her husband lay back down, his eyes pale. "I'd rather not set foot anywhere on that hill," he muttered.

"Fine. I'll go. In the morning. We can leave when I get back." She was still wrestling with the ties on the sack; hissing through her teeth, she straightened and gazed down at it for a moment. She pressed her lips together. It wouldn't do; if she tried to carry that sack over her shoulder, its seams would split. She would have to start over; she began pulling clothing from the sack. They were all such plain garments, light wool or brown linen, all except one gown as purple as a Caesar's cloak, a hidden treasure at the bottom of the sack. It was her only relic of the past, something she'd been permitted to take to the Subura only because she was wearing it when she walked there. "I'll never understand why you get the shivers every time I talk about going uphill." Her voice was sharp. Outside the window, children were still giggling. "My *first* husband and I had a villa up there."

"A small one."

"A *villa*. That's more than you've provided for me."

She began arranging bundles more carefully within the sack.

"He threw you out."

She stopped, her shoulders tensing. Her hands still. A few heartbeats, then she resumed filling the sack, though her hands moved more slowly.

"You're barren, Julia." There was a softness in the baker's voice. "You're barren, and he threw you out. Your equestrian husband threw you out. But with me you have never gone hungry."

She kept packing. Her eyes blinked back the burn of tears, then they spilled. Her husband watched her cry with his thin and sorrowful face, but he did not go to hold her. At last she forced the final bundle in, then leaned over the sack and let it out, her shoulders trembling. For once she wept not for the things she didn't have and couldn't be, but for the empty hole inside her where a child might have been. Often she'd seen other women carrying their round bellies in their hands as they moved in their slow, waddling gait—or seen them nursing tiny infants at their breasts. Her own were dry of milk, and her womb hollow within her. Hearing the laughter through the window, she leaned over the sack and cried, letting the tears fall on the tightly folded undergarments and bunched tunics, the simple garments that told the world she was a baker's wife. The low-caste Christians who occupied other rooms in their insula thought her husband something wonderful—a maker of bread. That didn't hold much weight with her. No amount of fresh bread had filled the hole within her or warmed the cold inside her.

Night fell over the Subura. Quietly, a few doors opened in the dark, and furtive shapes slipped out into the deadly streets, clad in dark cloaks and cowls. They went in pairs, or clustered quickly into small groups for fear of any prowling dead, and stole through the narrow alleys between tall buildings as silently as though they were God's watchmen come to inspect the world while its residents slept. But they were not watchmen; they were men and women of many ages and occupations, carrying a bit of bread beneath their cloaks, ready to barter it for hope. Those sliding along the sides of insulae on the wider streets found themselves joined by other figures (and they were not few) who had stolen out of homes uphill, slipping down from the villas of the well fed to join the weekly exodus.

The small groups passed through the Subura, heading downriver, until they had moved beyond the ancient boundary of Rome; they darted through the unlit streets between tall and decaying buildings until the buildings thinned and they came to a street that ended in a jumbled cliff of soft volcanic rock. There was a door in the rock face, and it stood open on its hinges; a man waited there, in a dark cowl and cloak like theirs, a torch in his hand. Beside him there was a vat of oil. The man asked a question of those who approached, and they murmured the correct answer, then dipped their torches (if they'd brought torches) into the oil, and the door warden lit them. With a last wary glance up the street, the dark-cloaked figures passed inside, slipping quietly into the Catacombs and down those long corridors lined with shelves on which rested hundreds of silent, shrouded cadavers—the dead of Rome's lower classes, interred here by families who could not afford a mausoleum on a hill. Those who hadn't brought torches had to walk in a darkness more complete than the void before God spoke the name of the earth, stumbling frequently over some unevenness in the earthen floor and leaning out a hand to catch themselves, feeling, with a shock, ribs or a long femur against their fingers. With the pestilence in Rome, one could not walk past the shelves of the dead—even these, the clean dead—without trembling.

There were several large caverns in the Catacombs, and the dark-robed people were gathering in the nearest of these. The cavern was packed with maybe a hundred living, men and women of several classes. In the flickering light of the torches some of them held, you could see here and there among the crowd the aquiline nose of the Roman patrician—the revered class, considered by birth and bloodline to be descendants of gods. But everyone attending, even and especially Father Polycarp himself, wore over their daily garments a dark robe and a cowl that most had now tossed back onto their shoulders. The clothes served to conceal them as they crept through the city to the entrances to the Catacombs. But the cowl and robe served a second purpose as well—they concealed class and station. Those gathered here had replaced their various costumes of caste and social connection with this simpler, shared garb. Here, unless you looked for features in a face, everyone was without adornment and without mark of wealth or poverty. Here, all of them were of one family.

Polycarp stood among them; they had made a little circle of empty space about the slab of rock where he stood. He carried no torch, and he clasped his hands behind him; sometimes, late at night, they trembled with approaching age. His voice remained strong, and as the last few, furtive members of the community of the Fish entered from those dark, open gaps in the wall that allowed the corridors to empty into this cavern, Polycarp raised his voice in song, leading them in the *Phos Hilaron*. It was a hymn to the nearness of God in the day's last light, a reminder to them all that though they worked in the dark, they waited for the sun to return.

As the people sang softly, they brought out from under their cloaks their offerings for the night, for the act of sharing that bound these people together, all these people who met so often now in secret. Few had come empty-handed; most had brought bread. A loaf, if they could afford it. If they couldn't, then something, even if it were only a bite of stale barley bread, perhaps the only morsel they had left to eat. The singing, then the hearing, then the sharing of bread—it was a rite that was becoming familiar through repeated use, though it was unlike anything that had been practiced in Rome before. As they sang they held the bread in their hands, lifted as though each meager piece was sacred. Perhaps for those of them that lived in the crowded, ravenous Subura, all food *was* sacred. And perhaps those who'd slipped down from the Palatine by cover of dark were relearning the holiness of bread from the passion they saw on their downhill neighbors' faces. After Father Polycarp spoke tonight and blessed their sharing of bread, they would each break the piece they held, whether it be a loaf or a smidgen, and they would pass the pieces around the gathering, until all had eaten.

"We can feed *on* each other," Polycarp had taught them on many such nights, "or we can feed each other and feed *with* each other." In the great Games of the Colosseum, the Emperor and father of Rome, *paterfamilias* of the family of Rome, would give out loaves of bread to the gathered crowds of his children, to assuage the sharpest bite of Rome's hunger so that the people might not rise in riot. But such bread was given to quiet the people, not to feed them or fill them. Polycarp, a father of this city within Rome, was interested in filling them. He would do so by teaching them to share bread with each other.

"I know that it has become a fearful thing to us, coming here through the dark streets," Polycarp told them now. His voice carried across the cavern, filling the silence that followed song. "But we must not fear the dead. Fear is a greater evil to us than death; our brothers and our sisters who can't yet sleep need our pity, not our terror." He lifted his hands, gesturing at the shelves on which silent corpses rested. "We mustn't fear the dead. They sleep. Those who now wake and walk can be given sleep. But we must understand—they walk not because they are unfed but because the *living* are unfed. My brothers and sisters, let the dead feed the dead. Rome builds vast mausoleums, houses grander than the houses of the living, and holds festivals, bringing food to the dead—food no one eats—while in the Subura, Rome's living starve." His voice softened and trembled with the passion of what he had to tell. The cavern became very quiet as the gathering strained to hear him.

"I will tell you a story," Polycarp said. "Long ago, the first man to be killed by a brother was tossed into a deep pit, his legs first broken with blows of a thick staff. There was water there in the pit but neither meat nor roots, and he starved, famished until he was little more than bones on the ground. It was a hungry and a horrific death. And his spirit could not rest; he rose lurching from the earth, moaning in his hunger. And when his brother came to gloat over the body, the famished dead devoured him, after which the brother also rose, half-eaten and ravenous with need." Polycarp gazed out, seeing the horror in those many eyes. "It is the hunger of the living that creates the restless dead," he said. "The dead themselves are here, all around us, sleeping. That is why we meet here, in the dark, among our sleeping dead, to share bread among the living. It is a reminder of who we must feed, if we wish our dead to rest."

The others' faces were uplifted, eyes shining in the torch-light. He saw Regina with her eyes alight and Marcus with his face grim but his eyes fierce with a young man's fealty. Polycarp smiled. He knew that beneath their robes, they each held a loaf from Piscus's ovens; Polycarp accepted bread in lieu of rent from the insula's baker, though neither the baker nor his wife, Julia, had yet joined the gathering underground. He let his gaze roam wider; he saw faces he knew from other insulae in the Subura or from the Forum; he saw a young man with one ear who served as a merchant's stable slave and, standing beside him, a senator's daughter. His heart warmed. Once, just three or four of them alone would meet here on the Sabbath each week. Now there were at least a hundred each time. Such gatherings had sprung up in cities across the world, meeting in secret places like this, under the earth in old cellars or places of burial. Communication between them was rare and treasured. As Polycarp gazed out at their faces, he found it a thing of great comfort to see so many together in one place.

"Listen to me," Polycarp called to the gathered brothers and sisters. "I will tell you about the Apostle's Gift. I will tell you about this thing that God will do through us for the city and for the world. How we will take from death its terror." His face glowed with passion. "Listen to me," he breathed. "Brothers and sisters, it is quiet here. No hunger here to distract us. All our lives, we feed on what leaves us hungry, drink from what leaves us thirsting. Because we are always left hungry and always thirsty, we begin to think that those visible objects of our hunger are what we need most. A loaf of bread, a pouch of coins, the respect of others, success, a woman's body, or a man's. Or even a person or a thing from times past, something lost and remembered that we crave. But it is not so. These are not what we need most. Our hunger thieves us from our true selves. Like a violent fever, the hunger eats away mind and spirit. In the end, everything that we truly are is gone. Only the hunger remains. Even other men and women are no longer anything but food to us, meat for our desires and obsessions. Then we are lost—unless some other brings a Gift. We cannot recover ourselves alone."

He gazed out over the gathering. So many faces, so many eyes glinting in the torchlight. The days to come might bring any good or any evil. Some of them might be eaten by the dead. Some of them might be found out and imprisoned by the Roman praetor. Some might face illness or doubt. But tonight, in the quiet of these underground tombs, they were gathered and ready. They had put aside the costumes of their daily lives. They had shared bread. They had opened their eyes and their ears. They'd begun to hope. They dared to hope.

"What is that Gift?" He smiled. "Seeing us, and loving us, as we truly are."

SOMEONE AT THE DOOR

AT SOME late hour of the following night, in the dream country, Polycarp found himself standing in a city populated by the innumerable starving dead and smoldering with crumbled buildings. With nothing to feed their hunger, no living flesh on which to gnaw, the dead jammed every road and every alley in the Subura; they lurched against each other in their thousand thousands. Never had he faced so many.

They pressed against the walls of the villa in which Polycarp took refuge, a villa with white walls and a pleasant garden in its atrium, high on the Palatine above the ruin of the earth. The door was shut against them, but the pounding of their bodies on the heavy cypress wood was loud, rhythmic, constant. The door rattled and shook, leaping in its hinges. Polycarp took a step toward the door and hesitated, his heart pounding. He did not want to face those lurching, clawing dead; his palms were sweating.

Yet the moaning of so many beings torn from life and torn from death—their suffering called to him. He could not stand idle at the sound of such misery.

He groaned and looked up, and, startled, he found the garden gone; instead he stood in a wheat field, the same field he'd known as a child in Thessaly, in Greece. That alerted him. There was some reason why he was here, some message. Something he must pay attention to.

The wheat was high above his head. The stalks tossed in the hissing of the wind, pressing against his body; behind him, distant yet too near, he heard the low wailing of the dead. He shivered, then began to *move*; he kept glancing at the sky, looking for something—he couldn't remember what. The sky was unhelpful, as gray as the unclean flesh of the dead. The very sky and earth were defiled.

There were faint voices far behind him, like a wind coming— and sharp, crackling sounds. He glanced over his shoulder and found that fire crackled through the wheat; soon smoke billowed about him, thick and choking. For a while he ran from the flames, rushing through the wheat as fear-maddened as a rhinoceros in the Colosseum; his sides burned, there wasn't enough air for his lungs. He stumbled and, in that instant, saw on a head of wheat before his eyes a small red beetle, its wings out though it stayed perched.

He stood still, his eyes fixed on that spot of color in the gray wheat.

He fought for breath.

There were noises behind him like beasts crashing through the wheat; a dark shadow rushed past him on the left. He forced himself to look away from the beetle. Glancing behind, he saw the wheat and the sky red with flame and, dark against the flame, running men and women, some of them on fire. Their hair and their clothes burning as they ran, so that they seemed angels in the instant of their fall, messengers of the world's end. They rushed toward him and past him. The reek of scorched hair and flesh hit his nostrils with a shock. The dead were back there as well, in the wheat; he could hear their moaning. Perhaps the walking corpses also were already burning, even as they hunted.

The red beetle. He had to follow it; it had always led him before. Its wings were out; yet it stayed perched. How could that be? This burning field where the dead and the living went up like torches in the wheat could *not* be where he was meant to be. Here he would burn, or be devoured.

He tore his eyes from the fire to look again to the beetle. Turning, he found himself staring—with shock—into the eyes of his master. Felt the master's hands on his shoulders, stopping him. "Stand, Polycarp," the Anointed One said.

———

Polycarp bolted awake on his pallet and rolled to his side. His bedclothes stuck to him with his sweat. He gasped for air, then got his elbows and knees under him and pushed himself up, ignoring the groan and cry of his aged body. Stand. A true dream—that had felt like a true dream. And the beetle had been it, emblem of truth.

Panting, he got to his feet. The scent of burning wheat and flesh still stung his nostrils.

A clamor at the door. Knocking. It sounded so loud in his ears. He pushed away the last trailing horrors of his dream, drew a blanket like a shawl about his shoulders, and stumbled to his door, which opened on the insula's narrow atrium. He pulled it open with a yank that nearly sprained his wrist.

"Marcus?" He squinted against the light from the oil lamp the youth held. "What is it, child?"

"Julia's gone!" His eyes were wide. "She must've left before we locked the insula, and—"

"Where's Regina?" With the dream still lingering in the dark behind him, and his joints screeching their anguish inside him, Polycarp couldn't keep the sharpness from his tone.

"I'll get her, father—"

"I'm here." The small, short woman called from her open door. She was in her nightdress, but she looked alert as she stepped out among the atrium's grasses and lilacs.

Above them, on the second, third, and fourth stories, a few faces peeked from their windows. Polycarp swallowed his alarm. "Quietly, daughter. Come inside."

Regina came to the door he held open, and they both entered. Marcus set the lamp on the bare floor by Polycarp's pallet, then knelt. Regina shut the door quietly, and the moment the door snicked shut, Marcus began talking, swiftly, as though to make a wall against fear, a wall made out of words. "There are so few of us. And now they'll know where we are, and they'll come, and—"

Polycarp lifted his hand. "Marcus, go to the larder." In the face of this peril, they would need courage and a strong reminder of who they were. "Bring me tomorrow's eucharist."

Marcus nodded jerkily, jumped to his feet. In a moment he'd vanished through Polycarp's one other door, which opened on a surprisingly well-stocked larder. It was possibly the only well-stocked larder in the Subura, and in a very real sense it was Polycarp's life work. Any coin that fell into Polycarp's hands, he soon translated into bread and meal to sustain the population of this midsized insula, as well as the hungry who came knocking at the door sometimes at dusk, offering their labor in return for food—or simply pleading.

Polycarp rubbed his temples for a moment. "What has happened, daughter?" He feared he already knew.

"Julia is gone. She informed. Marcus and I are sure of it." She spoke tersely. She often did. Her dark hair she wore in a bun, and she paid little heed to cosmetics, which in any case she did not need: she was without doubt the most striking woman Polycarp had ever seen. To apply no kohl to her eyelids belied her Eastern heritage, but she wished little remembrance of the past, either of her own person or of her people. Her years in Rome before Polycarp found her had been years of suffering, and from them she had learned to dread wearing signs of her beauty.

Polycarp took in her words now with reluctance and fatigue. Informed. Such things had happened before. But not in this insula.

"Father, at first we thought the dead took her."

He looked at her sharply.

She nodded. "There were dead in the alley on the insula's north side, earlier. Six of them. They were—*feeding*—on one of the crossroads brothers. One of the brothers!" She paled as she spoke of it. "You didn't see them, father, it was during your noon rest. They—they were tearing—things—entrails—out of his belly, and—" She paused.

He gave her time to gather herself; he folded his hands and prayed with his eyes open, his lips pressed together. Vivid before his eyes were the wasted cities and the fire in the grain. The empty houses where the dead waited behind silent windows, and no living things breathed or moved.

He would *not* let that world come to be. When the last day came and the sky rolled back at the sound of a trumpet, it must be the living, and not the dead, who lifted their arms and greeted his master's return.

This year, Polycarp had often come upon one or two dead in the streets and done what he could. A hush always fell when Polycarp confronted one of the shambling corpses, and afterward the citizens of the Subura parted to let the father pass, their eyes warm with awe. Polycarp had been watchful since the losses of the last winter. Seven or eight dead had attacked another insula, one farther upriver, where the holy widows kept their chastity and their own larder for the feeding of Rome's abandoned—particularly the Subura's children, the many without mothers. Breaking through the doors, the dead had overwhelmed the few who'd sprung up to defend the widows: a slave wielding a broom, a few unarmed patrician youths who had taken to visiting the Subura to aid the widows, and an elderly woman who took up a knife from the kitchen and barred its entrance, growling as loudly as the dead themselves. The dead had bitten many that night; Caius Lucius's guardsmen had not been far behind, burning the insula and several others near it, with the dead and the living within. During the assault and the torching, the guardsmen had found at least one youth from the upper castes there, which had frightened them. They hired informants now, seeking to know who in the Subura was speaking with people of the hill slopes.

Polycarp took a deep breath. The holy widows had been a community of mercy; their loss was a deep wound, one that hadn't really closed.

And now things appeared to be getting worse. A *crossroads brother* had been overwhelmed. Had been eaten. Not by one or two dead, but by six. Perhaps the crossroads brothers had left too many streets unwatched—those streets where the landlords of the Subura, who were themselves starving men, could no longer pay the brotherhoods' fees. With a chill, Polycarp wondered how many dead were walking out there.

"It is something I never wish to witness again," Regina said quietly. "Vergilius wanted to fight the dead, and Marcus wished to wake you, but I stopped them."

"You should have wakened me," Polycarp said quietly. Faintly, he heard Marcus opening cupboards in the larder.

Regina looked down, hiding her eyes.

Polycarp sighed. "You mustn't fear as much for me, or for the insula, Regina. We have to fear for the people—out there. Now those dead will be elsewhere, feeding. We cannot simply let them wander on, restless and devouring and unreprieved. If we do that, why are we here?"

Regina gave one brisk nod. "I'm sorry," she said.

"Tell me the rest, daughter."

Regina took a breath. "When we realized there were dead in the alley, we set a watch at the door. Piscus didn't come home. So we checked the rooms. All of them. I got the key and opened up their apartment, and neither of them were there, but their larder had been emptied, and many of their clothes were gone. They left," she finished simply.

Polycarp swore under his breath. Marcus would have looked shocked if he'd been able to hear from the larder, but Regina did not. She did look shaken, and pale. Polycarp reached for her and grasped her arm, putting as much strength into his voice as he could manage. "We will move, daughter. It is not the first time."

"We've grown too big to move." Her voice was very quiet.

"Nevertheless—" He stopped.

Clear in his ears he heard the words from his dream.

Stand, Polycarp.

He clutched his shawl tighter about his shoulders. Was *this* what the Anointed One had meant? That he must *not* move? If so, he could well imagine what fire was coming—the fire of execution pyres, lit by Roman guardsmen. His lips thinned. The red beetle had settled in the burning wheat. He had never ignored it before.

But in the dream, there had been *many* burning. Who else would suffer?

He thought of Julia's sharp voice and Piscus's silent manner and the large eyes that had earned him his nickname, Fish. *Ah, Julia, Piscus, why?*

"You are right," he said. "If they informed, then guardsmen may be here tonight, or in the morning. We cannot move everyone in that time, not without doing it visibly. And if there are still dead near the insula, it would be dangerous to try to move so many. We must stand whatever is coming." He looked to the larder, listened for a moment to the rattling of wood as Marcus fetched the communion cup. Marcus was so young. They were all so young.

"I have feared this day," Polycarp murmured.

"Father." Regina's voice was low, urgent. "We can't know what Julia and Piscus have told them, whose names were reported. Maybe the Romans know only that there are some of us here. We can burn or bury the scrolls, and the cup—"

"No," Polycarp growled. "If some of us are to burn, let us do it as who we are. Without the cup and the breaking of bread, we are nothing."

Regina seemed about to say something, but whatever it was she held back, for Marcus returned from the larder with a small basket and a flask of wine. The aroma of baked bread was faint, for the bread was a day old. Still, it was *this* bread, and the scent nourished Polycarp. His senses sprung awake at last.

"We are not crossroads brothers," he said. "We desire not Roman *pax*, order and safety, but *eirene*, peace: lives woven together into a fabric beautiful and tough that cannot be torn or unraveled." He sighed. "Julia didn't understand that." He considered Regina. "You and she were close," he said.

Regina glanced up. "Not close." She appeared to be choosing her words with care. "We shared a—a few words, sometimes. Neither of us had children. I worried for her." She closed her eyes a moment, then opened them, and they were hard. "Now she is gone, and we are still here."

"Yes. We are still here," Polycarp agreed. "Come. Let's set aside our fear and our grief, for a while." He glanced at Marcus, and the youth hesitated, then handed him the basket he held. He held the youth's eyes a moment, saw his fear under tight but fragile control. Young Marcus. Polycarp had grown fond of this fearful but desperately earnest boy. Less than a year ago, the youth had woken them all by pounding on the door of the insula. An illegitimate scion of one of the great families on the Palatine and raised among almost unspeakable wealth and privilege, in his boredom Marcus had fallen in with one of the rowdier bands of Palatine youths and gone carousing in the Subura for a lark, the night before he came to the insula; somehow he'd become separated from the others. Whatever had happened to him afterward, or whatever he'd seen, it left him shaken and changed. When Polycarp opened the door that next morning and saw the youth standing there disheveled, his face smudged with dirt and sweat, the young patrician blurted: "I am Marcus Antonius Caelius. They tell me you are trying to help Rome—make her better than she is. Even the Subura. I want to help."

Polycarp had blinked at the boy, only half awake. The name was known to him, and he was having difficulty understanding the youth's purpose in standing at his threshold. The boy was clad in a finely made toga, the regalia of a patrician, its elegant folds speaking of dignity, its white color speaking of an ancestry that the patricians chose to believe was in part divine. This whiteness could be achieved only by bleaching the cloth with urine collected by fullers from the Subura's inhabitants, an irony that occurred at least to Polycarp, though perhaps not to many patricians, whose slaves took the togas to the fullers' shops and brought them back so that no patrician ever had to smell the urine of his inferiors. Only by using the forgotten castes and keeping that use invisible could the patricians maintain the illusion that donning a toga conferred on them the dignity and half divinity they wished for, or that the performance of walking the Forum in their togas was anything more than just that—a performance.

In any case, Marcus's toga may have been an immaculate, patrician white the day before, but now the cloth was smeared with the grime of a night spent in the Subura, stained with a reality that had become, overnight, terribly visible to him.

Polycarp considered the boy. "How do you wish to help?"

Marcus just shook his head, as though bewildered at himself. "Just—help. I don't care how. However you need."

"Can you repair broken walls?"

"No."

"Can you cook?"

"No."

"Can you weave or sew?"

"No."

Polycarp looked the boy over. His skin was soft; possibly he had never even dressed himself. But he had no slaves with him now. "If I hand you some of our scarce funds," the father said quietly, "can you go to the market near the Fulvian Cistern each day and bring back bread and wine, and any fruit that doesn't look too rotten?"

The boy flushed. "That is a slave's work!"

"Yes, it is." Polycarp regarded him without letting his face show his mood. "We are all slaves here, young Marcus. Slaves of the One God who wishes to repair a broken city and bring peace to the living and the dead. He has bought us, we are his."

Marcus gazed inward for a long moment, and then something passed across his eyes. "I don't mind it." His tone went solemn. "The work. I won't mind it. All my life, I've been hungry—so hungry for my life to mean something. I think down here it might. Last night there was a—a *child*—starving. Her ribs—" Helplessness in his eyes; he wasn't able to get the words out.

"I'll send someone for her," Polycarp said softly.

"I don't think they'll find her." His hands were shaking. "She ran from me. She isn't there anymore."

Something ached in Polycarp, seeing the appeal in the boy's eyes. In their own way, the men and the women of the Palatine needed his larder and the teaching of the apostles, no less than the famished lives in the Subura did. Those who fed no one could feel as empty, as unfull, as those whom no one fed. As Polycarp swung the door wider and stepped to the side, a light of gratitude lit in Marcus's eyes.

"Come in, Marcus," Polycarp told him, "and tell us what you saw."

"Father." Marcus's voice was low as Polycarp took the basket. "The guardsmen might be on the way, even now."

Polycarp considered that as he lifted the cover of the basket and drew out a soft loaf. The bread was no longer warm from the oven that it must have left that afternoon; it was cool to the touch. "They might be, Marcus. But the Romans tend to do their violence in the open, by sunlight. In any case, our God is the same at night as he is in the day. I think we should remember that."

He lifted the bread high in both hands, though his hands shook and he couldn't keep them still. He prayed silently a moment, then murmured for the others to hear, "We who live do not nourish the dead. Our dead nourish us. On the night of his death, Yeshua, the Anointed One, took bread and broke it." Quickly, cleanly, Polycarp tore the loaf in two. "He said, 'Take, eat, for this bread is my body.'" One half he handed to Regina, the other to Marcus. Marcus lifted the bread in both hands to his mouth and nibbled at it. Regina tore hers in half and handed one half back to Polycarp. There was a shadow in her eyes now, and

Polycarp's throat tightened. Gently, he touched her cheek with his fingertips. "Take, eat, daughter," he said softly.

She looked up, and after a moment, she nodded slightly and smiled. Though faint, her smile appeared to change her eyes to the color of a summer pool. Polycarp found himself reminded of a favorite pond of his youth, one alive with frogs and vibrant weeds and adorned on both its surface and its pebbled floor with rich sunlight. Regina lifted her bread and began eating it. Polycarp watched her eyes, and with his gnarled, bent fingers, he tore off little pieces of his own bit of bread, one after the other, and brought them to his mouth. The taste of it filled him. He wet each piece in his mouth, chewed a few times, and swallowed. He felt the softness of Regina's hand brush his—one of those small comforts a person offers another that are nevertheless mighty comforts, because they foreshadow the blessedness of the new earth that is to come.

Yet the touch troubled him. An old warmth lit in his body, one he hadn't felt in a while. He didn't know why it was kindling now—perhaps it was the sweat and dread of his dream, and his body's need to feel alive and virile. Perhaps it was because of what he'd glimpsed in Regina's eyes when she gave him that smile.

If the Romans came, he at least would be seized. Even if he were to succeed in concealing or sheltering the others, which seemed unlikely, this could be his last night as a free man. Regina appeared acutely aware of this. He saw her hands tremble. There was so much in her heart that she had never spoken aloud, so much he would not acknowledge.

He reasoned with himself as he ate. *With this bread, I take into myself the body and the sacrifice and the love of our master. He has called me to do a task, a task that has become too large for me, it is true. But if I am to stand fast and do it, I must not allow myself distractions. I must permit this woman to remain a daughter to me and not a distraction. Else I shame our master and fail this task.*

For a few moments they ate silently. Polycarp felt Regina's eyes on him, and lifting his head, he returned the gaze. She looked away. At last he reached into the basket for the skin of wine and found that with the bread in his body he had the strength to lift it; Marcus reached in and took up the little wooden cup—wooden, for their master had been a carpenter—and held it steady as the old father poured the wine. Polycarp listened to the splash of it in the cup; the scent of it filled the little room with a hint of places far beyond this life-crammed Subura—vineyards open to the sun and wind, and quiet lakes beside which berries grew. It made him smile. He corked the wineskin and placed it reverently back in the basket, and covered it. Marcus handed him the cup. Polycarp's voice was stronger now as he lifted it and spoke the words of their rite.

"And he took up the wine and blessed it, and said, 'Take, drink, for this wine is my blood, spilled for you in a new Covenant with God. Do this as often as you are together, in remembrance of me.'" Gently he lowered the rim of the cup to his lips, sipped, then handed it to Regina. Again her fingers brushed his; he felt the warmth of them. She was a little flushed, and the soul he glimpsed through her eyes was troubled with many things. Hunger for a man to hold her but also for a father to shelter her, he could see that, had always seen it, though never had it been so near the surface of her eyes as tonight, and that concerned him. But there were other things there too. Fear—understandable. And shame, which he did not understand at all. After a moment she glanced down and sipped the wine.

Polycarp considered her. Regina was the gathering's only surviving deaconess; there had been two, but the other had been seized by the Romans in the month of Mars. She was a remarkable woman; besides her beauty and the sturdiness of her spirit, she possessed an education almost unknown in the Subura, something she had acquired in her youth. She was excellent at ciphering; she held the insula (and the gathering within it) together as though she were herself the owner. During the day, Regina ministered to the poorest in their community, bringing them food and talk, hearing their stories, and carrying some of these stories back to share with Polycarp. They worked closely together, and Polycarp trusted Regina; if she said a family on the Via Claudia XII had need, he listened and did what he could to answer the need. If she said a landowner on the Via Noctis was not withholding his promised tithe out of laziness but because one of the crossroads brotherhoods had been extorting his earnings from him until his own family was near starvation, Polycarp listened and tried to exert pressure on the brotherhoods.

Polycarp was the insula's heart, and Regina was its head; yet that seemed a strange way to put it, for Regina was a most deep-hearted woman. But her life had not always been as it was now.

The first time Polycarp had seen her, he'd been walking to the market by the Fulvian Cistern and had stopped, stunned. The woman who would later be the deaconess was kneeling outside the door of a cracked and graffitied insula, her head down, her wrists fastened with rough rope to a stump of an iron post. She'd been stripped to the waist, and her back was a thicket of welts. Something deep inside Polycarp growled when he saw that, even as something very like a torch's heat lit in his loins at the sight of her nakedness. He forced himself to focus not on the sight of her breasts but on the placard that had been tied about her neck and that now rested on her shoulders. *She is a slut,* the placard read, *and I put her from my house. You may cut her loose and have her, if you leave a copper in the dish. It is what she is worth.*

A small clay cup lay on its side by the woman's knees.

Polycarp stood there for a while, reading that placard and looking at the welts on the woman's back. It was not common in Rome to beat slaves so savagely, but such things happened in the Subura. Even free women were beaten so by their husbands, by men living lives miserable and without hope; it was not uncommon to be awakened in the night by screams from a nearby tenement. But then, one woke often to screams of murder or rape in the streets below one's windows, or stepped over a body at one's threshold in the morning to walk to the market. This was the Subura. Guardsmen rarely came here, and only the crossroads brotherhoods kept any real order.

This was a part of Rome where people who wished to hide hid in plain sight.

Polycarp moved across the street warily, uncertain it was wise to attract attention. He stood by the woman. She did not look up.

"What is your name, daughter?"

Her shoulders jerked when he called her that. Still, she did not look up. "Dora," she whispered. "Dora Syriacae."

His heart ached at the edge of defiance he heard under her whisper.

"Syriacae," he said. "This is a long way from Syria."

She was silent for a moment. Then she took a deep breath. "The master of this insula bought me from flesh thieves."

She was a pleasure slave then, and had no doubt been bought for the master's enjoyment or his sons'. "Why were you beaten, daughter?" he asked softly.

Her shoulders trembled briefly, and her voice rasped with pain and fear. "A tenant kissed me—touched me. Grabbed me as I walked by." She closed her eyes. "The master saw."

Her welts were many, and around them all the skin of her back was discolored. It must hurt her even to breathe. An ache and a discomfort grew in Polycarp's breast. It was clear to him what needed to be done. With the toe of his sandal he nudged the cup upright, and the ring of the coin against its clay interior brought the woman's head up, her eyes wide with hope and fear. Hope, because she clearly could not stay where she was, and who knew how long the master would leave her bound to that post, rejected, if no one bought her? Fear, because the beating you have already received is a known quantity, and a new master might be more cruel.

"You are Regina Romae," Polycarp said softly. "You have suffered too much under your old name, and it seems Rome, not Syria, is now your home. I ask you to put your old name away. Regina is a better one, I think, and you have a queen's strength, that is clear to me."

Her eyes searched him. "Am I yours?" she asked after a moment, and her voice broke.

"No." Polycarp sighed. "You are God's. It is his coin I have dropped into that cup, and he has bought you. As he bought me, a very long time ago. Though that was a different slavery, and a different coin that released me. Come." He bent and slipped a knife from beneath his tunic. Swiftly he cut the rope from her wrists. He spoke in a low voice, trying to ignore her soft breath near his face and the way it affected him. "No man owns you. You are free. I would be glad to give you a place to stay, if you need one. But you are no property of mine."

He took Regina's hands in his, chafing her wrists. She winced, and a cry escaped her lips. He wished to weep for her. He took his cloak and put it about her shoulders; it was heavy wool from the flocks of Transalpine Gaul and would have cost him much to purchase had it not been a gift. It was far too warm a garment for a summer in Rome, but other than in the middle of Augustus, Polycarp felt always a little chilled, however hot the day. Now Regina pressed her lips together tightly as the coarse wool brushed the welts on her back; tears started at her eyes. Yet she gave Polycarp a look of gratitude that was naked in its intensity, and she held it closed over her breasts, concealing herself. Polycarp nodded and lifted her to her feet. He was not a woman, but he could well understand the desire to hide from demanding eyes. He held her tightly until he was certain her legs were steady, and she made no protest.

"I will take the name Regina," she whispered, and suddenly Polycarp felt her small body shaking within the wool cloak. "Am I truly freed?"

"Yes." Polycarp took her shoulders in his hands and stepped back, looking at her face.

He did not offer to bring her to a clerk to get citizenship papers, nor did she ask. This was the Subura. No one had papers. Regina's eyes were looking elsewhere, into some other place. She was alone, he realized. Entirely alone, and realizing it. Polycarp simply held her shoulders, hoping the firmness of his hands would comfort her in her solitude.

She closed her eyes after a while. She might have been praying; her lips moved softly.

"I will come to your insula," she said.

"Good," he smiled. "There is an empty first-floor room that no one wants, because there was once a ghost there. But it is gone now, and restful, though no one will believe it. If that doesn't frighten you, you can stay there for a time. The rent I will attend to myself, until the next month. We will use the time finding you employment. I assure you, I am exceptionally good at finding things for people to do."

She stiffened. Her eyes took on a look of panic and, behind the panic, a gray shadow that Polycarp knew too well. Despair.

"No," he said quietly, and he put his arm about her and began walking her back up the street toward the insula. His trip to the market could wait. He whispered words for her ears alone, though others brushed by them in the street. His knife he still held unsheathed in his hand, and no one molested them as they walked. "No," he said, "I am not looking for a pleasure slave myself."

"Why are you doing this?" she whispered.

He glanced at her face. Considered telling her it was as his master would want. But that was not really a true answer. He might have passed her by if she had been some other slave. He sacrificed mightily for the people in his insula, both those of the gathering and those who were not—but he followed a strict policy of minding his own matters when he was out in the Subura. He pursed his lips a moment, then told her the truth, or as much of it as he knew. "I never had a daughter, or a wife. Even a sister. You might have been her. I thought of that when I saw you."

"But I am none of those." An edge of bitterness.

"No." He shook his head. "No, you aren't. Nor anything else I might want you to be. Whoever it is that you are, you may reveal it to me or not, with time, as you choose. Your body also is yours to conceal, or reveal to one who suits you. You may keep the cloak."

They walked silently for a while. When they reached the door of the insula, she glanced up at him, and he found that her eyes stirred things in him.

"Are you kind," she asked gently, "like an old grandfather—or are you only mad?"

"I have no idea. But doubtless one of those is true." He touched her cheek and smiled, and then stepped through the door, leaving it up to her whether to follow.

———

Now Polycarp settled back, folding his hands across his chest, and watched as Regina and Marcus shared the cup. What was going on with Regina tonight? It was rare to see her so unsettled or to see the desires of her heart shown so nakedly in her eyes. Marcus he understood: the boy was terrified, though now that he had eaten and sipped and shared in the Covenant, his face was calmer. But Regina—

Again he pressed his lips together tightly. Had his daughter had some part, unknowingly, in Julia's falling away? He couldn't imagine what that part that might be, but plainly something was profoundly awake in Regina's heart—and just as plainly, she was loosing the latches that she usually kept locked tight over her desire for him. He suspected that she had never fully reconciled in her own heart whether to approach Polycarp as a daughter or a lover, and she had kept her feelings under tight discipline. Now there were guardsmen coming for Polycarp, to take him from the insula, likely to suffer a painful death. They might not see each other again; indeed, the last moment might be this very breaking of bread, this drinking of wine. If there was something she must say, this could be the last moment to say it. He looked again at her eyes, and the plea he saw there pulled at his heart. Marcus didn't notice; he was looking at the door, perhaps wrestling down the last of his fears. Polycarp coughed and straightened. It was time to bring them all back to their task and sense of mission—himself included. Their strength must survive his death.

"My children," he rumbled, "our master calls us to repair what is broken, to heal what is ill, to bring good word to the despairing, to reclaim all that is lost." He drew in a ragged breath, for the pain in his hands was sharper now. "Our master wishes us to stand fast, no matter the peril, no matter how many fall away." He felt the bread in his belly, felt the comfort of it. "It is possible that when the guardsmen come, they will empty the insula. But it is also possible that they will be looking for me, and that when they find me they will not look too hard for others. We are already a city within this City. They will look for a Caesar. They likely know my name. But I am not our Caesar, who lives now in a heavenly city and not in this one. My arrest will change nothing." His voice hardened. "Marcus, there is an empty cellar beneath the larder.

The entry is cunningly disguised—you must look beneath the barrel of olive oil. Look where I have scratched the fish, and it will be apparent to you. I had it made after the raid on the widows."

"We won't abandon you."

"But you will heed me." Polycarp's voice hardened. "You will protect your brothers and sisters. Crowd into the cellar with those on the first and second floors. Those on the upper stories must pray. It is possible the Romans may tire of searching empty rooms and depart swiftly." He smiled grimly. "They will, after all, have found their 'Caesar.'"

"We should have you in the cellar," Marcus protested. "If it is you they are looking for, they will spend all their effort searching for you and take little heed of the rest of us. If we—"

A scuffling in the alley interrupted him. His head jerked up; he listened. Regina turned white. Marcus gasped. "They're here!" Every line in the boy's body was tense. If Roman guardsmen burst through that door now—at this moment—they would find them all unprepared, unhidden, sitting with the wine and the bread.

The very air in the room went cold and sharp with fear.

Polycarp growled low in his throat. Part of him had been waiting to hear this sound all night, he realized, ever since waking at Marcus's knock with his mind still caught in that dream. "Listen, Marcus. God gave you better ears than that."

There was no sound of marching in the alley, no clink of metal.

"The undead," Regina whispered.

Marcus jumped to his feet. Polycarp rose more slowly, stood unsteadily, and might have fallen, but Regina caught him, and he leaned on her for an instant before straightening, embarrassed. His body cried out for his bed. He was too old for the demands of this night. Yet he was the father of this gathering; he was the only one who could answer them.

He looked to the door, the outer door. The scraping of feet—many feet—half-dragged along stones outside. A thump and then a slide along the wall. Somewhere to the right, the sound of nails scratching against rock. For a long moment they listened to the sounds, hearts beating. Somewhere up the alley outside, a low moan. Polycarp heard Regina suck in her breath.

For a moment more the shock of it held them. This was not a visitation by one or two dead, or even by the pack Regina had spoken of. Perhaps that pack had lurched back into the alley again, but there were more of them now. Polycarp couldn't tell from the sounds how many, but surely more than ten. And these dead knew that there were living here—that moan confirmed it. Perhaps their voices had been heard through the door. Perhaps something else had drawn them to the alley. It didn't matter; they were here now.

"Father, don't!" Marcus whispered.

Polycarp had moved to the door. Now he turned. "Marcus, Regina." He stopped a moment, uncertain what to say. "What do you believe, Marcus? What do we know to be true? Nothing is broken that cannot be remade. Nothing is ill that cannot be healed, nothing captive that cannot be freed. That is what he taught us. I am going through that door, my son."

He gripped the boy's shoulder, saw both worship and fear in his eyes. They were the eyes of a young man witnessing his father at the brink of a cliff confronting harpies of Greek legend, and half the desire of his heart was to hide behind a boulder, and the other half was to grab his father by the shoulders and pull him back from the peril. Yet his eyes were dazed with the knowledge that were he to do so, he would lessen his father.

"Either I can meet them at the door, young Marcus," Polycarp told him, "or I can wait for them to break through. Except that they might not break through. They might go down to our neighbor's door. And that would be intolerable." He thought for a moment. "Go to the other rooms. Wake them, warn them, bring those you can to the cellar." That task was not too much for the boy's courage, he decided, and he would feel courageous doing it.

Marcus nodded once and, turning, almost bolted out of the room. After a moment Polycarp heard the inner door creak open and then shut. He drew in a breath, faced Regina.

She stood there with her face a mask of inexpressible pain, like one of the masks Attican actors wear in a tragedy.

"Ah, Regina," he rumbled, "please don't defy me in this. Either throw open that door, or move aside and stand behind me."

"Father, there are too many. Too many." Her voice was low and intense. "You'll be eaten!"

"Enough," he growled. "Move aside."

She sucked in her breath. "Wait." She pressed herself quickly to him, her arms going around his neck and her lips finding his. With a shock, he felt the softness of her breasts pressed to him under her tunic, the warmth of her. Her kiss was open mouthed, passionate, desperate. She smelled of love and fear. An unwelcome fire lit in his loins and spread to all his flesh.

Carefully he took her arms in his hands and detached himself from her, pushing her gently back.

"Be careful," she whispered, her eyes too full to look at.

"Regina," he whispered back. "Daughter."

Her eyes grew moist at the word. Frowning, Polycarp bent and took up the lamp of rancid oil. He held it high by his ear, just a little back so the flame would not obscure his vision. As he straightened, the taste of the sacrificial wine and the taste of Regina's kiss were still sweet in his mouth. He threw the latch on the door.

The alley was *filled* with dead. The light of the lamp Polycarp held brought them out of the dark, showing the gashes and bites in their gray skin in stark detail. For a moment his hand shook, and the light guttered. The dead slouched and slid along the wall of the insula toward him; several milling at the outlet to the Via Aquae Bruneae turned their heads with unnatural slowness, and their eyes reflected back the lamp. Their mouths opened, filling the alley with the low groaning of their hunger.

Never had he faced so many.

He sucked in his breath. That thought was so similar to his dream that it froze him. He stood in the door.

"*Father*!" Regina cried.

"Take the lamp," he muttered, and held it out to her without taking his eyes from the street. He felt the brush of her hand. Then the weight of the lamp was gone, and its light behind him cast his shadow, vast and dark, over a shuffling, broad-shouldered figure as it lurched in front of him and almost into him.

We must live lives of *unstoppable* hope, Polycarp told himself. That was the only way. Even if we cannot see above the wheat. Even here, in this place, where the walls of cramped buildings obscured people's sight of each other and of God's open sky and God's near presence no less completely than might the wind-tossed stalks of a harvest field. Even here, we must hope.

Polycarp clenched his teeth and stepped forward, lifting his hands, one gripping the corpse's throat, the other taking it by the shoulder. Others closed around him, their hands grasping at his clothes, their mouths reaching for him in a hunger too profound and unanswerable for them to voice it in any sound more articulate than the moaning that rose, breathy and loud, from deep in their bellies.

BRITTLE LIVES

SEVERAL MINUTES later, the dead lay about Polycarp crumpled and still, at least twenty of them, the flickering light of the oil lamp casting wild and careening shadows across their slack faces. The father swayed on his feet, like a tree chopped near the root; then he toppled and lay with his forehead to the stones. Regina let out a cry from the door to Polycarp's chamber, and the oil lamp she held tumbled from her hand and shattered in fragments of clay; the light went out, and everything in the alley was dark, the dead reduced to silhouettes. She froze, her hand whitened where she clutched the door.

She called to him softly. "Father!"

She heard him groan in the dark; the sound of it went right to her heart. As her eyes stung with tears, she ran from the door, darting up the alley to where he'd fallen, the grimed and smeared surface cold against her bare feet. She stumbled over the body of one of the dead and cried out, then caught herself on her hands. Everything in her blood screamed at her to run, before the thing she touched could twist and seize her ankle in its hard, inescapable jaws.

She had the sense, the terrible sense, that those dead might stand again, at any moment. But they lay still, they all lay still.

Crawling forward, shaking, she found Polycarp prone on the ground and knelt by him, taking him quickly in her arms. His chest was moving; he still breathed. Gently she ran her fingers over his face, his throat, his arms; he wasn't bleeding, he hadn't been bitten. But he made no response when she whispered, "Father, father." She clutched him fiercely to her, and her eyes burned. Overcome with the terror of the alley and the wonder of what she'd seen.

It had happened so fast, so fast. The corpse at the door had fallen, slipping to the side of the threshold, and Polycarp had stepped over it into the alley to confront the others, moving as unhesitantly as though he were walking to the market. Regina had stood in the door, fighting her own urge to hide, unwilling to leave him. Her lips still warm from kissing him, her heart in turmoil. She had never seen him use the Apostle's Gift before, and she hadn't seen what he'd done to the corpse at the door; it'd been hidden by Polycarp's back. She'd gazed out into the alley in the wavering light of the oil lamp, and she couldn't breathe for wonder.

Polycarp had moved among the dead with an intensity and grace, as though he were dancing. He laid his hand on each one, as gently as a parent blessing a son or a daughter. Each time he touched one's shoulder or its head, he gazed into its eyes. The first time, Regina gasped to see a living spirit flood back into those murky, dead eyes. For a moment a middle-aged woman gazed out through the eyes of the corpse, her eyes raw with regret and remembered pain. Polycarp held the woman's gaze a brief moment; then she let out a slow sigh and crumpled to the stones of the street.

Polycarp did that with each of them, his eyes deep with sorrow. He seemed to have no fear. One grasped his shoulder, pulling him back; he touched its hand and glanced back at it, and then a young man was gazing back at him. The man breathed a soft moan—not the hunger moan of the prowling dead, but the exhaustion-and-relief moan of a man letting go of a burden too long carried. With that sound he slipped to the earth and lay still, no breath stirring inside his gashed-open and half-eaten chest. One of the dead had gone for Polycarp's throat; he had caught the thing's neck in his hand and looked steadily into its eyes. Even as that one slid to the earth, two others seized upon Polycarp's arm, pulling him toward their teeth; the father simply touched them both on the head, looking in the eyes of one, then the other, as if witnessing and accepting each one's confession, in no more time than it would have taken to shout. As though each one's spirit had been bound deep within its body with chains of hunger and was now released at Polycarp's touch, escaping the body in a death sigh.

Regina had trembled as she watched from the door, her heart beating with a purely animal fear at the nearness of the dead; she could neither swing the door shut nor step through it. At the extremity of her fear, her face darkened with shame and anger. She was no Roman patrician bred on milk and water, to tumble from her chair at the first sight of something unsavory. Of Rome she may be, but of the Subura, where knives, not gossip, flashed across dinner tables. And her ancestry was Syrian, of a people whose bones were strong as the bones of the hills in which they lived. She bore old lines on her back, a savage record of what could be witnessed and what could be survived. The oil lamp shook as Regina's hand trembled, but she did *not* faint.

Now it was over. Her gorge heaved at the reek of the dead around them. In the dark of the alley where she knelt with the dead motionless about her, as restful as the bodies on their shelves in the Catacombs, Regina laid Polycarp gently to the stones and rested his head on her lap. Polycarp's head felt light, too light. The sight of his face shocked her, and she stared at him, the defiled dead abruptly forgotten.

In less time than a Roman hour, new wrinkles and crevasses had been carved into his cheeks, deeply, as though a sculptor had attacked his flesh with a chisel and a fine-edged knife. The skin about his eyes was sunken, and the shadows of the alley turned his face into an ancestral mask, an image of the ancient and honored fathers. His eyes were closed.

He looked old—*truly* old, for the first time.

"Father," she whispered, holding his head between her hands.

He hadn't been bitten.

He was alive.

He stirred slightly and began to murmur under his breath. He took no notice of her. His lips moved soundlessly and swiftly in prayer.

Something opened within her, a great well of helplessness, and she stood at the edge but refused to topple in. Squeezing her eyes shut against tears that she utterly rescinded and denied, she rocked slowly, caressing Polycarp's dry cheek with her hand. After a moment his lips stilled. His chest rose and fell. She drew in a breath, wondering if he was asleep. He looked it. Surely he had earned his sleep. She held his head, forgetful of the dead who had attacked or the Roman guardsmen who might. Caring only for this man, her father and her refuge, whom the night had nearly destroyed. She felt a little less fragile, seeing him sleep.

She had watched him sleep once before. On the first night after she'd been freed, the night when she'd discovered that she was still capable of loving. At first that had been a terrible night;

she'd lain awake on her cot shaking, her gaze fixed on the ceiling with its peeling paint. Everything had felt alien to her—the air in the room, the mattress beneath her back (thin, yet far better than what she was accustomed to—and clean, it was *clean*), the even thinner light from the window looking out on the atrium. The father, she knew, slept on the other side of the wall; once, she heard him rise and move about. She stiffened then, certain that everything she'd heard and seen and felt that day had been only delusion, as she'd feared, and that in a moment the old man would come to her with dry, grasping hands and demand what all men demand. But he only paced back and forth in his little room, and after a while she heard mumbling—words too soft to make out, if words they were. Perhaps he was talking to himself, or to his God. Then the sounds stopped, and there was silence. She dared not move.

As she lay there, an agony of suspense and a horror of that silence took hold of her, until her palms were sweating. At last she couldn't bear it; she got quietly to her feet and went to the wall. Pressed her ear to the plaster. Listened. She could hear each distinct beat of her own heart. She could hear the oceanic song of her own blood. But nothing else. No footfall, no stuttering snore. She bit her lip, holding back an urge to cry out, to shriek, to hear what reaction her cry would bring. In her nightshirt she tiptoed to the door—the inner door that opened on the insula's cramped but lush garden atrium. With a gentle push she swung the door open, grateful that its hinges were well oiled. She slipped out, pressed her body to the wall between her door and the father's. Her heart pounding. Searching the higher windows with wide eyes, her shoulders tensed with memory of the beatings that followed an excursion from one's cot.

But the night was quiet. A crescent moon had just risen over the roof of the insula; its light lay soft as milk on the leaves and closed buds of the garden. All the windows were darkened and silent; unlike the home of her former master, this was not a place that encouraged carousing after dark. Unable to keep her hands from shaking, Regina slid along the wall to Polycarp's door, hesitated, then touched her fingers to its handle. There was no window to peer into; only the door permitted any sight of Polycarp's chamber. Now her heart was violent in her breast, her mouth was dry. Praying that Polycarp had the hinges on *all* his doors oiled, she nudged the door open and slipped in.

She saw his shape—surprisingly small in the dark—curled on the pallet inside. Like a small boy, his knees drawn up near his chin. A blanket tossed aside and rumpled, but still tangled about one foot as though spurned in the anguish of a sudden dream. She'd left the door open a crack, and a thin line of moonlight lay across Polycarp's legs.

He was sleeping. Just sleeping.

The whole earth seemed to slide out from beneath Regina's feet; she felt as though she were falling from a great height. Slowly she lowered herself to her knees, hardly breathing. She kept her gaze fixed on the outline of the man on his pallet, on the slow rise and fall of his breath. He hadn't stirred when she entered; he didn't stir now. Whatever dreams had visited him, he'd dealt with them in silence, without outcry, and was now at rest.

Regina sat, drew up her own knees, hugged herself tightly. Everything that had happened this day—it was too much for her. Only this morning, she had been shivering in the street, her mind lashed by the pain of the welts on her back, by the shame of her nakedness. Waiting only for the next one who would use her. Now she watched this old man breathe. Her eyes were adjusting again to the dimness, after the moonlight; she could see his face, softened by sleep. He was not so old, not truly; whatever he had witnessed in life had carved savage lines about his eyes and lips prematurely, even as what she'd witnessed had left her own back marked.

He had demanded nothing of her this day. Nor had the few others she'd met in the insula. A younger man who lived on the second story had assessed her for a few moments with his eyes, but as he might assess a woman he wished to court, not one he wished to purchase. That had been a new and exhilarating and frightening moment for her, but this moment terrified her far more. She'd never sat beside a man who demanded nothing of her. That realization hit her fully now; she trembled in the dark. Drawing a shuddering breath, she reached back, ran her fingertips over the welts between her shoulders. She could feel them even through her nightdress; the soreness of her skin lit with fresh fire at her own cautious touch, and her face twisted in pain.

What was she?

What would it mean for her, to be the kind of woman who could relate to a man who demanded nothing of her?

She thought of women of the Subura she'd seen in the streets. Some were broken and pitiable, or small and wretched, but others walked proudly, though the clothes they wore were threadbare and little better than those of the slaves that worked in their homes. They walked proudly because some at least of their time they could devote to things of their own making or their own choosing.

Some few of them had never been beaten.

This day, she'd taken a new name, a free woman's name. When she was a child, her parents had named her Theodora, a "gift from the gods"; the slavers who'd abducted her kept the name but raped it of its intended meaning, using it instead to emphasize her body's beauty when they brought her to a private sale. The master who purchased her there shortened the name to Dora, tearing away syllables even as he tore away her history and the last of her childhood. Dora was a brief name, a diminutive name, a slave's name; it simply meant "a gift." As a slave, she was property. She might be gifted to whomever her master pleased; she could not gift herself.

But Polycarp had freed her and asked that she take the name Regina. "Queen," it meant, a giver of gifts: no longer a gift but a giver, and one who might give herself where she chose. The meaning of it did a violence in her heart: what would it mean to live in fulfillment of this new name? She no longer knew what she was.

The gentle strength of this sleeping man was unfamiliar and frightening; she didn't know how to respond to him. For the first time in several years, a thousand memories of her childhood home flooded into her, moments of tenderness from her grandfather and her mother, before the flesh thieves had stolen her away. Father Polycarp had touched her cheek this day, after wrapping a cloak about her in the street; her grandfather used to do that, when she was a little girl. No one had touched her so, since. She lifted her own hand to her face now and found it wet.

In the alley among the crumpled dead, Polycarp's eyes slitted open at last, pale as moonlight on water. For a moment he just drew in breath and air and gazed up at her. "Beloved daughter." His voice a hoarse croak.

She bent over him and brushed her lips across his brow. She felt his breath near her ear, then the whisper of his voice.

"Our lives are—so brittle," he rasped.

"Shhh," Regina whispered, cradling his head.

The father lifted his hand, gripped her fingers suddenly. His eyes focused on her; the breath labored in his chest, as though it took great effort to speak coherently after what he'd done, what he'd witnessed. The intensity of his eyes held her; though he was clearly fighting to voice these words through a fatigue that grappled with his spirit, his halting voice held the same passion and fierce intent with which he'd so often addressed the gathering in the Catacombs. She returned his tight grip on her hand. "Some things can never—be atoned for. Can only be—absolved, or—not. Without—that grace—all rotting, we are all—" His breath hissed between his teeth, as though for a moment it hurt him even to breathe.

"It's over," Regina whispered. "They're all at rest. You gave them the Gift, father." She tried to find words for the fullness of emotion inside her, so much fullness, so much she couldn't hold it. "You saved them."

"All of them?" he whispered.

"Yes, father." She lifted his hand, pressed the back of it to her lips. After a moment she glanced up, looking out across the alley filled with unmoving dead. Above them, a few furtive stars shone in a narrow crack of sky between the buildings leaning in on them. She thought of sleeping Rome in its thousands all about them, and shivered. "I have to get you inside," she whispered. "We have to hide you."

"No—there is no more hiding." The soft hiss of his breath. "Have to—stand."

"Father—" she gasped.

He gave her a small, grim smile, his eyes opening again. They were clearer now. He placed his hand over hers. At the tenderness of it, the dry warmth of his touch, she blinked back hot moisture from her eyes. She shook her head, appalled at what he was asking of her. Panic began to rise in her, panic at the shattering of everything that had held her and kept her safe these past four years in the insula, these years serving Polycarp. The sight of him sleeping, the need to care for him, to give *him* refuge—the gentle weight of his head in her lap—all of this had held the panic back. Now her body went cold with it.

"Daughter. The guardsmen—need to find me. And not you."

"I'm not *leaving* you."

"Regina." He looked at her, his voice very soft. The pain in his eyes made her gasp. "If you love me, daughter, *go inside*. Leave me here—to talk awhile with God." His eyes were still so pale, as though every inch of his body was in pain—though he lay so still. He lifted his hand to touch her hair, and she leaned her cheek into his fingers, her lip trembling. "Our God," he breathed, holding her eyes with his, "is the same here—at night—as he is by day in our rooms. We must submit when called, daughter. We must each of us submit, each of us surrender. We are all the redeemed slaves of God. Else—else, we are—" He gasped for air a moment; his gaze became intense, holding hers. "The gathering is as vulnerable to vices—pride, self-interest—as any other group of people. Daughter, hear me. Without our submission when called, we would become only a—only a mirror—of the Palatine. Only another kind of Senate. We must remain a gathering of servants. We must choose to live in this way." He breathed open-mouthed for a moment. "I know what I must do, daughter—and I must ready myself for it. But you—I would have you safe."

"No," she whispered, "no." His God asked too much! He asked of all of them too much! "I can't—" She forced the words out, something inside her tightening. "Father!" she pleaded. "Polycarp—"

She'd never called out his name before.

She felt that everything in her, all the pieces of herself that she'd moored so carefully, were coming apart on dark waters. The insula had long since become her refuge, and Polycarp in his acceptance of her had become her refuge also. Now both refuges had been violated—by the dead, by Julia's betrayal, by the guardsmen who might even now be coming down the narrow alleys. She gave a low, moaning cry; she might lose everything tonight, everything that meant anything to her. They might all be taken or be separated forever. These moments might be the last in which she would ever see Polycarp—how could she leave him?

Polycarp's fingers curled in her hair a moment. His pale eyes searched hers, and his cracked lips parted. "You are strong," he rasped. "Strong as a queen. The others—they need you, Regina. Go now."

She took his hand, turned the palm toward her and kissed it, her eyes squeezed shut against tears. Her shoulders shook with silent weeping. "Don't," she whispered.

"Regina, Polycarp, what's happened?" A call from the door. She jolted.

Marcus's voice.

Marcus. And the others. They needed her.

Strong as a queen.

She squeezed Polycarp's hand once, then let it go. She shifted the father's head from her lap and rose to her feet. She'd chosen to serve Polycarp and his God. It had been a free choice. Now they needed this of her. Her hands trembled. She wiped her eyes, took a steadying breath. Polycarp beside her was getting wearily to his knees; he turned from her, facing up the slope of the alley, then lowered his brow to the stones, an obeisance to the God he needed to speak with. All about them, the dead lay still, their spirits at rest, the bodies that'd been left behind no more now than driftwood washed into this alley by Death's river.

Regina's breast swelled with the force of her love for this man, her need for him. He meant to stand between the gathering and the Roman guardsmen, even as in the last hour he'd stood between them and the dead. How determined, how immovable he looked as he knelt among the dead, readying himself for whatever might come. Other men she had known, slave men and free: the tight-lipped and impoverished men of the insula who were so reluctantly rediscovering and reclaiming joy as they shared bread. The master who had enjoyed her body, lashing her at a whim or merely to distract himself from whatever pain or frustration he felt inadequate to face. These had been men who were not up to the task, men in whom there was no refuge, only the threat that if they wanted something of her they would bruise her in taking it, and that if she wanted something of them, they would crumple when leaned on. But Polycarp would never crumple. He could not be moved.

She could not let him down. He'd never let her down.

She walked to the insula door. Marcus waited there, and she could see Phineas and Vergilius behind him; no one had brought another lamp. She swung the door closed, with a last glance at Polycarp kneeling in the dark of the alley. Her hand trembled once, then she shut the door. She turned toward them, the wood of the door at her back. Their eyes were round with need in the dark.

"The father is at prayer." She cleared her throat. "Phineas, get a lamp." Her voice didn't waver, though she felt unsteady as a shrub with shallow roots in a high wind. "Vergilius, get everyone into the hiding place. Marcus, will you go to one of the second-story windows and keep watch tonight for the guardsmen?"

Only when they had gone from the room—Marcus giving her arm one brief squeeze before hurrying out—only then did she lean her head back against the door, closing her eyes and shuddering, biting her lip against the cries that she would not voice.

———

Regina had gone, but Polycarp knew he was *not* alone. He could hear the labored breathing of the great, dark-haired behemoth that crouched some distance behind him in the alley. He did not know if the creature approaching him had any corporeal reality, any more than the red beetle he had seen in his dream and several times in his waking life. But the *messages* brought by the beetle and the behemoth were real. Messages of truth and hope from the beetle, messages of fatigue and despair from the lumbering, misshapen beast that had now prowled into the alley. The messages they brought were desperately real, perhaps so real that they required some corporeal being to carry them, even if otherwise no such being would have existed.

As the thing approached, Polycarp did not look up but kept his brow pressed to a pavement stone smeared with offal and dried urine; he kept his eyes closed not from fear but from a weariness so poignant it wore at his bones. To give the dead rest, he'd needed to look first into each one's blind eyes and find beneath the gray scratches the remnant of the soul locked within the shambling corpse. He'd needed to witness each one's secrets, each one's sins, each one's suffering—all that each one had loved and feared and regretted in their brief lives. Only then might he absolve them and set them free and let the corpses slide lifeless to the alley floor. But he had needed to see each one's heart not through a glass darkly—the way he saw Regina's heart, say, or Marcus's, or even his *own* heart—but as clearly as *God* saw, without any veils to protect his mind from the pain of another's.

Our hearts are such small things. There is in the world both too much beauty and too much suffering for a human heart to hold.

Polycarp sobbed quietly as he rested on the mute stones, listening to the heavy paws and the wheezing breaths of the thing in the alley. Despair had come to visit him, as it had often done in the years since he came to Rome; each time, it was a little harder to send the beast away. Most often he heard the tread of its paws on nights such as this, after an encounter with the dead.

You are old, the creature whispered. *You are old, Polycarp. And there are too many hurts to heal. You are not sufficient for this task.*

"My master is sufficient," Polycarp murmured, too tired even to feel revolted at the grime he felt against his lips as they moved.

But you are here, and he isn't.

No. Polycarp braced his hands against the stones. *I am his hands, his feet. I must stand up.*

He swayed a moment, looking out at the tumbled bodies. In a moment of wild imagining he pictured them placing their hands to the street, even as he was doing, and lifting themselves up. Not as slouching, unsteady dead, but as the living called back.

Called back. Any spirit could be called back.

Go away, he told the behemoth. *I have no need of you and no time to listen to you, nor to the Adversary who sends you. You are unwanted here, as unnecessary as these bodies, these empty shells that carry no life.*

The creature Despair did not fall silent, but Polycarp kept it now at the edge of hearing. He needed to reflect on what had happened in this alley. How severely it had tired him, how vulnerable it had left him. He needed to pray, and think, without the pollution of Despair's whispered enticements.

He'd never considered having to face so many dead, more than a few at a time.

During the recent year of the pestilence, whenever Polycarp had come upon the dead in the Subura, he'd refused to conceal himself, though the approach of them made his palms sweat. Once, he'd stood in the path of a tall man lumbering down a street in the still dawn while the living peered out from their windows. The thing's entrails had spilled from a gash in its belly, and it was trailing them slickly behind it. Polycarp had stood and forced himself to breathe calmly even as the thing sensed him, raised its one unbroken arm, and let out that long, deep moan of unquenchable hunger. But as it lurched toward the father, it tripped in its own innards and lay moaning and twisting in a tangle of them, right in the street. Polycarp approached it slowly, then bent and touched the thing's side with his hand, saw the soul come back briefly into its eyes. Then the corpse went still and rested as silent as though it lay in a mausoleum and not on the grimed stones of a Suburan street.

Polycarp had sat looking at the body for a few moments. Then he bent to the side and vomited up into the street.

Another time he'd been walking home and had heard screams; he'd broken into a run, pouring on speed until he feared his heart would burst within him. He was no longer made for running. Others in the street ran the opposite way, away from the screams rather than toward them; someone hit him and he fell. He might've been trampled if there'd been more people. But there were only a few, and then the street was empty. He rolled onto his side, got up onto his hands, and looked up the street. There, at the open doorway of a jeweler's shop, two dead were feasting on the small, still-twitching body of a man who may have been the proprietor; his fingers wore many rings. They had dragged him half out of the shop and were sharing his arm between them, biting deep, then tearing the flesh away in long, bleeding strips. They did not look up as Polycarp got to his feet.

The two dead were a woman, young, and a small child whose eyes were as gray as the woman's and who tore into the flesh as ravenously.

Polycarp prayed without words as he walked toward them.

Afterward, when he was done, he crawled into the dark of the jeweler's shop and leaned against a great, wooden case that doubtless held locked within it many items of beauty. He drew up his knees like a boy does and rested his arms on them. Bowed his head. The dark was quiet and comfortable; he wanted rest as he had never wanted anything before. He had never even wanted a woman so much. He hadn't even wanted *God* so much. He just closed his eyes and breathed. In a while the tears came; he felt them cooling as they slid down his cheek.

Until this night in the alley, he had never experienced a greater strain than his encounter with the two dead at the jeweler's shop. When he'd set one hand on the child's shoulder and one hand on the woman's, and they had turned growling to bite at him, he'd looked into their eyes and *seen*—

He ached with what he'd seen. His breath caught in small sobs. He rocked, hitting the jewelry case with the back of his head.

When the child's spirit had looked out of his hungering body and gazed for the briefest of instants at Polycarp, the pain the father witnessed in him had been terrible. But the woman's suffering had been worse. In *her* eyes he'd seen the anguish of a woman who'd never been told she was beautiful, had in fact been told that she was of utterly no worth, unloved and unvalued by everything that breathed, whether mortal or immortal. The whole earth could fall through the hole in her and would not fill it. She had poured wine into that hole, and the touch of men, and even her nightly rape of that small boy—the one whose body Polycarp had found feeding on the jeweler beside her. And when the dead had come to her room, she'd put up no struggle as they fed on her and the boy. She had poured them into the hole too.

———

Bad as that hour had been, this night in the alley had been far worse. Too many dead who'd never had the chance to say farewell to their own pasts, to the tears that were never shed, the joys that were never consummated, the hungers that were never satisfied. His heart had not known there was so much pain, so much loss, in the earth. His head had known, but his heart hadn't known— not the way it knew tonight, after witnessing the unveiled anguish of twenty souls.

Polycarp bit down against a groan, strove to get his knees beneath him again, then had to stop, gasping for air. His ears caught a new sound in the alley, but he ignored it. For the moment all that mattered was the air moving in and out of his body. He tried to form words for a prayer and finally cried out in silence, pleading for respite. For recovery. For strength.

The sound—the new sound—intruded again. He focused on it.

A clinking of metal.

Muted, yet unmistakable in the stillness that had fallen over the tenements since the dead appeared.

Relief settled over Polycarp's shoulders like a warm blanket. *Thank you, master. Thank you. One more test now, one more task, then I can rest.* He heard the scrabbling of unsheathed claws on the stones as the dark beast fled the alley, running not because of the clink and clatter of Roman breastplates but because, as Polycarp breathed more evenly, there was no longer opportunity for it to speak.

The clinking grew near, then fell still, and a hard voice spoke above his head.

"We seek the insula where Polycarp hides. Is this it?"

Polycarp began to laugh softly, helplessly. Lifting his begrimed face from the ground, there among the bodies of the dead, he lifted his hands too. He reached for the pair of manacles the guardsmen held ready and for the rest from care they offered, even as in an earlier year of his life he might have lifted his hands toward a lover's face.

REGINA ROMAE

IN THE hours since the guardsmen had taken them from the insula, sleep hadn't come for Regina. She sat with her back to the rough boards of the wall in this prison shed she'd been tossed into, still in her nightdress. Her eyes on the locked, wooden door. Marcus's head she cradled in her lap; from time to time the boy moaned in the dark, stirring fitfully, and she stroked his hair. Having someone to care for helped her breathe calmly, kept her from shuddering into sobs. She had to keep it together.

There were bruises about Marcus's face, and Regina was careful not to touch them. While Regina and Vergilius had hurried the tenants from the first two stories into Polycarp's larder and into the hiding place, Marcus had been watching the alley from a high window. Seeing two of the guardsmen take Polycarp away, he'd wanted to run after them—he'd even taken up a dagger; she hadn't known he owned one. Regina had cried out to him to stop, to come to the hidden cellar; but he'd run to the door, reaching it even as the guardsmen burst through.

Regina had thrown herself before them, to give Vergilius time to shut the secret door in the larder—but it was too late. The guardsmen had come too soon; even as they rushed through the door, one of them caught sight of movement in the larder and shouted out; then Marcus was at the guardsmen with his fists, and they beat him until he lay still. Regina tried to bar their way into the larder with her body, though her heart hammered as they came at her; one seized her arm and she raked his face with her nails. With a bellow, he flung her to the floor on her back. Though she kicked at him as he bent, he shoved his knee into her belly and lashed her wrists before her with cord that bit savagely into her skin. She screamed; the man struck her. Then she lay still, dazed a moment, her head ringing with the pain of it—a terrible, gray moment where she thought she might pass out, where she didn't know whether it was a guardsman pinning her or her old master who used to crush her to the floor with his right hand balled into a fist, his left reaching for her body. Regina's breath came in short, frantic gasps.

The guardsman's voice came to her through a roaring in her ears—orders he was barking. "That larder. And every room. Search them."

The others. *The others*—they needed her. Marcus lay unmoving by the door.

"They're just tenants." She forced the words out, tasting blood on her lip.

"Maybe," one of the other guards snorted. "And maybe this is a rats' nest."

"We'll know quick enough," the guard who pinned her grunted. A blade scar sliced from his left temple across his nose to his jawbone on the right, giving his face a kind of savage beauty. His eyes were weary but without pity. The hardness in them dulled the edge of Regina's panic, enough for her to breathe. Her old master's eyes had been cruel, watery, self-indulgent. The eyes of this captor held only self-interest and determination. This man might strike a woman to quiet her—or strike a man for the same reason—but he would not do so for the pleasure of it. For a moment Regina focused on getting her breath back, regathering herself, as the guardsman turned his head toward the others. "There's no one here with more than a fist to swing. I'll take these two now—already sent Quintus and Lucullus back with the old man. You follow with whatever else you find. Praetor can sort it out. *Tenants*." His voice was thick with derision.

The other guards stepped past her into the larder, and she screamed and tried to throw herself at them. But she couldn't get out from under the man's knee; her hands were trapped so tightly that her wrists burned as she struggled. The man who had her snarled and got to his feet. He'd left a length of cord free when he tied her; now he dragged her to her knees using it, and his hand gripping her arm pulled her to her feet. Then he was pulling her behind him, leashed like a slave new from the docks, even as she screamed for the others to stay concealed. He tossed Marcus's limp form over his shoulder, took a firm hold on the leash, and pulled her stumbling out the door and past the restful dead. The insula fell behind, and the guardsman took them through the narrow streets of the Subura, uphill toward the richer parts of Rome.

Regina knew many residents of the slum must be watching from their windows, and she hung her head, hiding her face with her hair. She burned with the shame of being dragged so, in her nightdress, through the streets in the deep dark before dawn.

She tried to tell herself that she was Regina Romae, a deaconess of the gathering in Rome. But as she stumbled over the uneven stones, bruising her toes, and as her hands went numb, she didn't feel like Regina. She felt like Dora—that slave who'd so often found herself bound, helpless, in another's power. Something welled up in her breast and her throat, a desire to beg, to do anything to be freed of this terrible, biting rope. That feeling terrified her.

As they left the Subura, her captor stopped a moment. Regina glanced over her shoulder and gasped. Dark shapes were stumbling out of an alley and lurching into the street behind them. One of them let out a deep groan. Marcus stirred faintly on the guardsman's shoulder.

"Gods," the guardsman breathed. "So many. Gods."

He cursed and dragged her forward at a run, yanking on the cord so violently that she sprawled to the stones, smacking her shoulder and crying out. At the cry, more moans erupted behind them—down the street, but too near, too near! Regina kicked out in panic, tried to get her feet under her; a hard hand gripped her arm and wrenched her back to her feet.

Then they *ran*.

The stones battered her feet; she sobbed for breath. Her side burning, she began to pray to Polycarp's God. She cried out the *Phos Hilaron* in frantic Greek syllables; in this terror it was all she could think of. *Phos hilaron hagias doxes athanatou Patros*, she cried as they ran: a prayer for light and joy on a street where the buildings leaned so close that running over the stones was like racing through a tunnel in the earth.

Something grabbed at her ankle and she shrieked, falling again; something fell on her in the dark, and she felt a cold, dry hand clutch at her face. A hiss above her. She kicked wildly, writhing, a jagged stone beneath her cutting her back. Wetness trickled hot over her thighs, the reek of urine. A face above her, its mouth open, teeth bared.

Then the weight was lifted from her, and a man stood over her. A faint gleam of metal. Again the hiss, and then the chop of iron into flesh. Regina kept kicking, and the man above her swore. "Lie still, you slut."

She froze, the sound of his voice confirming that the shape that stood over her was living, not dead. Her heart pounded. She started repeating her name to herself, silently, again and again. She was *not* Dora. She was Regina. Regina Romae. The cords bit at her hands.

Another hiss, and she cried out, her mind going blank as her whole body flinched, anticipating the cut of teeth into her flesh. The man above her danced in place, and again she heard the chunk of metal into meat. A heavy figure fell across her feet and she twisted, kicking it off. It did not grasp her or bite. Then the guardsman's hands were on her arms, pulling her to her feet again.

She swayed. It was so dark. She could hear the dead wailing, very near. The man who held her was only a silhouette against the blind night. She moaned.

His hand struck her face.

Then the ground left her feet and she was over his shoulder, his hand on her rear. She felt the hard rhythm of his strides; he was walking very quickly. There was moaning loud behind them. She didn't kick; the pain in her face had cleared her mind. She sucked in short, sharp breaths, desperate for air.

She was Regina Romae. Regina Romae.

Anger and shame lit in her, a heat that drove away fear. Not in years had she shaken apart so badly. The warmth of her own urine on her leg made her furious. She could hear her own sobbing breaths, her quiet whimpers, and she clenched her teeth, stopping them. Lifting her head, she gazed into the dizzy night behind them. She could hear the dragging footsteps of the dead; she could hear their moans. They were close.

Then the guardsman carried her out from the close streets, and he strode up a long slope, the tenements of the Subura replaced by gardens and villas; without buildings leaning close overhead, there were stars, many stars, brilliant and sharp in the sky. In their light she saw the dead shamble out of the close-packed alleys and stumble uphill after them. They didn't move fast; the guardsman was young and strong, and, if unburdened, could outrun them. But now, bearing the weight of two captives, one on either shoulder—

Regina watched the dead with wide eyes. There were thirty, maybe forty. Still more shuffled after those. Dark figures in the starlight, barely separable one from another. Just shadow shapes that had lurched out of some child's nightmare with hunger and clutching hands and a need to kill. They moaned as they followed.

The sight shook her. What could even Polycarp do against so many? And how many more still shuffled in closed rooms in half the tenements by the river, waiting for a door to open, or tumbling by accident out the window to crawl up the street seeking someone to devour?

The guardsman's breath wheezed beneath her.

"Don't stop," Regina whispered. "Run, run."

She didn't know she'd spoken aloud, but the guardsman's steps quickened; the jostling of his shoulder against her belly deprived her of her own breath. She could only watch the dead as they lurched up the hill, nearly a hundred of them now. Their moaning filled the air. As though overnight the Tiber had become the Styx, and the boatman had confused his directions and was ferrying the dead over from the farther shore.

But the guardsman's sprint was brief; he began to pant and his pace flagged as the uphill road became steeper. Regina's heart beat wildly in her ears. Behind them, four of the dead had lurched ahead of the rest. Here on the Palatine slopes, the road was sunken, a wide channel to carry away sewage, with raised steps in the middle to keep the feet of affluent citizens dry. At this time of night, there was little fluid in the road, and even little scent, for water had been poured down it after sundown to cleanse the road. But the shin-high embankments to either side of the road served to confine and channel the dead, as long as the prey they sought was directly ahead. That kept most of the dead pressed tightly together; as the group shambled forward, they impeded each other.

But those four who were ahead climbed the road steadily, having more room, one of them slouching a little to the side, another with its arms lifted and reaching for its prey. The guardsman wheezed and stumbled to one knee.

"No!" Regina cried. "Get up, get up! They're right behind us!"

Her captor planted both of his palms against the moist pavement and gazed forward at the rising slope of the hill. With a roar like a beast, he thrust himself back to his feet, both captives still on his shoulders. One hand on each, he stumbled furiously up the incline.

The dead were only a few paces behind. They did not tire or stumble.

Regina fought her bonds, twisting her wrists, panting with fear as she tried to slip one hand free. She took care not to move her hips much; she didn't want to fall to the hard pavement, to lie there bound as the walking corpses closed in on her, their hands reaching for her. She strained and gritted her teeth and pulled at her wrists; pain flared in her lower arms. She couldn't get her hands free.

The guardsman was fighting for every step; the uphill sprint had wearied him. Perhaps, if given a moment to stop and breathe, he might recover enough to finish the climb quickly.

The dead would not give him a moment.

"Please," Regina whispered, "please."

One of the dead lurched close, its eyes dull, its teeth glinting in the starlight. Stretching out its arm, its fingers clutching at her. Regina tried to twist her head away, breathing in tiny gasps. She moaned through clenched teeth, tensing.

In the next instant the corpse's cold fingertips brushed *her hair*.

A dark blur crashed into the thing's head; the creature staggered to the side, hissed, then took a step back toward them; a man in leather armor shoved the guardsman with his captives behind him, then swung a great wooden cudgel, slamming it a second time into the corpse's head. This blow knocked the creature to its knees, even as the three other dead stumbled near.

Moaning—not a moan of pain but that long, low moan of hunger—the dead corpse began rising to its feet again. Their rescuer swung the cudgel, but now two more of the dead grabbed his arms, pulling him toward their mouths. He cursed and kicked one of them hard between the thighs with his boot, but the creature did not wince or move. Regina screamed as the corpse pressed its mouth to the soldier's wrist and bit deeply. Blood welled up around its teeth, dark in the night.

The guardsman slid his captives from his shoulders; Regina felt the pavement hit her back and rump hard, and sucked in her breath. The fourth walking corpse bent and snatched at her hair. But the guardsman's knife slid from its sheath in a song of metal, and he drove his blade into the creature's chest. That did not slow it. Regina cried out as she felt her head lifted by the hair, her wrists tied helplessly beneath her. The thing's face a shadow above her, its teeth reaching for her. She tried to speak, to beg, to scream—no sound came.

A blade shone for an instant before her face. One more hard tug on her hair and then the pull was gone; she fell back hard to the stones. She saw long strands of her hair still caught in the creature's hand, the ends severed.

The guardsman's rough hand grabbed her, dragged her a few feet up the road. As other feet pounded past her, she rolled to her side and retched into the street.

Several men were wrestling with the four dead; they had cudgels, and one or two had knives. She saw one cudgel come down again and again on a hairless head that kept snapping its jaws and hissing; skin and gray matter and tissue spewed from the growing wound in its skull, until the thing just fell to the side and lay crumpled like tattered clothes tossed into the drain.

Then it was over.

Four corpses lay still in the street, and one of the soldiers bent to wipe the mess from his cudgel on a tunic one of the bodies wore.

Regina retched again, tasting her vomit on her lips and in her mouth. She groaned. Her back ached from the impact of falling several times onto hard stone. She coughed and fought to stop her belly from heaving. Her hair, cut short on the left side of her head, got into her eyes. The moaning of the larger group of dead—who must be very near now—was loud. For a moment with one side of her face pressed to the street, she could hear their approach through the rock. She could hear both the moaning and the scraping of their feet. She began praying, whispering.

There were soldiers in the street, between her and Marcus and the dead. Several armored men. One knelt, clutching his arm. To her horror, blood ran from beneath his hand and spilled to the pavement like water from a fountain, an urgent stream of life leaving him. The man groaned something that Regina didn't quite catch, and then a new man stepped into view, tall and broad-shouldered, a giant with a high mane on his helmet. An officer, a centurion. There was no *gladius* at his belt, but he held a long cudgel with a jagged scrap of bronze fixed to the end.

He stood for a moment before the wounded legionnaire.

Behind him, Regina could see the slow-moving, steady advance of the dead. They were close enough to throw stones at, with accuracy. She rolled onto her back, glanced once at the star-pierced sky, once up the road to the high, quiet villas of the wealthy, sheltered among dark, tall cypresses. Marcus lay there in the road, near enough to touch if she weren't bound; his face was turned from her and he wasn't moving or making any sound, but she could see the rise and fall of his chest.

She had to protect him. She had to do something. She forced herself to breathe. There were armed men here—disciplined, trained legionnaires; she and Marcus would *not* be eaten. She just had to pull herself together, think, survive. She had to. How the cords *bit* at her wrists!

She glanced back down the street toward the dead in time to see the centurion raise his cudgel.

"You did your duty," the officer said.

The wounded man lifted his head and closed his eyes. Regina shut hers quickly as the cudgel came down.

When she opened them a moment later, the man lay in the street, his head caved in on one side, blood running, slow and dark, down the stones toward the staggering dead.

Her belly heaved again.

The centurion turned to her captor, who stood now to one side, his chest heaving as he recovered his breath. "Run past," the officer barked. "We'll divert them, lead them back toward the river."

Regina's captor panted, tried to force out words. "There may—be others—don't get caught—between—"

"I know my work, guardsman." The centurion's face was hard, and the anger in his eyes, cold and violent, made Regina flinch—though that restrained fury was directed not at her or at Marcus but at the guardsman who had trailed a crowd of walking dead up the hill toward the parts of Rome the centurion believed worthy of defending.

Turning from them, the centurion gestured quickly with his hand; men in armor but carrying only cudgels and staves moved past in a quick but orderly line. By law no soldiers who marched in any army of the state could carry sharp iron within the ancient boundary of Rome, so in the recent disorder the magistrates had hired mercenary guardsmen to keep the streets clean of dead; Regina's captor was one of these hired men. The centurion and these twenty were not. Their training had been brutal and without reprieve or rest, and they had been tested perhaps in the swamps of Germania or along Hadrian's Wall, at those distant frontiers where most of Rome's armies held watch, far from the Eternal City. Now, striking an uneasy truce between the security of Rome and the laws of Rome, this centurion and his volunteers had ventured into the city in their armor, taking up improvised weapons that held no blades.

They were few, but they were Roman soldiers. Where they marched, the world knelt.

Regina gazed at the hard eyes of the centurion, and for just a moment he looked at her. She caught her breath at what she saw. A kind of strength she'd seen before only in Polycarp's eyes. What this man said, he would do. The moaning of the dead was loud behind them, but she believed him. He would divert the dead from the hill.

She also saw that his eyes were not those of a man who expected to survive this night.

Grunting, the hired guardsman lifted her to her feet. "You'll have to run," he growled by her ear. She nodded. He tossed Marcus back over his shoulder, gripped her arm above the elbow, then pulled her with him as he broke into a fast walk. Swiftly, they left the legionnaires behind. She heard human cries and shouts amid the moaning of the undead, but she did not look back. She kept her eyes focused on the street above her, praying that she would not stumble or trip.

The Roman villas to either side of the narrow street were silent and dark. There were no windows, for on the Palatine Hill houses kept their windows on the inside, looking into the garden.

The outside was only a wall, closing out any sight of what walked in the street. Regina thought of the families in those homes, stirred from sleep by the wailing of the dead. Even at this moment perhaps a dozen mothers or nurses were clasping small children close, stroking their hair and whispering comfort into their ears. Perhaps a dozen slaves stood waiting by villa doors with staves or brooms in their hands, ordered to beat back the dead if the walking corpses should burst in. No lamps had been lit; no voices were raised in the dark. The men and women of upper Rome were simply waiting within their walls, silent and wide eyed, hoping the clamor in the street would pass them by, the way a tempest might pass by a forest of oaks.

Regina's sides burned, but she forced herself to match the guardsman's pace.

The moaning of the dead was farther behind now. She didn't dare cast a glance over her shoulder to see if the legionnaires had indeed led them away from the street. A glance back might mean tripping. She couldn't bear to lie helpless on the pavement again, not even briefly. With the dead falling behind, relieving the sharp edge of her terror, she began to worry for Marcus. She didn't know how badly he'd been hurt. He might need a poultice and a stay in bed; instead, he was being jounced about on a guardsman's shoulder.

She stubbed her toe hard on the stones, clenched her cry behind her teeth; the guardsman's hard yank on her arm kept her upright, kept her moving, though agony shot through her foot and up her leg.

"There it is," her captor breathed. "Justitia's temple."

Ahead of them, beyond the next villa, she saw a high, marble wall and, towering out of the courtyard behind it, the pillared façade of a high building, white and gleaming under the stars. Nestled against the outside of the wall was a smaller, blockier structure, an official's station. Several wooden sheds had been erected to either side of that station. A man leaned against the side of one, looking down the street at them. Another guardsman.

Regina tried to move her hands in her bonds, but she couldn't feel them; the cord had numbed them. Her captor dragged her toward one of the sheds. The other guardsman swung the door open, revealing a gaping, dark opening. It recalled to her heart the opening to the cargo hold of the slave ship that had brought her to this part of the world years ago. Her hands had been bound then too. Tears ran down her face unchecked. She'd been dragged uphill from the shattered refuge of the insula to this small shed that a Roman might toss a slave into. Of everything that had befallen her since she was pulled from the door of the insula into the street, nothing had terrified her as much as that dark opening of the shed. In her heart she cried out, though she kept her lips still. She didn't know where Polycarp was or what would be done with them—she cried his name silently as the guards pushed her through into the dark closeness of the shed. One of them— the new guard—caught her by the arms before she fell; she was pulled back against his body, and a rough hand slipped beneath her nightdress, groped her thigh with thick, seeking fingers. She flinched and made a high, keening sound that shamed her. Her body tensed like a branch bent back too far, ready to break at another touch.

"Time for that later, Decius," the guard who'd carried her said. "Reports to make, and I need you. Whole bloody Subura's full of dead—can't you hear them?"

The other guardsman grunted his assent and took his hand from her. In a moment she felt cold steel against her wrists, and then the cord parted, and her wrists were free; the guardsman shoved her to the straw. Marcus was thrown down beside her.

The door slammed to.

Regina lay panting, sobbing, on her belly in the dark. Only the freedom of her hands kept her from panic. She was not bound;

she was not in the slave hold. There was warm straw beneath her, not wood chips. This was not the past.

She pushed herself up on her hands, trying to breathe through the tightness in her body. Faintly, through the chinks in the shed's walls, she could hear the moaning of the dead as they hunted in the streets of the Subura, pitting the strength of their ravenous and unmet need against the discipline and order of the Roman soldiers.

———

Dawn came, a faint and furtive light between the boards of the shed. The distant moans had been silent now for some time. Perhaps the danger out there had passed. Perhaps not. The shivers of reaction from their panicked flight had come and gone, leaving Regina exhausted, hungry, weak. She sat with her back to the wall of the shed, still holding Marcus, who groaned from time to time but did not wake. Parts of her own body ached with stiffness and bruising. Her own odor was offensive to her; her skin was coated in a grease of sweat and dirt, and she yearned for a basin of water and a clean cloth. Her emotions were fierce animals within her, prowling and roaring, making her thoughts flee about. First, her horror at the rising of the dead en masse. Would even the battle discipline of the military men avail to stop the hungry dead? She knew Polycarp, who would bring the dead absolution and rest, would have saddened at the waste of the corpses that had been destroyed during the night. But surely Polycarp had never imagined having to contend with so many. Regina found her faith shaken. Suddenly the Apostle's Gift seemed a solution meant for a gentler world; this world was one of hunger, filled with those who would devour you—both among the dead and among the living.

But she pushed from her mind the memory of those moans of hunger and those terrible, grasping hands. Better to consider that unreal, a nightmare. Focus on what was at hand; there were closer, more intimate terrors clutching at her heart. Worry for Marcus. Worry for the others in the insula—had the guardsmen found their hiding place, had they kicked or broken their way into it before giving up the search? And fear for herself as she stared at the locked door and remembered the guardsman's hand on her body. Shame, heavy and hot in her breast; the guard had touched her as though she were a whore, a slave he might own and throw to the floor when he pleased. Men had touched her that way before; they had touched Dora that way. Regina trembled. She'd been dragged from the insula into the street; she'd been bound. However much she'd screamed or kicked, it had made no difference. Her freedom and her refuge and her new name—had any of it really been true, when it could be taken from her so easily?

The thought shook her.

Yet.

There was Polycarp.

Polycarp had loved her, called her daughter.

In his eyes, she had never been a slave.

When he'd touched her hair or brushed her cheek with the backs of his fingers, there had never been in that touch any demand for her to please him. Confronted with a man who didn't demand her, for the first time she'd found herself giving. At first, she'd given to him by doing little tasks about the insula or making tea for him, or carrying messages to his tenants. Later, she had done far more, keeping the accounts and listening to the tenants' troubles. She had learned to give to all of them, all who looked to her as a deaconess who might serve and love and shelter them, and not as a slave who must please and obey.

To Polycarp, she'd given everything that he'd accept from her. Now her breath caught, remembering; she had kissed him the night before. Before the dead, before the guardsmen. She'd pressed her lips to his, knowing that he might die when he stepped through that door into the alley. She had wanted to give even that, of herself. She'd never had the choice to give a kiss before, had never wanted to before.

"*Daughter*," he'd said, as though she'd embarrassed him.

She shut her eyes against a sting of tears, feeling the ache in her heart. Here in the dark of this shed, she heard more of her heart than she ever had before. She knew now that she yearned to make a free gift of herself, but this gift wouldn't be received, for it seemed clear to her now that Polycarp didn't need or desire a lover. He was a man accustomed to thinking of others as children to care for, and he had so many of these children, so many who needed his love. "*Daughter*," he'd said to her.

And now it was too late, in any case. Everything—everything—was shattered and lost. She blinked at the shreds of light let in by chinks in the wall of the shed, her heart bleak. She was crated here like an animal.

She groaned, her grief at Polycarp's absence sharp as glass within her. She needed him to hold her or to speak to her in that firm, calming voice of his. His voice always conveyed that he knew who he was and what he was doing. Just hearing him, she felt she knew who she was too. She needed that now. She needed him. She needed him to be *alive*.

Her throat tightened. She didn't know whether he had been simply knifed in the dark or was being held somewhere for a trial. He might even be in one of the other sheds she'd seen. She thought of calling out for him—but what would that serve, except to bring some reprisal for them both from the guardsmen outside? Yet the uncertainty tormented her. Where was he now? How had they treated him? She closed her eyes against the thin light. Even if Polycarp still lived, he was going to die—she was certain of that. She drew a few shuddering breaths, refused to cry. Marcus needed her. The youth was breathing raggedly on her lap.

Bitterly, she thought of Julia, wondered where the woman and her husband were now. Not in a shed, she was sure.

With a few words to the officers of the city, the baker's wife had shattered all their lives.

———

Regina had last seen Julia the morning of her disappearance. The baker had sent some bread with Regina to the Catacombs the night before, though neither he nor his wife had come to the gathering. They never did. The morning after, Regina had climbed the narrow, foot-worn steps to Julia's small, fourth-story apartment to thank her. She climbed slowly and with some tightness in her breast; she was never comfortable or at ease talking with Julia. The woman seemed stiff, unfriendly, and not very willing to partake of either conversation or companionship.

But then, Regina had reminded herself sternly, she knew a thing or two herself about what it was like to feel alone. She straightened her shoulders as she approached the door.

No answer came to her knock, but the door was ajar. After hesitating, she nudged it open, her heart beating with a sudden fear that something bad may have happened. Perhaps Julia had fainted or was ill.

"Julia?" she called softly.

The baker's wife sat at her windowsill, gazing out at the garden. Her head turned at the call, and Regina caught a glimpse of deep sorrow in the woman's eyes before she masked it. In her lap Julia held a bit of lace. Regina found her gaze held by it.

"It's very beautiful," Regina said.

Julia's eyes stayed cold. The silence stretched into something uncomfortable; Regina had the feeling that she'd burst in during some private moment too intimate to be shared—as though she'd interrupted Julia in the midst of a prayer or a confession.

"I came to thank you." Regina bit her lip, trying to think of the words she needed. "And your husband. For the bread."

"Well." Julia glanced down at the lace, her voice detached, distant. "We have enough to spare."

Regina heard a low murmur of voices from the garden below—a few people talking outside a door. She moved slowly toward Julia, giving the woman a smile and seating herself beside her on the wide sill, her back to the other side of the window, their knees almost touching. "Do you mind if I sit with you?"

When Julia didn't answer, Regina folded her hands gracefully in her lap and looked at the lace she held. "I never had that skill," she said softly. "My hands can't make anything beautiful. Though I was taught to dance, and—other things." Her eyes darkened, and she slammed a door shut in her mind against the shrieks of furious memories. She searched instead for older, less painful memories, ones rarely recollected, in order to fill the silence with small words. "But first, when I was young, very young, my grandfather taught me numbers. My parents didn't have any sons, and I was supposed to help my father at his shop. In Damascus." She smiled.

Julia let out her breath slowly. "This would have been for my child." Her fingers tightened about the lace. Those fingers were thick, but they must have moved with particular grace to make that small bit of beauty, that gift for someone who did not exist but was only a hope.

Regina's heart softened. She gazed at the other woman, as though seeing her for the first time. The baker's wife had been hurt, many times; it was in her eyes, a deep and weary conviction that life was a sequence of losses, and amid that weariness a still-flickering flame of yearning and need.

Regina recognized the yearning, and the weariness that came of having never had a child. Regina didn't think she herself *could* have one; her body carried scars inside, not just on her back. She had faced that. And in helping Polycarp she'd learned that she had many children, many people in this insula, and in others, who relied on her—for an occasional gift of bread from the larder, or for words of comfort, or for an ear and a listening heart, to bring their cares and needs to the father. She had a community and a home; what more could she need?

"Julia," she asked softly, "are you so unhappy?"

"What have I to be unhappy about?" Bitterness in her voice, sharp and lethal—though Regina sensed beneath it a woman so brittle she might break at a touch. "I have a man, and bread to eat."

"But it's not enough," Regina murmured. The bite in Julia's tone had startled her; she searched the other woman's face, her concern growing.

Julia's eyes lifted, found hers. They were dull with an old and harbored anger. "I was domina of my own house, girl. I don't suppose you have any idea what that means."

"No," Regina said after a moment. "I don't."

She waited.

Julia's shoulders trembled. She folded the lace, carefully, precisely. Her face struggled to hold in her emotion. "I want it back. I want it all back. I'd do anything for that. Give up anything. This— this place. I don't live here, I only breathe. I can't bear a child here, it's so filthy. Someone two stories down takes a shit, and I can smell it." Her voice was low and intense. She closed her eyes, tightly, and lowered her head, holding her breath against whatever was inside her wanting to shake her apart.

"I didn't know you felt like this." Regina reached out and took the other woman's hand, but Julia pulled her hand away quickly.

"Don't," she said. "Don't you touch me."

"Julia—" Regina fought to find something she could say. "Julia." Her heart beat with alarm. How long had she felt like this? What poison was in her heart?

"No. I'm done. I thought I could bear it, but I'm done." Julia straightened, her face becoming stone. "Please go."

Regina hesitated. The pain in Julia's voice was clear as a shout. Yet her anger was sharpening now to a knife's edge; Regina didn't think sitting here with her was helping her. "I'll speak to the father," she offered.

Julia's eyes flashed. "I don't want his pity, or yours."

Regina flushed. "It's not pity I'm offering—I worry for you."

"You." Julia's eyes burned now. "You worry for *me*. What are you?"

The coldness of her voice struck Regina hard.

"A slave," Julia hissed. "That's what. A slut who thinks herself the mistress of the insula. An uppity thing Polycarp puts up with because she's good with numbers."

Regina went white.

It was a moment before she could speak. "A slave?" Regina couldn't keep the distress from her voice. "I am a freed woman."

"You, girl, are a travesty." Julia set the lace beside her on the sill, her fingers trembling, then smoothed her dress. "This entire place is a travesty," she muttered.

Regina felt a surge of panic, fought it down. Her vulnerability terrified her. Julia's voice had taken on a cant and an intonation that she recognized. The consonants were sharper, the vowels shorter—it was not the way a woman of the Subura spoke. It was the way an equestrian spoke, a daughter of Rome's merchant classes, who strolled the Forum and claimed homes on the lower slopes of Rome's seven hills. Possibly Julia wasn't even aware of the change in her voice. Regina glanced at her cold face. Wondered if years ago, Julia had spoken in such a sharp, precise voice to her slaves.

She seemed suddenly a stranger in their insula.

Regina took a breath, tried to steady herself. Equestrians came to the gathering in the Catacombs. They were no different from the rest of the people, no different from the bakers or the tanners or the fresco painters. No different even from manumitted slaves.

And this insula, her insula, Polycarp's insula, was *not* the house of miserable years where Regina had been beaten, and Julia was not the domina of that house. She had nothing to fear.

"I would befriend you," Regina cried suddenly. "We all would, Julia. If you'd only come sit with us in the garden—or walk with us—or—why must you clutch your grief so tightly to your breast? Does it feel so good doing that?" Her face was flushed, her veins hot with adrenaline. "Come to dinner with us—tonight—please. Whatever you may think of us, you live here with us. Why stay locked away in this room?"

Julia's fingers trembled again, and she clutched the folds of her dress, stilling them. Watching her, Regina felt a chill of insight. Julia's grief was perhaps the one thing she owned, the one thing that told her who she was. The woman was so hurt and so alone that she'd forgotten how to love. Horror flickered in Regina's belly. She herself might have been like that. If Polycarp hadn't found her—she might have been like that.

"Please, come to dinner, Julia," she whispered. "Tonight. Phineas and Marcus and I are breaking bread together, and we'll invite the father, and I'll invite Cecilia and Portia. Just come. Don't stay up here."

"I have no intention of staying here." Julia's voice was very quiet. Something in her tone—some finality, some terrible certainty—brought Regina's head around. Her eyes widened. With a shock of clarity, she saw the window and the way Julia sat with her hips on the sill. How she would only need to lean back to topple from the sill and plummet to the garden earth four stories below. Regina thought quickly, her heart racing. Surely she was only imagining it. Julia couldn't mean to do that—she couldn't.

"You may go, girl," Julia said.

The blood rushed back into Regina's face. She was being dismissed, as one might dismiss a house slave. Her throat tightened; all the warmth left her body.

"Go," Julia hissed.

Regina wanted to say something, to protest, to plead with her, but so many feelings and fears were rushing through her body so quickly, leaving her racked and shaken. At last, she turned and fled, unable to find words, knowing only that she needed privacy now to recollect and regather herself. Leaving, she shut Julia's door with a quiet *snick*, blocking out the sight of the woman's cold, furious eyes. Old memories were rattling the doors in Regina's mind; she felt as though it took her whole being to hold those doors shut.

She walked as fast as she could down the steps and into the atrium and across the narrow garden toward her own first-story room. Glancing back over her shoulder as she moved around the lilacs, she caught sight of Julia still seated at the sill of her fourth-story window. Her cold hauteur had faded with Regina's departure; now the other woman sat with her head lowered. Framed in that window, she had the look of an animal in a cage. Not a beautiful woman but an elegant one, Julia had always seemed graceful in the way she moved and in her posture. She appeared slumped now, like one of the gazelles they keep in narrow pens beneath the Colosseum, to whet the appetite of lions who would later be loosed on the gladiators.

Perhaps this same insula that for Regina was a place of safety, with high walls to keep at bay the threat of memory, felt for Julia like a confinement. Beneath the current of her fear, Regina felt a sharp prick of fresh worry, as though she'd stepped on a thorn. Then she looked away.

———

She was the deaconess; she should've brought her worries at once to the father.

If only she'd told him.

But she'd been too shaken. Too shaken even for anger, or for anything other than hurrying to her own room, to its refuge and safety. Shutting the door, she'd leaned against it and hugged herself tightly. The words Julia had used fell on her like robbers then in the dim light of her room—*slave, slave, slut, slut*—and she whimpered through closed lips, then flushed in shame at the sound. She was *not* a slave. Not anymore. She mustn't act like one. After a few moments she stepped to the shelf along the back wall and plucked down a small flask of wine, one she kept there for mixing with water to drink. She opened the flask, nearly spilled it, her hands shaking. She allowed herself only a sip, then placed it back on the shelf.

Slave, slave.

After a while, her blood still loud in her ears, she knelt on her bedding on the floor and prayed aloud, though softly, sharing the secrets of her heart with Polycarp's God, that God he promised was always near and whose comforting presence Regina felt at rare times. The love Polycarp said his God had for the gathering, for his adopted children bought out of the slavery of their pasts, of their evils and their regrets—Regina knew about that love chiefly because of the love she saw Polycarp give to those in the gathering. But lacking the courage yet to speak her heart to Father Polycarp, she spoke instead to his God.

She prayed for most of the morning, concealed within her room. She prayed for the courage to believe in her freedom and for the courage not to flee when threatened. Blinking back tears, she prayed her gratitude that she was no longer in the master's house, no longer lashed or beaten or kicked from her bedding in the early hours, no longer answering to a name she did not want or laboring fiercely to delight and appease a man she hated. Even if she at times felt as though she were still in that insula, she wasn't. She was here. "Help me not to be scared," she whispered. "I want to help Polycarp, I want to make his work easier.

It is a good work. He is such a *good* man. I hadn't known there were such men, before I met him, before he saved me. But I am frightened, so frightened. I don't even know why. Please. I just—I need—I want to be free of my past."

Her heart roared awake inside her, like a lion lashed to the earth with hard cords, roaring in both fear and desperate hope. Without words, she laid out, vulnerably, the tangle of her feelings for Polycarp. Her face was wet with tears; this part of her prayer took a long time. It brought no answers, but a little comfort, for in thinking on Polycarp, the doors in her mind that had been rattling hard since Julia's cruel words touched her ears closed tightly and stilled at last.

Finally, Regina prayed for Julia.

Then she rose, her knees screaming in protest, and moved stiffly to her door and opened it. At the outer door of the insula, several of the tenants were talking in low, urgent voices. Marcus was there, and Vergilius. She walked to them, pale but composed, determined to be again the deaconess and not a frightened slave girl. Those were both roles she might play, and if her heart did not always know which role was truest of her, she did know which she preferred. So she walked to the men at the outer door with her shoulders straight and her steps graceful and certain.

It was after midday. Outside that door, six dead were feasting on a crossroads brother in the street.

———

Piscus did not come home to the insula that day, and for a time Regina and Marcus stood by the outer door talking about that, though Regina didn't share her altercation with Julia. There was a small slat in the door that could be slid back to let one's eyes look out into the narrow Suburan street, and from time to time, Marcus or Regina slid it back and peered out—but the dead had gone hours before and had dragged the remains of the crossroads brother with them. There was still a smear of blood on the stones.

When everyone else had returned to the insula from their day's work—all but Piscus—Regina took her copy of the master key (only she and Polycarp had copies, he as father, she as deaconess), and she went from room to room, knocking gently, unlocking and peering within if there was no answer. Marcus accompanied her for the first two stories, walking beside her in his tunic and brown cloak. Those were Suburan clothes, rough and torn through much use. Polycarp had loaned them to him the day Marcus first took a room in the insula. That had happened about two months after Marcus's initial visit to the insula door; in those two months, the young patrician had walked many times across the Subura to the market and back and had seen more things that had shaken him to the heart. At last, he went with Regina and Vergilius to one of the gatherings on the Sabbath, and when they returned to the insula he did not say goodnight to trudge his way warily back up the long slope to the Palatine. Instead he stood in the doorway of the insula beside Polycarp and Regina and Vergilius and slowly stripped off his toga, folded it neatly, and set it aside. Standing in his loincloth, he gazed down on it. "Sell it," he said hoarsely, lifting his eyes to Polycarp's. "I am no longer of the patrician Caelii. I am Marcus Antonius only. I cannot go back. When I am in my father's house, I am only playing my part; nothing is real. I will share my bread here instead. I'll spend what coin I have in my pockets to lease a room here. Father, set me to any task; I cannot go back. Not after what my eyes have witnessed."

So Marcus walked beside the deaconess now in simpler clothes, and with a simpler name, one stripped of a portion of its history, a history the boy repudiated, one he chose no longer to need or desire. Watching him from the corner of her eye, Regina found herself considering him with new respect. She'd considered him a child, a boy. Yet when he'd shrugged off his toga as another youth might shrug off a child's blanket, surely he had matured. She wondered why she hadn't thought about that before. Like herself, he had found a name, one he could own with dignity as a free man.

There was a girl, Ariadne, on the fourth floor, who still wept herself to sleep some nights because a tanner's son she'd wanted had married another. Ariadne had confided in Regina a week before, and Regina had told her that there were always other men and that all pains, even the most brutal ones, dull with time, becoming only scars, only memory. Now Regina cast a glance at Marcus, considering. The two would look well together. Marcus's steady heart and unwavering devotion would heal the girl's wounds. And Ariadne's demure demeanor—almost too respectful even for a girl of Rome—would help Marcus find his backbone. He needed someone who would look up to him, even worship him, reminding him of his worth. And Regina smiled slightly; she knew something that Marcus probably wouldn't know for some time: under the daintiness of that girl there was a hot fire in her spirit, one that would emerge at first in little flickers and at last in flame, once she felt truly secure in another's love. And she was intelligent. It was likely that whatever they did in life would be done together—that she would offer ideas and the drive to see things done, even as she made sure her husband felt strong and sufficient as a god.

Regina caught her breath. What was she thinking, imagining such a match? Marcus was a *patrician*. Of that caste with the gods of Rome in their bloodlines. Her lips thinned. A patrician might take a woman of the Subura for a slave, a slut to be cast aside after use to sleep on the floor by his bed, but never for a companion. A slow anger lit in her breast, making it difficult for her to breathe— then cooled as she glanced at Marcus again, saw the plain clothes he wore and the hardness in his eyes at odds with the soft lines of his face. No, he was not a patrician. He was Marcus. They'd eaten bread together. That hardness in his eyes meant the things he'd seen had taught him that the blood in his veins was less important to who he was than the Spirit he'd accepted into his heart. Everything else—from the clothes he chose to wear to the skin and features God had clothed him in, were only trappings that might either provide example of or disguise the man he truly was in his heart.

Regina's face heated with shame. Marcus had never looked askance at her or at any of the tenants, even the poorest. How could she think this of him, that he would spurn a Suburan woman because she lacked patrician ancestry?

She straightened and knocked at the next door. In any case, this was no time for matchmaking. As she exchanged a hurried word with the tenant who opened at her knock, ensuring all within were safe, worry bit at her insides. Who else might be missing, besides Julia and Piscus? And would there be any answer at the baker's door? There was no body in the atrium; the woman had not leapt from her window. That brought little relief; terrible and unnecessary as that death would be, it was surely better than being devoured by the dead, perhaps to rise later herself in irrevocable hunger. And the thought of it brought Regina a pang of guilt; she'd been avoiding thinking about Julia, even playing matchmaker in her head, but she needed to speak with Father Polycarp about Julia.

Regina found herself taking her time, her steps methodical and precise, not hurrying. Reluctant to reach the fourth story. Marcus began to fidget, getting antsy beside her; he clasped his hands behind him as if to control it. That brought Regina another small smile, another small distraction from her worry; whatever name he claimed, doubtless some things about Marcus would *always* be patrician, such as his concern for his own dignity. Yet she was certain his heart belonged no longer to the Palatine Hill but to Father Polycarp and his God.

"Please take the third floor, I'll take the fourth," she told him. There was no need to make him wait for her reluctance. "Just take note of any doors that don't answer; I'll come to those."

He nodded eagerly and moved toward the stairs. Regina let out a sigh and resumed her own walk. She finished the last couple stops on this second floor and then moved to the stairs herself; she could hear Marcus's rapid steps on the walkway around the third story.

As she moved along the fourth floor, each door was answered, a weary or a delighted or a troubled face peering out at her. A few words exchanged. "Peace and grace to you," Regina would murmur after a moment, then move on. As she checked the rooms, one door after another, her tension tightened in her breast. Everyone was here. No one lost, no one eaten. But no one had seen Julia and her husband come in tonight.

The Subura was not a place where men and women *chose* to be out after dark. Not, at least, if their business in the alleys was the kind that might be conducted by daylight.

Julia's door was the third from the end. As before, it was ajar. Regina felt a chill as she lifted her hand and gave a couple of hard raps on the thin pine of that door.

No answer to the knock.

Dread clenched about her heart.

"Julia?" she called.

No sound within. On the story below, Marcus's voice was lifted as though he were arguing with one of the tenants. He probably wasn't, though—he was often animated when he spoke, and especially when he was nervous.

"Julia?"

She threw open the door with a cry. "Julia!"

She wasn't there.

The room was empty.

Regina went in and stood by the table, her heart in her throat. Too empty. The room was too empty. There were empty shelves.

The closet doors were open, but there were only a couple of worn tunics on the rack within.

She'd packed.

Julia had packed her things. She hadn't thrown herself from the window. She hadn't been eaten by the dead. She'd *planned* this departure.

She'd—

A low, keening cry rose in Regina's throat. She pressed her fingertips over her lips and leaned back against the table. Everything came together in her mind like so many leaves swept by the wind into one pile against a low wall, the pile growing until it might almost overwhelm the stones. *I was domina of my own house— I want it back, I want it all back—I'd do anything for that—this whole place is a travesty—I have no intention of staying here.*

"Oh Julia," she moaned, "what have you done?"

In the shed, Regina wondered where that woman was now, and what things she and her husband had told the praetor and what things they'd held back. Perhaps they'd held nothing back. Perhaps even now Julia was walking through a villa garden, one of those opulent gardens she'd craved, with flowery vines hanging from orchard trees, and great marble sculptures of fauns and naiads. Or perhaps she was reclining in a veiled palanquin, visiting one of the Forum markets to buy new house slaves with her thirty pieces of silver. All of those luxuries, all of those trappings—Julia would use them to tell herself who she was. In the Subura, where Regina and Marcus had found their names, Julia had been without family or identity, cast out from the life she'd valued; perhaps she had felt nameless, only a face among a thousand faces.

If only Regina had realized what Julia had been talking about—what she'd been, in her way, trying to confess to her.

Regina moaned softly and leaned her head back against the boards of the shed wall. Her breast felt tight. Difficult to take full breaths in this small shed, this holding place. She closed her eyelids and forced herself to breathe evenly. She'd been sold, like a slave—they all had.

She tried to think. She was the keeper of accounts, the observer and solver of problems, the deaconess. She had to think. What would become of them? Who had been arrested from the insula—and were they to be questioned or were they to be condemned? Where had they taken the father—what had they done with him?

Her eyes burned. Marcus stirred slightly, and she stroked his hair soothingly, holding in her tears. She knew at least one thing. Marcus lay beaten in her lap, and he needed her. She didn't know who else had been arrested, whether those in the larder had been taken, or some of those who'd hidden in their upper-story rooms while the guardsmen slammed through the door, or only herself and Marcus. But for Marcus Antonius at least, she was still the deaconess of the gathering in Rome. He was hurt, and he needed her.

At that moment there was a rattle in the lock.

Her eyes shot open.

It seemed to take a long time for the lock to turn, and as the rattling continued, her heart pounded. For a moment she was terrified that the lock wasn't turning because it was one of the dead at the door; memories of the night before fell on her. She watched the door, unable to see anything. Then the door swung open, and two men stood there. Living men. She stiffened, recognizing one—the man who had touched her. Framed in that door, he looked large as a Celt. The other she hadn't seen before; he was young, only a few years older than Marcus. They gazed in at her, perhaps taking in the sight of the smudges of dirt on her face, the bruise on her left cheekbone, and Marcus unconscious with his head in her lap.

"Look at the whore," the larger guardsman muttered to the other.

Regina's throat tightened. "I am a prisoner in this shed," her voice trembled, "but I will not take that name. I am a free woman."

"You." The guardsman stabbed his finger at her. "Are a cultist. A desecrator. You'll shut your mouth and let us have what we came for."

She stiffened, her pulse pounding in her throat. Quickly she tensed up, ready to fight. Something in the back of her mind started to scream as the large man moved toward her, his companion staying by the door.

But as he bent over her, he only seized Marcus by the arms and hauled him to his feet. The boy was still breathing raggedly, but his eyes fluttered open. The man began to muscle him to the door.

Regina leapt to her feet, her fright of the moment before forgotten in the face of a more terrible fear—that of separation. "*Where are you taking him*?"

The guardsman glanced over his shoulder, smirking at her. "He's a patrician, isn't he? Imagine that, skulking about with you rats. This little *fellator* will stand on the jury. Maybe he'll remember who he's supposed to be."

Regina spat on the guardsman's cheek; the man backhanded her. She fell to the straw, her head ringing, the left side of her face burning. She lay dazed. She heard Marcus moan her name faintly, then a scuffling sound as he was dragged from the shed. The slap of the door against the jamb. Then it was dark again, with only the thin shivers of light through the chinks in the wall.

Alone, Regina curled up and sobbed quietly.

This little shed was too much like that cargo hold she'd been chained in—so long ago—on the tossing sea journey from Syria to Italia. The clink of the chains, the leering faces of the flesh thieves who'd stolen her, crowding her into the hold with other

Syrian girls they thought desirable and marketable. Their hands on her body, grasping and bruising her. That whole journey had been a fever, a nightmare; her mind hadn't been right afterward, not for several years, not until Father Polycarp had come, clothing her and granting her a room to herself, with an open window.

Now that room was gone. All those she'd cared for and who'd cared for her were gone. She was as alone here as she'd been in the galley. The soiled straw scratched at her arms.

A while later, she lifted herself on her elbows, rolled, sat up. She breathed slowly. Wiped at her eyes with her fingers. She didn't know what would become of her when night came again. But whatever would be done to her, she would not meet it weeping. Forcing her hands not to tremble, she smoothed her dress, filthied from the streets and the straw. Then ran her fingers through her hair. When the guardsmen came for her, she would be ready.

"I am no whore," she whispered.

Another rattle in the lock. This time Regina stood to meet it, lifted her chin. She was a woman of Rome and a woman of the gathering. She had reason to be proud.

The shorter guardsman entered, and she could hear a man laughing somewhere outside. He laughed back, then swung the door shut. Then he stood before her and drew aside his cloak; she watched his face warily but didn't move. He took something out from under his cloak, pressed it into her hand. Her eyes widened as she felt the warmth of a fresh loaf of bread against her fingers. "What is this?" she breathed, searching his eyes.

"You are not alone." Breathing quickly, the guardsman took her other hand and drew with his finger against her palm the shape of a fish.

It was all she could do not to cry out. "Thank you," she gasped. She tore a small piece of the bread away and chewed it for a moment. The bread was still soft and moist, and easily swallowed. "Where is he? The father?"

"Another shed, not far. He is well; sometimes the men at his door can hear him praying. They say there will be a trial tomorrow."

Regina felt she might faint. She swayed slightly on her feet, clenched her hands around the bread. He was alive. Father Polycarp—her Polycarp—was alive. Thank God. He was alive.

"Can you take a message to him?"

The guardsman was silent a few moments, then shook his head. "I don't believe so. I have no business at his shed, and I could pretend I'd come to gawk at the prisoner, but—they wouldn't let me in." He paused. "I should tell you there are nine others. In the other sheds. Nine from your insula. I don't know if you knew."

Regina's heart missed a beat. "Others," she whispered. "Who?"

"I'm sorry. I don't know their names. I will see if I can find out."

Regina reeled at this news that confirmed all her fears. Others. Nine of them. How would the gathering survive this? And what would become of those who depended on the gathering? What about the men who came to Polycarp's larder to get bread for their children? What about old Flora, whose water jar Regina carried?

Yet Polycarp lived. And there was a friend among the guards.

Regina tried to gather herself; so many feelings pounded through her that she felt dizzy. She tore the loaf in half, handed one half to the guardsman, and for a few moments they ate together in silence. The man brought out from beneath his garments a tiny flask and held it, waiting. This kindness was unlooked for; it was something to hold onto. It occurred to her to doubt him, to suspect some trap for her. But Roman justice needed no trap to convict her. She *had* to trust; this sudden hope was too sharp in her breast.

"Thank you," Regina breathed, between swallows of soft bread. "This is of God."

"It is," the guardsman whispered. "I'll bring you word—what news I can—before the trial begins."

She placed her small hand over his. "Don't endanger yourself."

He shook his head. "No. No danger. If I come in here a few times, the others will simply think I'm using you." His face flushed in the dim light. "You must cry out, once or twice."

Regina nodded and sucked in a breath. After a moment she expelled it in a short, shrieking cry. Then another. The guardsman jumped. "How's that?" she whispered.

"Convincing." He passed the tiny flask to her, and she took a gulp gratefully, then sputtered and choked for a moment. It held wine, not water; it stung the back of her throat.

"I am sorry for the indignity of this," the guardsman muttered. "There's little I can do to ease it without suspicion. A hired guardsman isn't usually attentive to the needs of a slave."

Her eyes burned; she risked another sip, swallowed. "I am free."

"They will choose to believe you are not."

Regina nodded, handed the flask back in hands that shook—not from fear now but from excitement. "I don't remember your face from the gathering in the Catacombs."

"I was only there once." His face lifted. "But I have never forgotten it. The words he said. About the Gift."

Regina leaned in a little, whispering more intensely. "You are right to help us. The Apostle's Gift—it is *real*. I have seen it. I've seen what he has done. And the other things he teaches—that we each have a gift, no matter who we are or what class—those things are real too. You are right about me—I was a slave. Maybe I still am, to this day, though I fight my chains each morning. But

I too have a gift. I keep accounts for our insula. And you have a gift. One needs only look at your eyes to see it. I don't know what yours is. Maybe," she lifted the last of her bread, "maybe your gift is ministering to prisoners." She smiled. "I only tell you this because you need to know, whatever happens at that trial. His words are true."

"I believe it," he whispered. "Cry out again, domina—as though we are finishing our love—and then I have to go."

She did her best, though her face burned to make such sounds in the presence of a man who was not her lover. But in her heart a warmth and a strength was welling up. *Domina*, he'd called her. Lady of this house. Though this "house" was only a shed with dirty straw, he saw her within it as its keeper, not as a slave or a prisoner—despite his words earlier. She feared speaking again, for the gratitude in her was so strong it might spill from her in sobs or unintelligible sounds.

This next day might contain any peril. She might yet be beaten and raped. She and those confined in the other sheds might be burned alive or executed in any number of terrible ways. She didn't know yet what had become of those in the hiding place at the insula—save that nine were in prison sheds like this one. It was possible the Roman praetor might hunt through all the streets and insulae of Rome for those of the gathering. It was possible the hunt could spread to every city in the Empire. This had happened once before; it could happen again. Yet her hands trembled with hope. As long as a Roman guardsman could believe in the Gift and in the message, and bring bread to a prisoner who was without status or citizenship, as long as that could happen, the gathering was alive. In hiding, without refuge, yet fiercely alive. Suddenly she was certain that Polycarp was not weeping in his own shed, that he was standing and waiting for what would come, with that unbending strength of his. Her face flushed; she burned with shame at her vulnerability and her tears. She was the deaconess; Polycarp depended on *her*. The others in their sheds depended on her. This guardsman, in his way, depended on her. How could she have been so entirely without hope, so lost, weeping in the straw?

"Thank you," she managed to whisper. "What is your name?"

"I am Brutus Secundus."

"I will remember it, Brutus Secundus. You are blessed among the gathering for your kindness."

She tore a small stretch of cloth away from the hem of her ruined nightdress. After wetting it in a little wine from the flask, she began to scrub at her face and arms with it, cleaning the grime from her skin.

"I'll bring a cloth later." Brutus considered her a moment. "In fact, I'll bring a bucket of water if you wish it." Seeing her look, he added, "It won't be hard to explain. You're from the Subura. I need only tell the other guardsmen that I want my slut washed before I have her." He flushed in the dark. "Forgive the words, domina. We are rough men, and most of Rome looks down on us, even when Rome needs us. So we are used to looking down on the Subura; it can feel good knowing there *is* someone for us to look down on. It is not how *I* think, but it is how most of us think." He cast a glance at the filthy straw. "Yet no one should have to sleep in this. I'll bring water."

She understood the gift he was giving her, and why he'd used those words, though they had made the doors in her memory shift a moment on their hinges. *My* slut, he'd said. Brutus was offering her protection from the other men and asking nothing in return. Even as Polycarp had done, housing her in a room in his insula.

She nodded, her eyes moist. "Thank you," she whispered again. "Thank you."

Though she stood in peril for her life, though she'd been separated from Polycarp and Marcus and all the others, for the first time since the moaning of the dead in the alley she felt some measure of safety.

She let the dirtied cloth fall to the straw; she didn't dare tear away more of her dress. It was some relief, at least, and though she still smelled, with the sudden cleanness of her face she felt more capable, more sufficient for the needs of the day.

She drew in a breath, met Brutus's eyes. "I know Polycarp is guarded. If you have opportunity to speak to the others, please tell them that Regina and Polycarp stand firm. Tell them they must stand firm too. Tell them the gathering persists. That nothing is broken, nothing is ended. Please tell them this."

CAIUS LUCIUS JUSTUS

THAT NIGHT, the night before the trial, silence filled Caius's villa, dark and palpable. As no one had approached Livius's room for hours, the moaning within had ceased. That silence should have been a relief, a cool drink after a hot wind. Yet instead, the silence was menacing, a violence on the ears. It seemed a promise of fresh wailing, waiting only for the stumbling of one's foot to provoke a muffled curse or an unsteady tremble of one's hand to send a cup clattering to the polished marble floor. Such sounds as these might wake the horror that lay chained behind Livius's door. The slaves had performed their evening's duties in fear and now shivered on their pallets, waiting for uneasy dreams to take them.

In the praetor's study, Caius sat at his desk, his hand making anxious, jerking movements as he sketched the Latin letters of the last order he hoped to give as urban praetor and senior magistrate of the city. His hand had cramped, and now he clutched the stylus with a desperation that didn't suit the dignity of his office. He had already begun the order over again, twice. Had labored half the night on it. He stopped frequently, his expression grim. In the thunderous silence, he listened for sounds from his son's chamber, but heard nothing.

Once, he left his study and passed like a shadow through the sleeping villa until he reached his son's door. He reached for the handle. Stopped. Waited there awhile.

Caius's palms were sweating. He found it difficult to breathe. Horror of what waited on the other side of the door swept through him, shaking him like a fever. It was not grief but raw, animal *horror*. He felt that whether he turned the handle and went inside (though this he'd done a thousand times before) or turned from the door and fled, either way he would be stuck, body and spirit, into madness—if he did *anything* but stay very, very still and wait for this horror to pass.

As slowly as the creeping of a snail through the garden, rationality returned. His heartbeat slowed. For a moment he was dizzy; then he leaned against the wall by the door.

The horror would *not* pass, he realized. It would not end, not ever. Not unless he destroyed the body of his son.

But he could not do that. He couldn't.

The order he must write awaited, yet he avoided returning to the study. He left his son's door now and went to the slaves' quarters, woke one of them with a kick in the dark, sent him to bring wine to his study. Then Caius went and stood in the atrium to wait, gazing up at the stars. He had not looked at the stars for—a long time. Not since Livius had died.

The stars were lovely and cold, and he thought perhaps he had *never* seen them before, not truly. He gazed at them with his head tilted back, hands clasped behind his back in Roman fashion. Erect and dignified. His throat was tight. He could almost hear Scipia his wife laughing in the garden, as she used to. Grief welled up so full inside him that he could hardly breathe.

Scipia. How different his life was without her. Her laughter and the flash of her eyes had always distracted him from his duty, yet driven him too to excel at it. Tonight, on the eve of the trial, she would have known just what to say to quiet the troubles in his heart.

He had first seen her on the marble steps of the Senate House, wishing her aged father well as he climbed to a legislative battle over some question of public land. Caius had been one of the younger senators of his faction, possessing little rank then, only the great prestige afforded him by his family name and the dignity of a successful term as a minor official in the northern wars. He recalled standing at the doors of the House, gazing down the steps at that radiant woman, where she stood straight and slender as a statue of Rome on the steps. Caius had never been a hesitant man, and he'd presented the matter to his father in the most direct terms over dinner. A cold and unaffectionate man, with all that mattered to him concealed within an impenetrable shell of propriety and caution, Marcellus Lucius Justus had responded only with a grunt. But that had been enough. At dawn the next day, the older Lucius Justus had walked across the Palatine to the house of the Luculli and had made the marriage arrangements.

For Caius, that had been a year of Fortuna's favoring; a wedding, the softness of Scipia's lips on his, and then the miracle of her belly's gentle growth. In the Senate, Caius had spoken with passion and clarity of the need to return to traditions now fallen into disuse, to preserve the ways of their fathers. At home, he'd prayed beneath the masks of his *di parentes* and sat long in the evenings with his hand on Scipia's belly, awaiting patiently some kick or nudge from the child she would give him, the next of his family.

But Fortuna had played him false. His wife's death at Livius's birth had meant the absence of any good Roman mother to instruct Caius's son in how to live a pious life, one of proper respect for the honored fathers and fear of the Roman gods, piety that might have kept Livius safe from the Eastern superstitions that had so infected Rome. Caius himself had little to offer his son; his own father had barely spoken more than a few words to him during his childhood and his youth, and as an adult Caius had found that he was more at ease debating in the Senate or hiring advocates for the Roman courts than he was devoting time to his son at home. Buying a Greek slave girl to serve as nurse to young Livius had seemed a reasonable action to take when Scipia died, but the girl had filled Livius's mind with every kind of superstition, and Caius had sold her off in a fury before the boy was five. Buying her had been a mistake; he realized now he should have instead remarried, and at once. A quick remarriage would have meant suffering some loss of *dignitas,* but it would have been better for the boy.

And there might have been other children, if he had.

Perhaps he should *still* remarry.

He gazed up, his memories bitter within him. How beautiful those stars were, yet how violent and how cold.

A sudden wailing came to him on the night air, and he shuddered, his reflections shattered. The very sound he most dreaded: the moaning of the dead. But it did not come from behind his son's door. It was muffled by the walls of the villa. Perhaps far away. Sweat ran down Caius's face. In the night, that moaning brought a terror that could not be reckoned with or disciplined away. By day, the praetor might deal with the rising of the dead as a crisis to be met and addressed with dignity and action; by night, in this home so full of the presence and the memories of his own dead, the cries of those corpses outside were a dissolution of everything a man could be certain of. He should hear silence broken by occasional cries of birds or even a distant hum of human noise from the Subura, if he stepped out into the atrium and listened acutely. Or the sound of the wind in the cypresses on the far slope, above the Forum. There was a certain way Rome was supposed to sound, at night. No more. The wailing of the dead made what lay outside his walls in the dark uncertain. It was as though some wind had come and torn away the city he knew, leaving only moaning, chaotic darkness outside.

There was only one refuge left to him: his study, a tiny, enclosed trap of a space. Where that unfinished order awaited him. He walked back to it now, leaving the garden, and found that shutting his study door and drawing slats down over the window only muted the moans of the dead a little; he could still hear them, faint but persistent.

Before shutting the door, Caius retrieved the small silver tray left at the study's threshold by the slave he'd kicked awake, and he set it carefully on the desk; it carried a silver goblet filled with wine and a fresh bottle of ink. Caius could remember a time when such obedience and perfect discipline would have brought him pleasure, when seeing a slave leap to perform a task promptly and properly had been as cooling to his temperament as a glass of the best wine in the city. He took no pleasure in it now.

He sat at his desk. Everything was coming apart. The events of the day had speared deep into his chest. That corpse-woman crashing through his door, hands lifted and growling with a hunger to bite and tear apart everything that mattered in Rome. Polycarp's unapologetic defiance of Roman tradition, And an hour before that, Caius's interview with the slave the Christians called a "deaconess," whose words had pried inside him and found where he was vulnerable: his shame at having failed his son and having failed even his wife's memory.

He closed all of that off inside him, breathed raggedly. *Dignitas.* Duty. What was the hour? He had to finish writing that order. He reached again for his stylus and ink. Lifting the stylus in his hand, he looked at the small Latin letters his father had carved into it, before Caius was born: the family name. Caius felt the pressure of his ancestors' eyes, the open, vacant eyes of those dozens of masks, though they hung in his son's room and not in this one. They had abandoned him, those ancestors, yet still he felt the weight of their demands. Impossible, unanswerable demands.

Muttering under his breath, he hastened to make the small, angular letters of the Latin script on the parchment he'd started earlier. His mouth was dry and his eyes bloodshot; he kept lifting one hand to scrub at them with his knuckles. He did not know how late it was. He labored over the order.

When Caius finished at last, he felt hollow, like bark with no wood inside it, a cypress scored and burned out by lightning. Shaking from lack of sleep, his hands folded the parchment, and he set it carefully aside to take with him in the morning. He rose groaning from his seat and took up the oil lamp from his desk (its reek had filled the small study); he took up also the goblet of wine his slave had brought and which he hadn't touched yet. Gently he carried both out with him. He had one more duty to perform this night.

For a mercy, the dead, both inside and outside his villa, were quiet. Walking stiffly against his weariness, Caius went first to the atrium, to the apricot tree that stood in the northwest corner with a marble dryad embracing it. Scipia had loved that tree and that dryad, but Caius was too tired now to mourn her. He had burned himself out; he was finished. In another day, everything would be finished. Reaching up, he plucked two apricots from the branches—two golden fruit, August ripe—and, making a fold in his garment, he carried them with him, with the oil lamp in one hand, the goblet in the other.

As in most patrician families, Caius Lucius lived near his dead, and his dead slept near their living; the mausoleum was a great marble enclosure just outside the villa and nearly as large as it. A little path led from the back door of his villa up through lush shrubs and flowering beds to the great marble gate of that place of stillness. Caius murmured a prayer to Janus, god of doors, and a word of respect to the *di parentes* who had fathered his family, then slid open the gate and slipped into the courtyard of their house.

The garden within had grown wilder than the garden in his atrium; it was overrun with tangled vines and clinging flowers, and the small pond near the path was choked with nenuphars. Unpruned branches overhung the little path that wound among the shrubs and the marble chambers of the dead—all their houses, each with a door shut tightly. The many generations of his dead. Caius stopped at the doorstep of his grandfather's resting place and looked around. It was not *his* work to keep either this court-yard or his own atrium tidy—that was a slave's work. But it came to him suddenly that he had no garden slave to tend his estate. The thought made him sigh. Another failure. How mournful this garden of the dead looked. Untended. He was as complicit as any Christian in Rome in the neglect of the dead.

He poured the wine gently, spilling a little of it on the mar-ble steps. Then he set the cup down and placed the two apri-cots beside it. Wearily he sat on the doorstep but kept his back straight; he was in the presence of his ancestral dead, and though their censure would be silent, here *dignitas* was more important than ever.

"I let the hearth fire go out," he said quietly. "The night my son was born. I shamed you. But still I bring you food and wine the night before every Ides and the night before every Kalends, as the men of this family have done for six hundred years." His voice trembled. "Tomorrow I will seek justice against the man who has offended all Rome's dead. And once that is achieved, I will seek justice against myself, as I ought to have done months ago. For I also have guilt toward you, honored fathers. I also must make atonement." He lowered his eyes. "I fear it, *di parentes*. And I have shamed you too with my fear." He hadn't had the courage to end it before. Death without leaving behind a son to tend the hearth fire for him could mean eternity as a wandering, wasted spirit. But he knew now that he was already living as a wandering shade. Unrestful death could not be that much worse than this faded, empty life—and it would have one crucial difference. Having cast himself upon his sword, he'd have regained his honor.

He glanced about the garden, his eyes bleak. "No son will bring food and wine for me, and no scion of our family will bring you food on the next Kalends. I hope my actions tomorrow will bring you rest and atone for my breach of duty this next Kalends; I know there will be no rest for me. I ask for your blessing, *di parentes*. I have never needed it more."

Caius lowered his head, as a son receiving a blessing. A breeze caught at the cypresses along one wall; he heard the soughing in the high branches. There was no moaning of the dead.

Once, the silence of his own ancestors after a prayer would have chilled him, signifying as it might a removal of their protection over his house. But now he knew there were worse things to hear from his dead than silence.

———

As the sun lifted above the cypresses and the morning haze, promising the hottest day the summer had yet brought to Rome, Caius stepped down from the villa door into the street between two lines of standing, respectful lictors. He'd slept little and his body was heavy beneath the precisely draped folds of his toga, but at the sight of his lictors he straightened his shoulders. They were a visible reminder of his duty, his last duty to Rome. He must hurry to a brief bath; then he had a shrine to visit and the sacrifice of a bull to oversee, so that the gods would attend the day's trial at least partly appeased and in a good mood. Afterward, he'd repair to the temple of Justitia, where in a few hours the day's jurors would be gathering, ceremonially washing their hands and faces at the gate to enter clean into the presence of Justice.

Here, at Caius's own doorstep, the urban praetor looked out at the gentle curve of the street and at the cypresses that half hid the grounds of neighboring villas. A few other patricians were about; he saw two men in pristine togas walking slowly along the hill and, moving the other way, four bronzed slaves carrying on their shoulders the weight of a palanquin, behind whose colored veils reclined some Roman domina or some daughter of high family. Somewhere a raven called. Everything Caius saw was perfectly placed, perfectly cultivated. Every person he saw wore their clothing well; every tree wore its foliage well, trimmed and lovely. Everything here was as Rome should be, the very Rome he used to serve with love rather than weariness. For the first time in many days, he took a moment's comfort in this well-disciplined set upon which the intrigues and debates of Roman family and Roman policy were played out. Caius drew in a deep breath, tasting the warm August air; it carried the scent of lilacs from the villa gardens and, beneath that heavy perfume, the sharper, resin tang of cypresses.

Tucked neatly into the sash across his toga was the parchment he'd folded up before leaving his study this morning. That parchment would keep this Rome, his Rome, safe and clean. There must be no more violated villas, no more Roman girls stumbling down the street without a palanquin and without air in their lungs, to claw through the doors of state officials.

"This is the day on which all depends." He said the words aloud and nodded to his lictors. "Stand tall; look well. Not even a hair out of place. Today, remember that you are Romans attending Roman justice and ensuring Roman peace in a barbarous and degraded world."

"Yes, praetor," one of them said.

"The Roman dead rise furious at dishonor." His face was hard. "Today we will show them that their sons are still worthy of them."

"Yes, praetor."

Caius nodded again and stepped forth into the street. But almost immediately he stopped; his heart gave a lurch. Near enough to shout at, a figure had just come around the corner of the villa across the street and was stumbling unevenly along its wall. Its left side fell against the marble, and it stumbled along a little farther with its shoulder against the stone.

Caius's throat clenched; he held back a moan of horror. He held up his hand to halt the lictors.

Caius watched, every sense alert, as the figure dragged itself along the wall. It was a man, young, perhaps twenty. A breastplate on his chest, bloodstained. A sandal on one foot, the other bare. Thick leather. Military grade. But the man carried no weapon. His hair was cropped short, his face pale. There was a bloody wound on his arm.

Caius held his breath; he could sense the lictors holding theirs. But there was no scent of death in his nostrils. The blood on the man's arm looked fresh. He stared ahead sightlessly, but his skin didn't have the gray pallor of the dead. The military dress was an oddity.

"Soldier!" Caius's voice carried across the street.

The man's head turned, too slowly. Then he left the wall and staggered into the street toward them, one hand lifted, a moan from his lips. Caius tensed. The lictors drew back.

Then the moan became a word. "*He—eelp—*"

Caius let out his breath slowly. His legs felt suddenly weak; he forced himself not to buckle. "Get him," he snapped.

But even as a couple of his lictors stepped forward, the soldier missed his step, his body tilting to the side in a curiously graceful motion; then he fell. Cursing, Caius broke into a run, coming quickly to the man's side. Several of his lictors gathered in a helpless circle about the man; others hung back. Caius's pulse sped up. He didn't understand how this bloodied, stumbling soldier had come to the Palatine or why, but this was a Roman soldier dying in the street. He reached the man where he lay panting on the stones, then stopped sharp, everything in him going cold, as his eyes found the wound on the man's arm.

The wound was a half-moon circle of teeth marks.

As he had in that hour when a dead patrician girl had broken into his station by the temple, Caius took note of details. The man's face was flushed with fever, he was shaking. His lips kept moving as though he would speak, but his eyes were glassy. And that livid mark on his arm—Caius had seen such wounds before. On his son's body, and on the bodies of house slaves he'd sent to tend his son.

The bite. The wound that meant restless death.

The man moaned again—a sound of helplessness and anguish, not of hunger—and his eyes, horribly glazed, gazed up at Caius.

"Water," he moaned.

"Where did you come from?" Caius hissed.

"Water—please—tribune—"

"What has happened? Where did you come from? How were you bitten?" His voice sharp with urgency.

"Tribune," the man groaned. He twisted onto his side, shaking. "Tribune!"

"I am not your tribune. You are in the streets of Rome. Explain yourself."

The man's eyes fixed on some point just past Caius's ear. The praetor could feel heat radiating from the man's body as though a sun were barely concealed beneath the thin sheen of his flesh.

"Centurion—Licinius Albus sent me—find the tribune—tell him—" A spasm of coughing.

"Tell him what?" Caius demanded. The lictors shuffled their feet and stayed well back from the dying man. There were whites around their eyes. They could all see the bite.

"We fought them," the man choked, his hands convulsing in the grip of the fever. "We fought them—the risen fathers. Fought them. They pinned us—yesterday morning—in a small insula. Held out as long as we could. Not just forty, tribune. Not just forty. More came. Many. We fought them. The risen fathers. Water—please—water."

Caius's blood ran cold at both the mention of many dead at the riverside insulae and at the mention of Roman soldiers within the boundaries of the city. He thought of the medals on his wall, the rusted *gladius* in his study: military battles were to be fought along the Rhine or the Danube, never the Tiber. Battles in Rome were to be fought in the Senate House, if at all. Much good that the Senate ever did. The thought of legionnaires within the city chilled him. Yet for a single, dizzying instant, Caius's mind grasped what he might do with a legion of Rome's best at his call. Cleanse every insula in Rome of its dead in the space of a single evening. His hands shook as though he was fevered himself. No. No, he was not a Caesar. The last time a man had unloosed a thousand legionnaires within the boundary of Rome, the city had been torn in two. That must never happen again. What purging had to be done, must be done with limited civil forces, easily controlled and easily dispensed with when they were no longer useful.

The praetor took a slow breath, the momentary vision passing from him. "Where is your centurion?"

"Eaten." The man's lips curved in a terrible, fevered grin. "Tore him out through the—window. All those—hands. Couldn't stop them. Eaten—eaten."

Silence settled in the street, broken after a moment as another cough racked the man's body. Caius listened, straining to hear sounds above the low hum of human noise by the river far downhill. He could hear no moan of the dead. Yet he remembered the wailing in the night; the silence now seemed as ominous as the silence outside Livius's door—as though the dead were waiting only for some misstep or shouted word to wake them and bring them groaning up the hill.

Caius crouched beside the feverish soldier, took a better look at him. He had a scar across the bridge of his nose; it cut across his right cheek almost to the ear—a remnant of some battle fought on some far frontier against a living enemy who bled when you cut him and who tried to cut you back. The skin of this legionnaire's face was blotchy and dry, every hint of moisture baked from his flesh by the fever within him.

"Your centurion brought armed legionnaires into Rome, I take it." Caius spoke quietly, for this man's ears only. His tone low and intense. "I am not surprised that the gods dealt with him harshly for that impiety and that disrespect for our law. This is a civil problem that needs a civil solution. It is not a military problem." Caius glanced up at one of his lictors and nodded. As the togate man stepped near, Caius reached for the fallen soldier's hip, drew from its sheath the long knife he found there. The soldier was convulsing again, his arms clutched to his breast. Caius spoke through a tightened, dry throat. "May you find Elysium," he murmured, then drew the knife swiftly across the man's throat. Blood flowed out around the blade; Caius was careful not to let it touch his skin. The man gurgled and was still.

Breathing hoarsely, Caius rose to his feet. "Take this," he murmured, passing the hilt to the lictor who stood by him. "Go within and summon my slaves." The lictor stepped away; Caius did not take his eyes from the dead man, whose blood had pooled about his head. "The head must be destroyed," he said softly, to no one in particular. His hand strayed to the folded parchment at his side. Caius's certainty of what had to be done tightened and solidified into a small rock inside him. In the darkness of his study the night before, he'd been assailed with doubts and many strange thoughts. Now he was certain.

Arrests and trials and prayers to the gods weren't enough to contain this festering, hungering pestilence; the insult to Rome's fathers must be removed, must be utterly cut out of the city, as a surgeon might cut a tumor from a man's leg. Caius would burn the thread of Polycarp's life, then hand the parchment to his lictors, issuing an order against the Subura that would be executed in blood. It would happen swiftly, but it would happen one district at a time, so that all the districts would not rise together in a general riot. Wherever they found dead, the guardsmen of the city were to put everyone in that building or that street to death. Many of the living would perish—but they were only people of the Subura. Illiterate lawbreakers and blasphemers of the gods.

He could think only of his son's door and the terrible, fragile silence behind it. No more patrician families need lose their sons or their daughters to this atrocity.

He heard the creak of the villa door opening behind him and turned to see the lictor he'd sent reemerging onto his doorstep, attended by two of the villa's male slaves. Caius spared them only a glance. "Clean this body from the street. One of you run for a surgeon. The brain must be cut away cleanly, then the head sewn up. I weary of burning the bodies of good Roman men and women. This one fought in Rome's wars; let him be interred with honor—as soon as his family can be found. Make haste."

And with that, Caius stepped around the body and moved down the street, his lictors flanking him.

Anger seethed in him; he would see justice done this day.

Someone must atone for the dishonor done to the neglected fathers. For the hearth fires whose coals had gone cold. For the little shrines whose marble steps were dry and unstained by wine because those who should tend them had become cultists.

He would see Polycarp burn like a sacrifice. He would watch the old Greek's flesh curl and blacken in the heat. And then, when this duty was completed, he would hand his secret order to the lictors and would go home. He would then have done all that he could, all that he must do as a father to the Roman people in the Emperor's absence; he would be free then to focus on his duties to his own home and to atone for his own personal loss of honor. He would lock the gate of his villa and walk to his son's room and wish him well. Then to his study. There he would take down from its place on the wall the sword that had rested there since the days of his military service in Dacia, before his son's birth. He would slide the blade from its leather, look for a few moments at the reflection of his cold face in the gleaming metal, then set the hilt against the floor.

He would quietly fall on his sword. And it would be over. His honor recovered.

After he watched Polycarp burn.

POLYCARP ON THE IDES OF AUGUSTUS

THE GATES to the temple of Justitia swung open, revealing the carefully prepared theater of the day: a sunlit courtyard with a floor of dust and gravel, the temple itself at the far end gleaming white (the marble freshly washed). Before the temple, the white curule seat where Caius the praetor sat, the lictors in a row behind him before the temple steps, holding bundles of rods tied with ceremonial cord, representing state authority to discipline and punish. To the right, a narrow pit in the earth where a fire might be lit; to the left, rows of benches and carefully groomed, togate men seated on them. Many leapt to their feet as the guardsmen pulled Polycarp through the gate, and in an instant the low hum of conversation in the courtyard was shattered by cries of rage and fear:

"Desecrator!"

"You make our youth turn from their ancestors!"

"You starve our dead!"

"You famish our temples and shrines!"

"You sicken Rome!"

"I lost my *wife* to you, you filthy *fellator*!"

And one man who must surely have been the youngest there beat his chest with his hand and yelled: "Give us back our fathers' Rome!"

Polycarp let the shouts wash over him. He heard in their voices the anguish of their spiritual crisis. In the past few days, they had heard the moaning of the dead nearer their doors; the dead had attacked the very Palatine by night. Patrician Rome had wakened and looked about in horror. They didn't know what was happening or why; they knew only that they were threatened.

As the jurors on their benches clamored for his blood, Polycarp looked about him. Though considerably smaller, this courtyard was an arena not unlike the Circus Maximus where other leaders of the gathering had once been tossed to the chained dead. Before Rome had built any Circus or Colosseum or public arena, gladiators had performed their games at family feasts in the villas of the Palatine, their gory deaths a sacrifice to honor the ancestors of that family. In the same way, the deaths of the Christians in that evil time had been meant to honor and appease the disrespected, wrathful, and rising dead. Now, this day, the dead were restless again, and the guardsmen led Polycarp before the screaming jurors as a sacrifice to their dead. Before bringing him in, they'd first given him a clean white tunic to wear, then replaced the manacles on his wrists. He wore the costume of a culprit, but it occurred to him that it was also the costume of the ritual sacrifice, with perhaps one difference in the details. When a Roman bull was brought to the altar, temple attendants pulled the bull in with but a bit of white string about its horns. Polycarp felt the heaviness of the chains depending from his wrists—did they need so much metal to restrain one old man?

Polycarp looked at Caius where he sat across the long court-yard, stern and cold. Then he glanced past the praetor's curule chair, letting his gaze settle on the tall statue of Justitia where she stood at the top of the steps, one hand upraised as if to forbid entry, the other holding a great pair of scales, and a diadem on her brow—as though to suggest that in Rome, which in previous centuries had been governed by no king or queen or emperor but only a senate of men who trusted to their own hearts and minds to find consensus, that here Justice alone was regal.

How lovely, that marble face. A fold of stone cunningly con-trived to resemble soft fabric covered her eyes. Justitia seemed calm, impassive, and entirely unmoved by the cries of the jury. A wry smile tugged at Polycarp's lips. "This is not what I imagined your temple would sound like, Justitia," he murmured.

At a hard shove against his back, Polycarp nearly lost his footing.

"Be silent, desecrator," the guardsman barked.

Holding his peace, Polycarp focused for a moment simply on walking over the sand toward Caius's seat. He ignored the heat of the sand beneath his feet. Heavy on his shoulders sat the fatigue of having looked into the eyes of the walking dead, and his body was sore; he growled low in his throat. He *must* have the strength for this day. He had a role to play, lines to speak. Not those Caius expected, perhaps. He had been playing his part on a larger stage long before this day, a stage the shape and size of a city—but this day would likely be his final act. To the Greeks and the Romans both, the world itself was a stage on which the theater of history was played out for the entertainment and delight of the gods. Men and women quarreled and fought and died on that stage, until the god descended in a machine to intervene at the end of the drama. But as a father of the gathering, Polycarp saw the stage differently. On this stage, men and women who knew God could play the active part of the device that would carry into the theater the *deus ex machina*, the god in the machine. Their role was that of God's machine, God's body. They were his hands and his feet, stepping in not just at the end but at the very moment in the drama in which they found themselves placed. Through the gathering, God might intervene early to transform the grisly sets of the Subura and the cold, remote sets of the Palatine into new places, and to change the players' costumed garb to represent miraculous transformations within their characters.

This day had been long rehearsed. Now Polycarp hoped he could call at least a few of the others in this arena—the jurors, the lictors—to play the parts they truly needed to play, to see their togas and their carefully groomed hair, and these very manacles Polycarp himself wore, for the costumes they in fact were.

Polycarp had prepared himself. All the previous night, he'd waited in a cramped shed with little sleep and no company but the occasional, distant moans of wandering dead downhill by the river. A long time he'd lain awake on the straw, listening for those groaning cries. His eyes stung with tears. In the dark, he contemplated the misery of the earth. Those moaning things by the Tiber bank had been men and women, fearing and loving and craving. Locked into little tenements that crowded narrow water browned with human waste, in life they'd hungered and found no answer to their hunger. Now that hunger had been translated into something eternal. At one point during the night, Polycarp had pressed his hands hard over his ears, unable to bear any more. He'd turned his face into the straw and wept. He was old; it came to him suddenly that he needed to find another, some other to care for the gathering. In the next day he might be dead. He didn't think about the fire pit; he thought only of the weakness of his body and the emptiness of his hands, which held no bread, could never hold enough bread to feed those who needed it. And within every set of eyes he'd seen, living and dead, there had been broken lives, so many. What had his life been worth, when the gathering was so small, the hunger so great? In those cries in the night, he heard all of Rome suffering, and he was spent.

Toward dawn as he lay half awake, he'd heard a new sound: the raucous cries of geese rising in the distance above their nests at the river. He listened, his eyes wide in the dark. The dead must be disturbing the geese, as the Celts had disturbed them in the chill at dawn, centuries ago. Perhaps those cries were cries of warning. Perhaps the cries of the geese were no less a sign than the beetle in the field of wheat—were there Romans in the city even now lying awake, listening, even as he was?

The morning light brought resolution. Polycarp's guards gave him no food and little to drink, but did bring a basin of shallow water to wash his face. He cupped his hands in it, brought the water to his face. The coolness of it had brought fresh life to him; he recalled his baptism in Thessaly. His master was sufficient to this day, even if he himself was not.

Now, as he neared the temple end of the courtyard accompanied by a guardsman, Polycarp turned his head and gave the jurors a more searching look, and caught his breath. Among them was a face he knew. On the back benches, huddled in on himself, silent, sat Marcus Antonius. The boy's bowed shoulders bore a toga in the patrician cut, and Polycarp sorrowed to see it. What was in the boy's heart, forced to wear the uniform of all that he'd rejected? It was plain to see that he did not sit there dressed so of his own accord. The boy's face was dark with bruises. His sullen eyes gazed at the temple grounds; as though ashamed of where he sat and what he wore, he didn't look at the father.

Polycarp let out his breath slowly. *Ah, Marcus, Marcus.* Something began to ache in his chest. How bad had the raid on the insula been? Had the hiding place in his larder been found? Had Regina made it out? Had anyone? A momentary guilt sat queasily in his belly. Regina had wanted him to hide all signs of their faith, conceal themselves entirely; he had refused that extremity. What pain had his choices brought now to her and the others?

The guardsman's hand clutched Polycarp's arm, and the old man stopped, straightened. He was a few steps before the curule seat. Turning his eyes from Marcus's face, he could feel the intensity of Caius's gaze. For Marcus, at least, he must stand tall and represent the gathering well. With an inner growl, he reminded himself: his God was the same within the walls of this temple as he was outside of them. A man who served him must stand no less steadily here than elsewhere.

"Polycarp of Larissa, then of Smyrna, now of Rome." Caius's voice was coldly formal. He'd assumed the voice of the praetor urbanus, with the full weight of Roman tradition and Roman justice behind him. "You are called to give answer before the People of Rome in the presence and precinct of the goddess Justitia."

"And I have come, Caius Lucius." Polycarp made a show of looking about the temple grounds. Then he shook his head slightly, as though bewildered. "Where are the advocates?"

"You are a Greek." The praetor's voice was sharp. "And you have lived many years in the Subura, surrounded by the most disreputable persons. Your citizenship cannot be verified. Therefore none are needed; the jury requires only a questioning of the accused and the confirming testimony of two witnesses."

"I see. But you are wrong, Caius Lucius Justus. I do have an advocate, and one who will speak directly to the hearts of the jurors. Maybe they will listen. Maybe they will not." He shook his head. "Where are your witnesses, then?"

"In good time." Caius waved his hand in dismissal. "First there are questions I intend to ask. It would be best for the admissions to come from your lips. The offenses for which you stand here carry a capital penalty, but I would offer you the opportunity to die well, Polycarp."

The corner of Polycarp's lip curved. "I thank you for that respect, Caius. I hope I have lived well enough to die well." He bowed his head slightly. The chains were heavy about his wrists, and it was difficult in the heat to stay standing; he longed for a chair. But his comfort did not matter. What mattered this day was that he stand with dignity and bear witness only to things that were true, whatever the threat. His words must plant seeds in dry hearts. Those jurors would likely burn him, but he might yet with his words wake them to the futility and falsehood of the roles they played. Something might begin here that would continue in conversations and disputes and questionings around every family room in patrician Rome. It was not only those jurors on their benches who listened. His words here would matter to every member of the gathering in Rome wherever they now hid, whether in Suburan insulae or merchants' houses or high villas. His words would matter to every member of every gathering hidden in cities across the world and to every gathering in centuries yet unborn. Before so vast an audience, he must stand without giving thought to the weakness of his body or the possibilities of failure. "Ask your questions of me. I am ready."

The praetor stood very straight, Roman straight, in his seat; his white marble chair had no back. Chairs with ornately carved backs were for barbarian princes and slothful magistrates in frontier towns. A Roman wanted no prop to hold him up.

Caius watched him intently. "You do not deny that you are a leader of the followers of the rabbi from Palestine?"

"No, I do not deny it. Why should I?"

"And that you have, often and frequently, led others, both citizens and otherwise, to these strange beliefs?"

The jurors leaned forward on their benches, the low rustle of their togas and the low murmur of their voices sounding like the coming of a flood, rushing slowly nearer out of the distance.

Polycarp paused and lifted his head. For a moment his eyes shone bright. "I am an old man, Caius."

"Answer the question—"

"—I *am* answering the question." He swallowed his anger; he must not allow this praetor, who stank of fear and eagerness for blood, to prod him. "But I am old, and I talk—slowly. Also because I am old, I like to have company when I break my bread and when I go to worship. I used to have old men like myself to talk with, but now I am the only one left. Sometimes it is good to have young people who will pass you a bowl of wine and listen to your stories."

He looked at the jurors. Many of them wore frowns of discomfort. The youth who had beaten his chest with his hand and cried out *Give us back our fathers' Rome!* looked stunned, as though he'd been slapped. One middle-aged man on the back bench was chewing on his cheek—as though chewing on unexpected thoughts—much as a goat might chew its cud while resting in the pastures of Thessaly. Marcus appeared to be holding his breath.

Polycarp's words gave their anger nothing to feed on. He could see in their faces and in the way some of them turned to whisper to each other that he was not what they'd expected. After all, they had come not to perform the true duty of a jury but to see with their own eyes the desecrator, the one who starved the dead of food and then touched the dead with his hands. They had come for a quick trial and a quick killing.

It was harder to grasp the iron spear of rage in clenched fists when you had confronting you no visible monster but only an old man who talked about his life, one not unlike the grandfathers in their own families, those men who were soon to join the honored dead and to whom those families looked for wisdom and moral grounding. It was likely that when the jurors heard stories of the desecrators—those who led astray the youth of Rome and woke the resting dead—they didn't think of them in the shape of an old man. The accused who now stood before them on the sand: was he a betrayal, a perversion of everything they looked to in an aged man, or was he one of their elders calling them to account? Their faces bore the confusion of this moment.

"You will not deceive us with the smooth rhetoric of a Greek, Polycarp." Caius's voice, clear and cold, cut through the rustle of noise, his words a reminder that it was at least not a *Roman* elder to whom they listened. "You will answer questions with an *I do* or an *I do not*, with the plainness that the good citizens of our jury expect. We are not here to hear your stories but to do justice."

"I see." Polycarp met Caius's eyes, and after a moment the Roman blinked and looked quickly away. Polycarp sighed. In that brief gaze, he'd seen a grief that would howl like a wolf in the hills, if it were not tightly chained and muzzled; the praetor had blinked before he could see more. Caius was not a youth, but he was too young to carry such a weight of sorrow and remorse within him. How had he been hurt so badly? Had he no wife to soothe his cares? No children to bring him the healing of laughter? He had no gathering to confess his sins and his suffering to, and his gods were impatient with confessions.

"What else do you have to ask?" Polycarp said.

Caius looked shaken, as though he'd sensed Polycarp's searching of his heart. He drew a breath, but his voice now was hoarse. "Polycarp, do you teach to others the perverse religion of the Jews, taking from them the religion of our fathers?"

Polycarp would have liked to quibble with *teach, perverse, Jews,* and *taking,* but decided there was nothing to be gained in it. It was a simple enough question. "I do."

"Do you teach them by eating the flesh and drinking the blood of your cult's dead founder, that they can attain immortality?"

They were speaking different languages and different scripts, the praetor and the father. Polycarp held the silence a moment— the murmur from the jury was getting ugly again—"I do. However—"

"Do you then consume flesh and blood?"

"I consume bread and wine." Polycarp's voice became a growl.

"An *I do* or an *I do not* will suffice, Polycarp. Do you take into your body flesh and blood?"

"I do not."

"Do your followers?"

"Certainly not."

"And is it untrue that you meet for your rites among the bodies of the Roman dead?"

A weight of dread settled over Polycarp. So Julia had revealed that. He'd feared it. The Catacombs might be watched in the future. It seemed certain now that he would not be a lone sacrifice. As in the time of Nero, there might be widespread arrests. Rome had burned once in a time of plague, and his people had burned even after the other fires were put out. Was that what his dream had foreboded? He could hear the muffled click of Despair's claws on the sandy ground. A glance across the courtyard showed the great beast settling into a crouch beside the cold fire pit. The beast was hungry.

A strange feeling of continuity came over him as he gazed across the dusty courtyard at the Roman praetor. How many had stood here—not in this walled compound, but in a hundred arenas like it, in different cities, questioned in different languages yet speaking the same lines he now must speak, held because they had devoted themselves to sharing bread and had denounced those who kept their larders locked, or because they had shared at times with their neighbors a fierce certainty that there were some things that locked doors and high walls and hired swords cannot turn back—and a fierce hope that something else *could*.

He remembered Paul, who'd worn chains much like these a few generations ago. He remembered Yirmiyahu before the king of Yerusalem and Daniel before the princes of Babylon. He glanced once at Marcus, who sat with lowered head on the jury, wondering if he too might one day have to stand in chains like his. He wondered who else would stand and give witness, after him. His lips were dry with thirst, and the heat against his scalp made his body want to sway where it stood, but he stood firm, and his heart hardened within him. This was the crucial day: he would not be standing here if his master did not have something for him to say and something for that jury to hear. He believed that. He had to. He turned his back on the beast and the pit.

"It is true," he murmured, "that we meet in whatever places seem safest."

"Your own words convict you." Caius's lip curled, though his eyes remained unsettled. "I give you this chance, Polycarp, to make amends. Do you now recant your superstition and pledge to do what you can to return the children you have corrupted to the ways of their fathers?" Recant. A hard knot of anger burned in Polycarp's chest. "Forty years and six I have served my master, and in all that time he has treated me well. Why should I turn my back and blaspheme him now?" He faced the jury, his voice rising, his patience fraying. "In our father Peter's time," Polycarp declared before Caius could interrupt him, "the Emperor of Rome threw many of the gathering into the Colosseum, where they were eaten. Your fathers wished to believe that those who died in the Colosseum were bread to satisfy the ancestors. Now we all stand here again, in this arena. Your praetor intends my death to atone for the dishonor you believe my gathering has done to your ancestors. And just as the Emperor casts bread to the crowds, your praetor intends to cast some bread to you, good jurors. Because you are hungry. You are in crisis. It is hoped that my death may relieve the bite of your hunger for certainty and safety, and that it may relieve the bite of the dead's hunger for honor. I fear you are much deceived. My death is not the bread you need. Nor are you the people in Rome who need bread most."

Polycarp grunted as though dismissing the jury and turned to the curule chair, his voice stern now. "But come, let us finish these games, Caius Lucius Justus. I do not know how long my body can stand on this hot sand."

Caius observed him a moment with narrowed eyes. The jury seemed to be holding its breath. The youth who'd called out was frowning as though a forest had sprung into being in the soil of his mind and he was now trying to find his way through it. The man of middle age was still chewing slowly on his cheek, watching the father now with a cold, concentrated look, as though to say, *Your words do not move me, old Greek.* Marcus still looked weary, resigned. Polycarp sighed softly. Though it was the others he must persuade, it was Marcus's heart that mattered to him most. It was painful to see him so. He would like to put some strength into the boy's heart, some firmness into his back. He yearned to call out to the boy: *Remember you are a child of God, Marcus. He has wakened you and adopted you from your old life. He has fed you, bread and wine. He has clothed you in his love, a finer garment than any toga. He has commissioned you, equipping you with a gift invisible yet potent: your desire to seek out truth, whatever the cost, and prune from your life all that is untrue. You are brave, my son, and you have been adopted into the family of the bravest, by one who is* paterfamilias *to all who live and breathe. Take pride in your sonship. No son of our God need lower his head at the world's scorn or its bruising. Remember who you are, my son.*

But of course he could not call those words across the sand. He could only speak the words that were right for this day and this place, and hope that Marcus heard in them the words he could not say and found strength.

Caius stirred. "So be it." His eyes were dark. "Guardsmen! The first witness. Bring her."

There was a rustle; someone was being brought out from around the back of the temple. A murmur passed through the jury as a woman was led out into the courtyard—without chains.

It was Julia. Plump and red faced in the heat, she avoided looking at Polycarp, but went to stand a few strides to his left, between him and the jury. Her garments were finer than he recalled—she wore thick-soled, freshly made sandals and a gown of purple, with pearls about her throat. Though her face shone with sweat, she looked very much like an equestrian merchant's wife, and not a baker's. Polycarp glanced about, but did not see Piscus. Perhaps he was waiting behind the temple too. Two witnesses, Caius had said.

Well. Now the test truly began.

"Julia," Caius said quietly. "You carry an august name, the name of one of our most revered houses. A caprice and a prideful overreaching on your parents' part, I expect. But today you can show that you merit such a name as that of the Julii. Your words will help us decide on a just verdict and just action, and will aid us in protecting Rome."

Julia's shoulders were very tense. Polycarp watched her, a flicker of anger swiftly dampened by sorrow. The line of her shoulders spoke of pain from old wounds reopened, of regret, of bitterness directed against herself and others. He marveled that the jury could not see the way she stood; to his eyes, her pain this day was so visible, it hurt to gaze at her. What Pandora's box had she unlocked within her breast when she left the insula?

"You stand in the precinct of the goddess Justitia," Caius was intoning. "Will you speak truth and verity?"

"I will." Julia's voice was firm, calm. None of the tension in her shoulders made it into her tone.

"You lived for some time in Polycarp's insula, did you not?"

"I did. For half a year. My husband rented another place before that."

Caius watched her, his eyes hard and cold. "And what did you see there?"

She lifted her head. "There were maybe fifteen, maybe twenty in that insula who never poured libations for the honored dead, never whispered a prayer to Janus when they went out or came in, never took any fruit or wine to our insula's shrine. I tried to go there, but the door to the shrine was locked."

Polycarp gave a start. Could that be true? He had not locked the old shrine, nor asked anyone to. The thought troubled him. He knew what it was to be barred from the public worship of one's God.

"The shrine was important to me," Julia continued, her voice a little shrill. "There was a time when I prayed every evening for a child."

Caius lifted his hand. "What did you do?"

"My husband and I made a little shrine in our room and concealed it."

There was a furious mutter from one of the jurors.

"Why did you conceal it?" Caius asked.

"I was afraid," she said simply.

"Why were you afraid, Julia?" Caius murmured. "Surely the honoring of Rome's dead and of Roman gods needs no concealment."

She lifted a trembling hand to her face, rubbed her temple a moment with her fingertips. "I'm sorry," she said. "I don't like to talk about it." She closed her eyes. "Most of the time, I stayed in our room with my husband. You don't know what it was like, living there." She opened her eyes wide. "You can't imagine it."

"It is the jury's duty to imagine it," Caius said. "Tell us the rest, Julia. Leave nothing out."

Julia took a breath. "They are all mad, Caius Lucius, jurors. The old Greek is the maddest of them. In that insula, everything is—it's upside down. A pleasure slave keeps the insula's accounts and presumes to look in on everyone. Yet a young patrician man, one of a high and ancient and revered family—" For an instant she cast a glare toward Marcus, who was looking at her with horror. There was a naked fury in Julia's eyes, a *real* fury, not a play-acted one, as though Marcus's abandonment of his toga at the insula had been a personal betrayal of her, of her hopes and beliefs, of things that mattered to her. And she couldn't keep the fury entirely from her voice. "He is sent three times a week to the market to fetch bread, like the lowest, nameless slave. And then, that bread he brings, they give it out to—to *beggars* and layabouts and thieves while they themselves adjourn to secret meetings in Polycarp's room or in despoiled Roman tombs, even in the very Catacombs beneath the city, to eat their own secret meals. They themselves speak of dining there, in the dark, on flesh and blood."

Silence fell. The jurors looked breathless, as though Julia's testimony had ridden them into wild country at full gallop. Polycarp focused on Julia—how she stood in her bright gown. He watched as her chin lifted. Clearly the role she played now was that of the offended domina, stiff with horror at her night's discovery of some evil rite performed by her house slaves when they thought the family asleep. Some handling of snakes, or some chanting in a circle, some remnant of whatever magic had been native to their conquered tribe. To the offended domina, Polycarp and the tenants of his insula were doubtless lower than the house slaves; though free, the men and women of the Subura slept on thinner blankets, dressed less well, dined less well. And perhaps, the domina might think, perhaps what secret rites these half-Romans might perform after dark would be more barbarous than any a few Germanic or Dacian slaves might dream of.

"Flesh and blood? Boar's flesh, perhaps?" There was a violence beneath the cold in Caius's voice. "Or mutton?"

"No. Human flesh." She paused. "Desecrated flesh. They speak of eating the bodies of their dead."

A growl from the jurors now, deep and bestial, a growl that rose from their bellies. Marcus looked even more pale.

"The desecrated dead," Caius repeated. He leaned forward, his eyes fierce. "You had better tell us more."

She hesitated, then shrank back, as though it had occurred to her, abruptly, how very serious the allegations she made actually were. She glanced at blind Justitia, her eyes wary. "That is all I know," she murmured. "It is terrible enough. They would share the flesh in their gatherings at night. The old Greek teaches that the living mustn't feed the dead; the dead must feed the living. Is it any wonder our affronted dead arise?"

Looking at Julia now, Polycarp realized suddenly that she'd *always* borne false witness. She'd pretended to be a tenant content in the insula, a baker's wife, when her heart was elsewhere. Before that, on some villa on the Palatine, she'd perhaps pretended to be a good and devoted wife to her first husband. She was always playing a part, always wearing a purple gown. Without disguise, naked, she might be too terrified to breathe; perhaps she had not even looked at her own heart in that way, unclothed, unveiled. She wanted others to see what she chose to show them; perhaps she wanted to see only what she showed herself. He wondered suddenly what had taught her, long ago, that she needed such veils. He wondered who she really was, what she really hungered for.

His dread grew heavier. Here was one he had not helped, one he hadn't fed. He could hear the rising anger of the jury as she spoke—and faintly, beneath it, another sound: the low cry of the dead, many of them, somewhere below on the hill. But nearer than they'd sounded last night. The sound had a strange quality, as though their moaning had actually been audible for some time, though only barely, heard by the ear but unnoticed, and had suddenly become louder and more clear. That chilled him. He listened a moment, forgetting the witness and the jury.

They were climbing the hill. Dead did not often do that; they moved down streets toward the river, like water, their shuffling feet taking the easiest paths, unless they heard or smelled the living and gave chase, uphill or down. Perhaps now, one or two of the dead, or a few, had sensed some pedestrian on the high streets and stumbled toward him; perhaps, fleeing uphill, he was pulling dead after him—first a few, then a larger group that followed those.

Or perhaps they had heard the furious cries of the jury, carried toward the river on some ill wind.

Whatever had caught their notice, they were coming. Perhaps, hearing that low hunting moan, a few undead would break free of villas and gardens along the Palatine streets and join the swarm moving up the slope, until they came onward like a reeking tide, like the dead in his dream, a multitude decaying and hungry without reprieve. A few of the jurors had noticed the moaning now; several of them glanced up, and a shudder passed through them. But after a moment they turned their attention back to Julia, though with pale faces; in the past few days, they'd heard such distant moans too often for that sound to toss them into outright panic now.

Off to Polycarp's right, by the fire pit, came the slow, slouching sound of a great beast shifting its weight.

You stand condemned, Despair whispered.

"Yes." Polycarp was sweating in the sun. Convicted not by that jury but by the baker's wife and by the cries of those dead. His larder had been too small, his voice too soft. He'd done too little. This day he was called to account for those he'd failed.

Yet something in him toughened, baked hard by the sun. He *did* stand here as a sacrifice. Not the sacrifice Caius wanted, an appeasement of the furious dead. Another kind of sacrifice. Glancing at the faces of the jury, he didn't think he would be able to avoid a severe verdict or that his body would escape the flames. But his master while he lived had once said that a seed must fall to the ground, split, and die in order for a mighty tree to be born. His failures might be redeemed in this moment if the words with which he met his death could yet plant those seeds in the jurors' hearts, seeds that would later bear fruit. Maybe it was too late, with the starving dead loosed in the city. Yet he had to hope. When the evils of the world sprang out of Pandora's box in the old story, all that remained at the bottom was hope. "A fragile thing," he murmured to himself, "but it is all we have. We *have* to hope. Against the madness of the world, we have to hope. And even if I were without hope, still this is where I've been told to stand. My master is still sufficient. As long as I stand here in his stead."

"Speak loud enough for us to hear," Caius broke in sharply.

"Very well." Polycarp lifted his voice. The courtyard shimmered in the sun's heat. "This wearies me. There are no advocates present to question young Julia, no one to read in her testimony where there is truth and where falsehood. In such an absence, of what use are her words to you?" He faced Julia, whose face was contorted in the grip of her emotions. "I grieve for your pain, daughter. I regret that you found no home with us." It was the only apology he knew how to make.

"I'm not your daughter," she hissed. "My father was an equestrian, a man of worth."

"I do not doubt it." Polycarp coughed to clear his throat, which was terribly dry. "But it is not ownership of a State Horse that makes a father a man of worth, but whom he chooses to feed and how he chooses to feed them." He glanced at the jury, saw Marcus watching him now with eyes that shone with pride amid a bruised and sleep-deprived face. Polycarp took a little strength from that. "Manius Curius," he told the jurors, "lived in a cottage and devoted himself to the growing of turnips. Yet he was one of Rome's first men, whom all in Rome still revere. And I know of another just man, a writer of laws, who once left a palace to live in a desert tent, that he might teach a starving tribe to gather bread from the ground."

"Enough," Caius snapped, the sharpness of his voice cracking across the walled ground. "Jurors, your pardon, but I must hasten these proceedings. There are dead on the hill—we can hear them. Be without fear: I have guardsmen in the street to meet them. But we who are here must proceed swiftly, hasten this trial and the rites that follow, to do justice on the one who has caused Rome so much harm, bringing this dishonor, this plague, and this evil upon us. I don't plan to tarry over tales and trivialities." He turned to the accused.

"Polycarp, your violence upon Rome, upon its traditions and its health and upon the Roman peace, will be suffered no longer. I can bring another witness to confirm what Julia has told us, but I would rather avoid the delay. As the appointed magistrate of the city, I require you to recant your perverse beliefs and submit yourself to our judgment. I will ask again. Polycarp, father of the tomb despoilers, the god destroyers, the atheists, do you recant?"

But once again Polycarp had stopped listening. Or rather, he was listening again to the dead. They were nearer. There were faint shouts and cries that subsided quickly, smothered beneath the growing noise of the long, drawn-out wailing of the approaching corpses. Far too much like his dream of the dead city and the wheat.

The sun was beating hard on Polycarp's bald head, and the dust and grit beneath his feet swam for a moment under his gaze. He looked up, glancing sideways at the sun, taking its measure. The blaze of it made it difficult to think. If only that sun was a little kinder, a little more like the sun he'd known in Thessaly. He smiled faintly, remembering how he had once, as a boy of twelve summers, felt that kinder sun on the back of his neck as he sat at the edge of his parents' wheat field. He had burned that day, but hadn't noticed; his entire mind and being had been focused on a large red beetle crawling across the back of his hand. It had landed there of its own accord, and its little wings had snapped back under its shell, translating it in an instant from a flying blur of red into a small creature that crawled across the surface of the earth as men and women do. He stared at it, holding his breath. Then he got slowly, slowly to his feet, taking the utmost care not to dislodge his find. With exaggerated caution, placing one foot at a time, he moved along the edge of the field, fearful—so fearful— that the beetle would fly away. His heart was louder and more violent in his chest than he'd ever felt it before. He glanced up, could see his mother standing by the threshold of the house.

She knelt by him when he reached her, the beetle still perched on his hand. It had crawled over the webbing between two fingers (tickling him so that he nearly jumped) and then along his palm as he tilted his hand carefully to keep it from falling.

"What did you bring me?" his mother asked, her smile warming his entire world.

Without speaking, he simply held his hand a little higher, for her to look.

"A beetle?" She cupped Polycarp's hands in hers, holding his hand steady as the little creature crawled along his palm, teasing his skin with its tiny legs. "Symbol of truth and eternity," she said. "My grandmother from Kemet taught me that when I was a girl." She laughed softly as she passed her mothers' knowledge to her son, her one child (Polycarp had never had a sister), a gift as sustaining as a head of ripe wheat, as precious as a berry. And even as she laughed, the beetle's wings flickered out of its shell, tiny and fragile. Polycarp held his breath, and his mother fell silent, watching.

The wings trembled once, twice. Then the beetle flitted from the boy's hand, zipping into the air. Polycarp watched, his mouth open, as the beetle flitted to a smooth white stone, its color stark against the rock. From there, the beetle flew to an ear of wheat at the edge of the field. It clung to the ear, and the wings flickered back into its shell.

"The world is full of truth and life," his mother whispered. They were speaking in Greek, that melodic language that, as an old man, Polycarp still thought in sometimes, even after decades of using mostly Latin. *Aletheia kai zoe*, his mother had sung to him: *truth and life*. "Polycarp, my little Polycarp, you must find what is true. But you cannot hold it in your hand or keep it captive: it will fly. Truth always does. And you must follow when it does, wherever it leads you."

"Where will it fly, mother?"

"I don't know," she laughed. "But you must follow it. It might fly across the river, or over the fields, or up that cliff over there. It doesn't matter. It will take you to the one thing you need today, the one thing you need to do. Trust it. It is sacred."

He nodded and sprang from her, chasing the beetle. He slowed as he approached the field, holding his hands before him, almost cupped, ready to catch it. He stepped carefully toward the ear of wheat, higher than his head, where the beetle rested. But when he was only a few steps away, it flickered deeper into the field.

For a moment he paused, looked at the tossing sea of wheat. Then he threw himself into the grain, moving quickly but stealthily, as boys sometimes do. He could hear, so faintly, the hum of its wings. It would stop, then start again, that sound. He followed it. His body felt alive and taut; if he had to jump to catch the beetle, he felt he could jump high as the sun. Something more life-filled and vibrant than blood pulsed through him.

In the summers in Greece, with the wheat stirring in the breeze and the sky open as a woman's heart, every youth knows in his blood that he is a god, immortal, uncontainable, with a world to roam. Polycarp's heart beat in his ears as he pursued the small beetle, the tiny hum of its wings the kind of lullaby that seduces flowers into dreaming of bees. He stalked through the wheat.

Then stopped. Breathing hard.

He waited. Quick, urgent heartbeats.

He'd lost the sound.

Horror seized at him; he looked about urgently at the endless wheat—a great expanse of grain higher than his head, nothing visible but the high stalks. A breeze passed through, making the heads of wheat caress his face and arms.

Must he turn back now, return to his mother's arms?

Could he even *find* his way back?

He looked to the sky, hoping to catch a glimpse of the beetle. But there was only the sun: its heat above him something palpable he could feel, a weight on his face.

———

When he lowered his eyes from the sun, he met Caius's stern, hard look. The dead were moaning; he could smell Caius's fear. He called to mind Caius's question of a moment before. "No, I will not recant," he murmured, lifting a chained hand and passing it across his eyes to clear away the stinging sweat. "I am an old man, and perhaps I fear death more than I did when I was young. But there are other things worthier of my fear. Why should I lose myself in the wheat for you, Caius Lucius?"

Polycarp straightened and turned his back to the praetor, faced the jurors. "Now I will give *my* testimony. And you will listen, for I am the oldest one present, and I have seen more of life—and death—than any of you. It is likely I have seen things you could hardly believe."

His voice was very clear. In that moment his *dignitas*—the most important of qualities to any Roman—was so great, so intensely visible, that no one spoke or interrupted him. Even Caius remained silent now while Polycarp spoke, though the praetor's body grew tense as a bow stretched taut to the point of snapping.

Polycarp spread his manacled hands as wide as he could; an ell of chain restrained them. Among the jurors, Marcus was gazing at him out of a bruised face with that same look Polycarp had seen in his eyes the night he went to confront the dead in the alley. The look of a man who wanted to leap in front of his father and shield him, but could not see a way to do so. Polycarp smiled faintly, for him.

"You are greatly misinformed about who I am and what I have been doing," he said. "I am Polycarp. I was born in Larissa, Thessaly, a Roman citizen of Greek blood. I was born a second time in baptism in Smyrna, where for some time I served a small gathering of both citizens and noncitizens, both rich and poor, who were devoted to the sharing of bread, the teaching of our master's apostles, and to prayer and fellowship. While I was there, a message came to us from the holy widows in Rome, describing to us the severe hunger suffered in the Subura. There were many tears as it was read, for matters in Smyrna are not as bad as here in Rome, and your brothers and your sisters in smaller cities have compassion for you who live in this great one.

"Hearing the message, the elders among us appointed me to go to Rome as an apostle, and with the appointment was passed to me the Apostle's Gift. Perhaps you wonder what I mean by this; I will tell you. We of the gathering worship One God, the Giver of Life, the Giver of Gifts.

"There are many gifts, and no one who encounters the Spirit of God is without one. Some are given gifts for teaching, or for healing, or for perceiving things that are yet to come. The gift entrusted to me was that of apostleship, for I was sent out to witness and to see to and see into the souls, living and dead, who suffer in this city, to hear their griefs and to absolve them.

"I will tell you about this Gift. It is to see with God's eyes, to hear with God's ears. It can only be given to one who is first willing to look and hear. One with the Gift sees through all veils, through all garments and costumes. If one of you were to come join me on this sand, take my arm, meet my eyes, you would find me gazing not only beneath your toga to the man beneath it, but through every cerement you've wrapped about your heart. It might be a terrifying experience for you—to have your every regret, your every fear and secret hope, naked and seen. But in that moment, if you were willing, you might also see your own self just as nakedly. You might be forgiven. You might lay all those secrets down and be as one who runs naked and free on the grass. That is a very great Gift, though a fearful one."

Polycarp let his gaze move across the jury, but each of them lowered their eyes, a few with their faces terribly pale. He gave a small nod. "It is a fearful thing, yet something each of us yearns for—to be naked before God or before another human being. To be intimate and loved for who we truly are. And if this is so with you who live, it is so, too, with the dead. Think of how burdened your hearts are. Those who die so burdened yearn and hunger even in death. Desiring intimacy, they rise and devour, for consuming another is the only way they know to take another into themselves. But I think there is one very great difference between the dead and the living. If I were to touch one of the dead and gaze into its eyes, it would be far readier than any of you to lay down its burdens and rest."

A murmur rose among the jury. The young man who'd cried out the loudest when Polycarp was brought in now hissed through his teeth, his eyes dark with horror.

"Yes," Polycarp said quietly. "It is a terrible thing to touch the dead. In the land in which the gathering was born, that touch would make you unclean; you would be cast out. And it is true that if one of the dead should feed on you, the fever will come and you will burn and die, then walk restless yourself, because the fever-death gives you no time to unveil your so carefully hidden heart to any of your brothers or your sisters, and in that way prepare for the last river crossing that is death. But what other way do we have to calm the restless dead, other than to embrace them? Do you really think that destroying these walking bodies by the sword does your dead more honor? Or that the only way to deal with that which wishes to consume you is to flee it or destroy it? Deer and fanged beasts live in such a way; men and women must not.

"My brothers on the jury, I give witness that my touching of the dead does not spread the fever, nor do I enter into your tombs with any purpose to wake or desecrate those who sleep. Why should I? The restlessness of the dead disturbs me as much as it does you. May God will that my testimony satisfies your ears better than this incoherent witness about despoiled tombs or rumors of midnight feedings. And that brings me to the other accusation I've heard today. Let us speak of that.

"I am accused of eating flesh and drinking blood. I would laugh at the absurdity of this, but you take it seriously. Very well. There is much flesh and much blood in Rome. Have someone visit my larder. See if there is less bread and grain there than one might expect. Ask the market by the Fulvian Cistern if I buy from them less often than another man."

The jurors were shifting in their seats uneasily; their faces told him too plainly that they did not believe him, or did not want to; with the wailing of the dead audible in their ears, they wanted very badly to have someone to blame. Polycarp shook his head, barely restraining the frustration that burned in him. The heat of the sun on his head, the heat of the sand beneath his feet, made patience difficult; sweat was pouring down his back beneath his tunic. "But you will not," he said. "You do not care to. Because the real accusation is that I have taken 'your fathers' Rome' from you, and that because of me, your fathers rise from their mausoleums in wrath to devour their sons, as did Uranus in the old story they tell in the country of my birth. Caius Lucius Justus, and men of the jury, if your fathers and your kin who are dead are wrathful, it is not at me. Give you back your fathers' Rome, you cry. In your fathers' Rome, men treated their own gods and their temples— and aging men, for that matter—with more respect and less noise. Why should I expect to be left in peace to serve my God with those who'll serve with me, when you are so neglectful of yours?"

The benches erupted at that, and again the temple was a clamor of angry voices. Polycarp shouted over them. "I am not done, fellow citizens—I am *not* done!—I grant you!—I grant you, it is possible that the gathering may one day stand guilty of great crimes, for though assembled by God, we are a fellowship of men and women, and we are as broken as we are beautiful. But the gathering I serve does not stand guilty today. You wish to believe that we who worship differently are therefore a different kind of people, a people capable of any sacrilege and therefore deserving of any punishment. But your wishing does not make it so! You make so much of the fact that I come to you here from the Subura. It is pointless. The distinctions you make, make fools of you. Patrician, plebian." He turned, held the youngest juror's gaze with his. "You wear the toga; I wear the simpler tunic of the people. It means nothing. Stripped of it, you and I look the same—just two men hungering and thirsting. It is only a garment. What matters is the heart." He took his sleeve between his chained hands, tried to tear it; the cloth was stubborn. "Look at it. Look at it!" he cried. "A thousand threads—different threads—woven together so they cannot break. That is what we are to be. We are to be one cloth, one body, one gathering. Patrician! Plebian!" he shouted. "You weaken Rome with your distinctions. Rome now is not one whole cloth but layers, castes, one sitting atop the other. It needs only a strong wind, and the separated layers of the city will be tossing in the air, tumbling and helpless. We cannot survive unwoven from each other. You have to understand that.

"Listen to *that* in the streets outside. Those walking *mouths* are there because you have not fed your people, and because men and women and children, Roman or otherwise, die daily, unnoticed, in the Subura. If you *had* no Subura, you would have no region for the dead to fester. What can be plainer than that? That is what you should be talking about among yourselves. The choices of your past have come home to you. They are at the gate. Maybe it is too late to recover anything. But maybe it is not."

He raised his voice, a fire burning in his heart. The words seemed to pour through him now as though from some other place, and for an instant he wondered if this was what it had been like for the prophets of old, proclaiming words God himself had given to their ears. He felt like a tunnel through which a backdraft of flame was rushing, scorching his insides, yet exhilarating in its wild energy.

"We are *all* on trial," he cried. "Our dead are here to demand answers, and we are out of time. We have to choose, now, this day. Will we have a City divided into the eaters and the eaten—a City populated in the end only by the hungry dead!—or will we build a City where we break bread together, *all of us*, Roman and Greek and Syrian, male and female, master and slave, not feeding *on* each other but feeding and sustaining each other? Give me your verdict, please, then let me rest. The past few days have been more exhausting than any in my life. I will admit that I would rather die in my bed than in a fire. But now, if you can't manage to look at the truth and decide what to do about it, I am done talking with you."

Julia was gazing at him, appalled, as though he were some kind of creature she had never seen before, whose behaviors and postures were utterly alien to anything she might expect or know how to interpret.

Polycarp merely turned aside and gazed at the statue of Justitia. His eyes glanced behind her, at the pillars of the temple and the door behind them, which must lead to the inner alcoves and the inner court, where sacrifices were made. He longed to see some small flicker of red, a beetle crawling on the marble steps, perhaps, or flitting past Justitia's blindfolded face. Some sign, some confirmation that he was this moment standing where he needed to be. He had said the words that poured into him and through him; he could think of nothing more to say. Yet he didn't think anyone had heeded him. What good was it doing, that he stood here? He kept his eyes from the cold fire pit, wondering how soon it would be lit. The dead were moaning outside, and the jury were talking among themselves in heated voices. He felt unutterably weary.

"Citizens, calm yourselves!" Caius's voice broke the air. "Guardsmen, bring the other witness."

Polycarp pressed his hand to his head; the sun was very hot on his brow. And the dead. Those moans—there might be a few corpses now literally in the very street outside. Or perhaps in a house near at hand. But he could *hear* them. So little time.

The jurors had turned in their seats to watch the second witness approach; a guardsman was escorting a woman over from where she must have been standing behind the jurors' benches. The woman was short, but she stood with incredible dignity and poise. Yet her eyes brimmed with unshed tears, and the hand she held over her heart was clutched too tightly about the torn fabric of her nightdress. She stared straight ahead, as though terrible things were to her left and to her right, as though she knew that she could only keep walking forward if she chose not to look at them.

Polycarp swayed suddenly on his feet.

He knew her.

Perhaps better than anyone in Rome, he knew this woman.

If she was here to witness against him, if she had broken, then surely all his work was broken. How would the gathering in Rome hold, if neither he nor she were left to care for it? How could the gathering anywhere hold? Her presence here was a spear through his breast, and the anguish of it a blow that all but knocked him out of the world of light and heat into some far other place, cold and dark.

The woman was Regina.

ALETHEIA KAI ZOE

THE DAY before. An open square just outside the walled compound of Justitia's temple.

Regina shrieked again as the three-bladed whip tore into her back. The pain and heat of it flashed through her body; her legs buckled, giving out beneath her. For a moment she hung limp from the post by her chained wrists, panting, waiting for the pain to dull. Her nightdress hung in tatters from her shoulders.

The guardsman wielding that whip meant to break her.

She bit her lip hard, clenching her teeth. Over and over in her mind, above the screaming of her body's pain, she recited what she knew to be true, what she held to be true. *I am Regina Romae. I am a deaconess of the gathering in Rome. I am no slave; I give refuge and comfort for the lost. These bonds, this pain, they do not make me a slave. I am Regina Romae.*

The lash struck her again, and she jerked and screamed through her teeth. The whole world melted into the heat of the blow, and when she came to, she was sobbing, on her knees, hanging again from her wrists. A rough hand seized her hair, tugged her head back, the guardsman's breath hot on her throat. "Writhe for me, little slut," he hissed, and forcing her face toward his, he kissed her, assaulting her mouth. He tasted of bad wine, smelled of sweat. She screamed in helpless fury, but his lips smothered the sound. She fought him, thrashing, but his hand held her head still until he was done. Then he dropped her head back and stepped away, chuckling. Hot rage seared through her as she panted for breath. If she could only wipe the taste of him from her lips—but her wrists were confined high over her head, manacles biting into them. She spat into the dust.

The lash struck her across her hips, and she jerked again, then hung sobbing, panting. God, it *hurt*! Her face was wet with perspiration and tears. She found the rage within her, seized it, fed it. She was Regina Romae. She was the deaconess of the gathering in Rome.

The lash tore another scream from her throat.

She was Regina Romae. She provided refuge. She would not break.

"*God!*" she cried. The blades of the whip had struck her side, flicking around to sting her breast. She twisted away from the blow, sobbing, her face burning at the guardsman's laughter. For years, her bitterness and shame at her past had remained only a tiny seed, one she didn't allow to sprout but was unable to discard entirely. Now her captivity had made that wild seed burst into weed and flower; with a violence and a voracity that stunned her, it had grown into a raging thorn plant twining about her heart and lungs, threatening to strangle her.

She hung in a haze of pain and didn't feel or hear the guardsman step toward her—but the manacles sprang open and she slid to the dust, where she lay panting. Her back was a great blaze of heat, with lines of fire traced over it, crossing old scars. Dazed, she stared at the dust and drew in what air she could. She heard the sound of quiet whimpering and, realizing the sound was her, she pressed her lips together. She closed her eyes, started to pray silently to Polycarp's God. She felt footsteps near her body and tensed.

"Can I see her?" A woman's voice, not far away. The voice was familiar to her, but her thoughts were too scattered to give the voice a name.

"Why not, domina? I'll get her on her feet."

Large hands gripped her arms, and she was pulled up. The world swung about her for a moment, and she vomited; it splashed in the dust and grit. By some blessing she didn't get any on her body or on her torn and soiled nightdress, but her lips were slick with it, and her mouth tasted filthy to her. Cursing, the guardsman released her arms, leaving her to sway on her feet. She heard him walk away and then stop. Regina found that her dizziness had faded now that she'd retched, and she started working up enough saliva to spit.

"You're pathetic." The other woman's voice.

She opened her eyes. That woman standing before her—she knew her.

"Julia," she said flatly.

The baker's wife stood there with her arms folded beneath her breasts. She was no longer dressed as a woman of the Subura; she wore a gown of fine purple fabric, rarest of colors. In fact it was too rare—it was the kind of gown a woman of the equestrian class might wear if she wished to be seen as having patrician blood somewhere in her line.

Julia's eyes shone with a cold and bitter joy. She looked Regina over, assessing her, much as a domina might assess one of her house slaves who'd just received a beating for some infraction. Regina's face burned.

"I wonder if you have any idea," Julia said, "how sickening it was to me to see a slave girl queening it over the insula?"

"Brought—" Regina swayed, steadied, found her voice again. A cold, hard knot formed inside her. "I brought your husband broth when he was sick. I listened—tried to—when you felt alone."

"So you performed a slave's services, once or twice, and you think I should be *grateful*." Her eyes blazed. "Uppity slut. I know, you were happy there. In that—place. And you think I should've been happy too. Right? I suppose you *were* happy. After what you were, anything would be a step up. But I'm not like you, girl. My first husband—we *lived* on the lower slopes. We had a *villa*. We had two slaves. And all of that was *taken* from me. All of it." She blinked back tears furiously. "Do you think I *enjoyed* taking gifts of—of broth and—and pity—from that mad old man? Do you think I *enjoyed* living there? Do you think after what I've been, that I'd be *grateful* to you?"

"No." Her tone was cold. All the warmth had left her body. Julia's accent was equestrian again, and for an instant, at the sound of it, chains fell from the locks of closed doors in Regina's mind, and shrieking memories beat upon the doors like a thousand screaming dead. But then her blood drummed loud in her ears, louder than Julia's petty tone, and with the roar of her blood she heard Polycarp's deep voice, as though he stood before the doors in her memory, between her and the past that would devour her. His voice, telling her she was Regina of Rome, queenly and loved. And free. Brutus's softer voice, calling her *domina, domina*. And her own mind was still chanting ceaselessly against the brutal pain in her back, chanting the words, *I am Regina Romae, I am Regina Romae*.

The rattling of the doors stilled.

Rage burned hot in her body, rage so fierce she forgot even the pain that seared her. "No," she hissed. "No, you aren't like me." She lifted her head, meeting the other woman's eyes. How hateful the sight of Julia's cold smile seemed to her, and how small. "I'm bound here for your amusement, and I see you *are* amused. But I know who I am now. I *know* who I am. You—that gown you wear is nothing more than a costume. A part you'd like to play. It doesn't change who you *are*, Julia."

Julia's face contorted. "The praetor didn't order you lashed," she blurted. "*I* asked the guardsman for that."

Regina smiled thinly. "How nicely did you ask him, Julia?"

With a small shriek, Julia drew back her hand for a slap, but Regina was quicker; she caught the other woman by the wrist, tightened her fingers cruelly. For a moment she held Julia's eyes with hers. Everything in her became hard ice. "Don't—*ever*—touch me."

She squeezed her grip, and Julia's face twisted in pain. Regina held her eyes. "You should leave Rome, Julia. Tonight."

Then a hand clamped over Regina's shoulder, and she cried out as the hard fingers crushed down on a welt. Regina released her grip on Julia, hissing through her teeth. White as death, Julia backed away. Her mouth worked as though she wanted to say something. After a moment, though, she just turned and moved away at a brisk clip, retreating without a glance over her shoulder.

The guardsman turned Regina, and she glared up at him. Drew the back of her hand across her lips, wiping away flecks of vomit. At least the vomit had cleaned his kiss out of her mouth. "What now?" she asked coldly.

His eyes narrowed. Without warning, he struck her.

She found herself on her belly in the dust, her ear and the right side of her face ringing. She retched again, then sobbed with pain.

"Mouthy bitch." The guardsman's hand gripped her hair, lifted her to her knees. Her vision was a little gray, and the ringing in her ear was louder. "Be glad you're Brutus's," the man muttered.

Then the world dimmed fast as a flame dying at the end of a wick, and she blacked out.

"I am sorry," Brutus whispered, his back against the door in the darkened shed. "I am so sorry."

Regina lay on the straw. For the moment she lacked the strength to rise, even to her knees. She didn't look at Brutus but stared at the boards of the roof. She was not a whore. No matter how many times they whipped her, she was not a whore. She was Regina Romae, and there were people who looked to her and depended on her. Brutus was looking to her, at this very moment. "Your hand didn't wield the lash," she murmured.

"My hand didn't prevent it."

"Stop," she whispered. "Please just stop. I blame you for nothing." She shifted slightly and immediately regretted even that small movement; the pain that lit in her back forced a moan from her. She was breathing hard for a moment. The strength she'd shown when driving Julia from the courtyard had passed; tossed into the dark of this shed, shaking from pain and reaction, she was again awash with fears of what would happen—to her, to Polycarp, to all of them.

"You're the only reason I'm not raped and beaten whenever one of them is bored," she whispered. "Don't blame yourself for the things you can't do anything about."

At this moment she couldn't bear the thought of comforting another human being. She needed the guardsman to be a strong presence, someone to lean on for a moment while she recovered her breath.

Brutus came and sat by her.

"I used to watch my father beat this girl," he said quietly. "One of the house slaves. Her flesh would be cut up—so badly. I used to bring her wine afterward, hoping it would help. I will never forget her eyes." His voice was thick with remembered pain. "I was very young, domina. I would have liked to have stayed my father's hand, though it would have dishonored him, and myself. I would have liked to have said, *No more, no more. This is unjust, father.* When I heard Father Polycarp speak that one night, I understood why—why I'd wanted to stop my father so badly. But the truth is I never did."

They were silent for a while, he with his guilt, she with her pain and her struggle to retain her certainty of herself. It was as though a pit had opened beneath her and she was falling in. Polycarp would be tried and burned; the ten prisoners from the insula would likely be burned afterward without trial, herself among them. She had no refuge other than the kindness of this guardsman who knew the sign of the fish. And she lay in filthy straw in a tattered garment, beaten like a whore, and could extend refuge to no one.

She had not felt such an emptiness, such a weight of helplessness in many years, not even when she'd been carried bound up the streets of the Palatine with the hungering dead in pursuit. Her eyes were sore with crying. Every part of her body was sore, the outside and the inside. She thought of the prisoners in the other sheds. She knew each of them by name; she'd sat with them many afternoons, listening to their hopes and fears. She'd held the women close while they wept for the brutality and poverty of their lives. She'd given the men words of hope and courage when she found their shoulders slumped and their eyes defeated. She had given them advice when they had disputes or were simply angry with each other. She'd brought bread or broth up to them when they were sick. She had lifted their cares to her shoulders and carried them with her to Polycarp, all through the four years she'd lived as Regina Romae, the deaconess. She had been their refuge, as Polycarp had been hers. She was responsible for them. Her hands trembled. They were her children, yet she could do nothing to save them. The despair of it racked her, tore her more savagely than the whip had.

"Is Marcus all right?" she whispered.

"He is."

Another silence. Anger began to crackle again in her heart. "Julia came," she whispered. "To see me. After the lashing."

"The spy?" Brutus's voice dripped with loathing. "I'm surprised she's still in Rome."

That caught her attention. "Why?"

A low growl beside her, in the dark. "Caius deeded to her husband a villa in Arpinum, one that's been city property for a while."

Regina's hands curled, making claws of her fingers. A villa. All for a villa of her own. "I think she's a witness," she said after a while. "At the trial. I think that's why she's here."

"The praetor doesn't even need witnesses. With the dead on the hill, everyone's crying out for blood, someone to blame. He'll burn the father tomorrow. He won't need witnesses to get a majority vote from the jury, and a majority vote is the most he'll need, because he'll claim that without papers, the father has no citizenship." He grunted. "But he does *want* witnesses. We're supposed to talk with all the prisoners about it."

"About witnessing?" She looked on him with horror.

Brutus gazed back at her, in the dark. "Caius is offering freedom—for the witness. On condition of exile from Rome after the trial. No one's taking him up on it."

She laughed softly, then wept as the laughter made her welts burn again. "He doesn't understand. We can't be bought."

"He bought Julia."

"That's different," she murmured. "She's not of the gathering. She just lived at our insula. Polycarp gave her a place to stay when her husband shut her from his villa, and later she married a baker, who moved in with her." Her anger cooled as abruptly as it had risen, and she found only sorrow in its place. "She was never really happy. I thought it was because she missed her first husband on his hill. I didn't understand her, Brutus."

He watched her a moment. "Don't blame yourself for the things you can't do anything about," he said.

Regina began to cry softly. "I'm sorry," she sobbed after a moment. "I'm sorry." She turned on her side to try to hide her face, but moaned sharply at the pain.

She heard him shift in the dark. "Is there anything I can bring you, deaconess? There are other things in the station to eat besides bread and wine. I can bring you something more, I think. Decius and the others—they'll just think I'm—infatuated."

She smiled amid her tears. He was trying to cheer her. But she needed more right now than a pastry to eat. "Pray with me," she whispered.

He took her hand in his; his was large and calloused. Softly as though he might break them, he murmured the words:

Phos hilaron hagias doxes, athanatou Patros,
ouraniou, hagiou, makaros, Iesou Christe

"Joyous light of the deathless Father's holy glory..." The words fortified her heart; in this dark shed with its dirty straw, they seemed especially precious. So many times in the evenings, she had seen Polycarp stand in the insula's tiny atrium by the lilacs, looking at the sky, intoning those words in a Greek so musical you could cry listening to it. She gripped Brutus's hand briefly and managed the next words of the prayer with only one quick break in her voice:

elthontes epi ten heliou dysin, idontes phos hesperinon,
hymnoumen Patera, Hyion, kai Hagion Pneuma, Theon.

"Having come upon the sun's setting, having seen the evening light, we praise in song…" Brutus whispered back:

Axion se en pasi kairois hymneisthai phonais aisiais

And Regina recited the final line, her voice strengthening:

Hyie Theou, zoen ho didous, dio ho kosmos se doxazei.

"Worthy it is at all times in all seasons to praise you with glad voices, God's Son, Giver of Gifts, Giver of Life, for which the world glorifies you."

God is the Giver, she whispered in her heart. *Made in God's likeness, we are not mere gifts to be given but givers ourselves. We are givers: we must remember we are givers.*

"Thank you," she told Brutus, then added to the prayer: "I trust you can hear us, for I know Polycarp trusts you and that you hear him. Be our refuge in this hour."

A calm settled over her; freed of its despair, her mind began to plan. For a few moments she didn't even feel the pain in her body; she simply tallied accounts in her mind, as she so often had as deaconess in the insula. Then everything clicked into place with total clarity.

"Brutus," she said, "you must get me in to see Caius Lucius."

He shifted beside her. "Why?"

"You said he wants witnesses."

"He does. What are you thinking, domina?"

Deep beneath the calm that lay over her, something within her ran screaming into the smallest corner of her mind at the prospect of what she had to do. The rest of her was cold and still and clear.

"I need to be there in the temple when Polycarp is tried," she said. "I need to be a witness."

In the silence, she could hear Brutus breathing in the dark.

"Someone needs to counter Julia's testimony," she explained, "someone needs to stand with him. I need to be there—tell Caius Lucius I will stand witness. Tell him I will say whatever he pleases. I was a slave once; he will believe it of me. Tell him the lashing broke me. If you have to, tell him you had me, that you beat me afterward, until I begged to be a witness. I don't care what you say—just please get him to see me."

Brutus's eyes were pale, and for a long moment he chewed the inside of his cheek. When he spoke, his tone was hesitant. "These lies are the same as the ones I tell to the other guardsmen—that I come to the shed to make you my whore. But it troubles me to lie to the urban praetor. I heard the father speak once. He said, 'better to die than to speak untruth.'"

Regina's eyes flashed. "I will speak a small lie to one man so that I can speak the truth to many. This thing has to be done." Panic welled up within her. She *had* to be there, at that trial. "Brutus. Brother. Please. We are all God's actors on this stage of the world. There is a time when we must tear aside all the masks, let everyone see each other as they really are. That time's tomorrow, at that trial. But we have to wear our costumes, play our parts, until then—to get there. Please." Her voice quivered but did not break. "Please—you must do this. Please. The father mustn't stand alone." With a moan of pain, she lifted herself from the straw; Brutus pressed a hand to her back and helped her sit up, though his touch on the welts made her scream again.

She sat there, breathing. Then she lifted her shoulders, took a graceful sitting posture, folded her hands in her lap. "Will you do it?" she whispered against the pain.

"I will," he murmured.

Regina closed her eyes, the relief nearly unbearable. Polycarp. She would see Polycarp. When he defended the gathering, she would stand beside him.

Brutus looked at her in the dark. There was a touch of awe in his tone. "I never knew a woman could be so brave."

"Then you haven't known many women. We endure much for the ones we love." She drew a slow breath. "Please go now and tell the praetor."

He hesitated.

"Please, Brutus. I want to be alone."

When he'd left, Regina sat very still for a while in this shed that had become an unexpected refuge, guarded as it was by Brutus, a quiet place where she could rest in the dark and search her own heart. She searched her heart now. She had been a slave once. She had been a slave a long time. A man had come and freed her, given her a warm coat and a place of safety. He had reached into the empty dark and found her heart there and cupped it in his hands and pulled her near, to where there was light and warmth. She closed her eyes. The full import of what was going to happen slammed into her there, in the dark. She almost couldn't breathe with the dread of it. Fresh tears burned her eyes. They were going to kill him. Father Polycarp. Her Polycarp. They were going to burn him. And likely her as well, and the others, all those imprisoned in the other sheds. Phineas, who wrote letters every week to his three sisters in Nola and who amused and sometimes annoyed his neighbors with his obsessive fear of balding. Philemon, with his paints and his longing for a wife. Hadassah the Jewess, who had the most beautiful singing voice, though no one outside the insula had ever heard it. They were all so precious to her. Their need for her in this hour called to her. She was Regina Romae, and the men and the women of the gathering depended on her. That was the truest thing she knew, and the truth of their need, and the truth of hers—a sign of the need of every living person for shelter and succor—lit in her like a fire. Alone in the dark, she wept quietly, and prepared herself.

It was a surprisingly small office for the urban praetor, hardly much larger than the shed, and Regina found she had to close her eyes and force slower breathing; the walls seemed to close in on her. She stood before the praetor's desk with her arms at her sides. Each time she took a breath, the slight movement lit fires in her back. Her face was still moist from her tears, and it was all she could do to stand and keep from wincing. But she stood very straight. She would show no weakness she did not have to.

She considered him. The praetor's toga was perfectly, impeccably draped about him, as though he meant to appear as flawless and orderly as a marble statue—but his face was dark about the eyes, and his left eye was bloodshot. This was a man who clearly didn't sleep much. Nor did he look up from his scrolls and scraps of parchment. He did that to intimidate her, she supposed. As though she were barely worth notice.

Her fingers gripped the dirtied fabric of her nightdress firmly. She would *not* be intimidated.

"Our informant had mentioned you to me as one Dora Syriacae, a manumitted slave." Now he did glance up, his eyes cold. He leaned forward slightly in his seat.

"A manumitted slave." He said the words slowly. "Yet you have no papers on your person. So I must express my doubt, Dora, that you are really free. Are you?"

"I have been free since the day I met Polycarp," Regina said softly.

Yet she was breathing too fast. Now that she was here, standing before this togate incarnation of patrician Rome, feeling his judging eyes on her as he sat beneath the rows of his medals and behind the hard weight of his official desk, she found that she was standing again over a dark pit of doubt. Did she believe the words of the hymn she'd sung with Brutus? Did she believe in the promise of a restored world to come, a world made new— justice for the impoverished and the homeless no less than for the residents of hill-slope villas, the dead at peace, loved ones long parted brought back together? In that moment, standing before the praetor's desk, with the lines of the lash on her back and fresh on her heart last night's memory of the shambling dead and the nightmarish proximity of that long-ago cargo hold on a half-floundering slave ship, she didn't know. She gripped the fabric at her hips more tightly. Perhaps the world was, after all, only what the Romans said it was: a world where the strong used the weak and the cunning used the naïve, among both gods and mortals. A world where things lost remained lost, and things eaten remained eaten. She wanted to cry out at the horror of it; she pressed her lips into a thin line.

"I am free," she said.

She *must* believe, because Polycarp did. To voice or acknowledge her doubts now would be a betrayal of him.

"Perhaps I *am* unimportant to you," she said, with forced calm. "No more than a former slave whose legality you question. But I can be useful to you, Caius Lucius. I would like to serve as a witness, in return for proper papers." His face showed no change in expression; neither did she blink. She kept her voice measured and rational. "Father Polycarp is an elderly man. His *dignitas* is very great. Is it usual to bring old men and wise to a trial? You may not be able to convict him without some ignominy, Caius Lucius."

"I'll manage," Caius said drily.

She looked at his eyes, found something there that startled her. "You haven't seen him yet," she breathed.

He frowned as though puzzled by her manner. "Seeing his followers first is instructive." A note of caution now in his tone.

Regina laughed suddenly; it welled up inside her, in a flood of relief, and she couldn't keep it silent. Caius's face darkened, and strength rushed back into Regina, a pouring like water into a cup, until she was filled with it. For a moment she kept laughing. How he sat there—so proud! Like the Nemean lion after feasting on an antelope. She fought for breath and loosened her fingers, letting the folds of her nightdress slip free from her hands. For a moment she stood straight as a queen. Well. Caius Lucius was about to meet *Polycarp* and no antelope. Let him condemn the father if he dared. Regina's face shone; her heart was so full. Polycarp was greater than this small and frightened man. He was greater than the dead that had pursued her the previous night. He and his God. He was greater than the slave ship that had carried her—for he'd taught her that she might have a new name. Even when this little praetor burned her man, Polycarp would still be greater than this moment, and she was suddenly, fiercely certain that the gathering would never forget his memory. She took full breaths. She *believed*.

Caius's face had flushed. He lifted his hand; Brutus took a step toward Regina. She lowered her eyes, her head. Her heart racing. Her laughter had endangered her. She must appear the frightened slave. "Pardon me," she whispered, taking the flame of hope within her and cupping it in her hands, trying to dampen its light to other eyes. "I meant no disrespect, praetor urbanus. I laugh because I am near fainting. I have been lashed, Caius Lucius Justus, and left without food or water. The strain is very great, too much for a woman."

His eyes were watchful. Regina thought fast. She had come playing the role Caius expected to see her in, but the praetor was a shrewd man. Now she had to look every inch the broken slave. "I know you're suspicious of me, Caius Lucius," she said softly. "But

I—I don't—I don't want to be a slave again. I can't. I *can't*." Her face twisted; she summoned to the surface of her heart the very real pain that the thought of a return to slavery caused her, and trembling, she showed that pain to Caius openly, vulnerably. The risk of it—of being so vulnerable before this man—made it difficult for her to breathe. Regina let her hair cover her face, keeping her expression hidden. That afforded her some sense of shelter from his eyes and perhaps only made her appear more broken.

She felt the praetor's gaze on her for a long, silent moment.

"You'll have your papers," the praetor muttered at last. She heard him sigh. "You are right that we need witnesses. This trial must be conducted with all the proper piety. You will confess," he suggested, "that you have all eaten flesh, at his behest."

Her shoulders jerked slightly. "I will."

"You will also give witness that he abducted young Romans of good family, that he—"

"I will say whatever will please you, Caius Lucius," she whispered. "For the price I've mentioned."

Caius sat very still, measuring her with his eyes. "Very good."

Regina lifted her own eyes. The praetor's face was pale; no, this man didn't sleep much. Or laugh. Or smile. To her surprise, she felt a stab of pity for Julia, but it was a cold pity. Julia too had stood before this man's eyes. But when Julia had stood in this place, she had taken the praetor's judgment, his assessment of her, and taken it into her heart. Regina could well imagine how Caius Lucius Justus had gazed at Julia, the baker's wife and once the wife of an equestrian merchant of the lower slopes. Caius would have seen a woman who had tumbled downhill, draining into the Subura, a decayed citizen, barely a Roman, barely more than a riverside whore. How his eyes must have tormented Julia! With what rage Julia must have hurried then to find someone lower than herself, someone who could be lashed and judged in her stead. With what need she must have begged the guardsman to chain Regina to the whipping post. How desperate Julia must be now, how fierce her hope that a purple gown and a spacious villa would make her the domina she longed to be. But being a domina was not a matter of the clothes you wore or the space you inhabited. It was a matter of your relationships with others, how you treated others in the shared theater of your lives. It was about your capacity to give gifts and inspire others to give too.

Caius's cold eyes shook Regina too. But Polycarp had not looked at her so. Strengthened by her pity, Regina met the praetor's eyes for an instant, looked *in* them rather than *at* them. Saw the empty pain, like the reflection of a desert—and a vulnerability deeper than her own. As their eyes met, Caius's brow creased. He leaned hard on his desk, and something shut just behind his eyes, sealing away the emotion. Yet he kept gazing at her—not judging now, but intense, focused.

"How odd," he murmured after a moment. "You almost remind me of—" His lips thinned.

"Who was she, dominus?" Regina asked. She shivered once at using the word *dominus*—it nearly caught in her throat. But she had a tight grip on herself now; her four years of freedom would not crumble about her at a single word. And the word, like her deferent tone, had the effect she hoped for: it set Caius at ease. He looked distracted. As though he were confiding in a house slave in a moment of indiscretion. Perhaps it was the first time he'd confided in anyone in many years. It was perhaps the first time in years that he'd spoken with a woman beyond offering a polite greeting as he passed in the Forum.

"My wife," he said softly, after a few moments had passed. "She was my wife." He did not even seem to notice that Regina was still there; he was speaking to something or someone he heard in the silence of his own heart.

Regina noted again the medals on the wall, the perfectly swept floor, the crispness of the toga Caius wore, though his face showed the strain of little sleep. A moment's sadness found her. Whoever that woman had been, she surely would not have wanted to be mourned in this way—coldly and without memory of joy.

"I grieve with you," she said.

Even as Caius's eyes kindled, she knew that had been the wrong thing to say and the wrong tone to say it in. This was not a room in Polycarp's insula, and this man was not one of Polycarp's tenants. This man was proud and lethal, and he did not recognize in her a deaconess to confide in.

"Do you?" His voice was like unsheathed steel. No longer was he distracted or bemused; his entire body was tensed.

"I—" Regina groped for something to say, something she might have said, if she were truly a slave. Panic ran cold through Regina's body. What if in that lapse of caution, in presuming an intimacy with the praetor, what if she had tossed away her chance? "Forgive me."

"How *dare* you pity me," the praetor hissed. "You are nothing but a *pleasure slave*—wearing her mistress's nightdress! You grieve with me? You?" His face went livid, and Regina's heart beat frantically as Caius rose to his feet, his body taut with fury. "Get out of here," he said. "Slave. I serve *Rome*. I have *fought* in her wars. I've cleaned her streets. I've seen her most unmentionable parts and draped my cloak about her naked shoulders. I've lost family to her, lost honor, lost—" He paused, panting. For a moment he shook, visibly. His voice sank almost to a whisper as he wrestled with something within himself. "I have not served her these many years to frivol away my time conversing with whores and desecrators of tombs." He gestured for the guardsman. "She knows her task. Get her out of here."

Her task. The trial. Regina lowered her head, slave-like, but she'd gone breathless with relief. She was not just to be tossed back into the shed; she would be at the trial, she would have the chance to speak, to see Polycarp, to stand at his side. Dizzied, she felt Brutus's touch at her arm, as though to steer her, but he didn't close his grip. As Caius lowered his eyes to his papers, dismissing her, she took careful steps toward the door, not wishing to fall. She would see Polycarp. She would be able to speak for him. Her blood ran hot with elation; she lifted her head, even as Brutus guided her through the door and into the fierce August sunlight. She had done it! Whatever happened to her now, it would happen to her at Polycarp's side. She would defend him, and the gathering, speaking the truths Rome didn't want to hear. Let them *try* to silence her then! She was no slave. She might have only a moment, but she would take that moment. And speak what was in her heart, before all the world.

In the sunbaked arena of Justitia's courtyard, all eyes were on the drama being played out on the sand: the cold, furious eyes of the urban praetor; the eyes of the guardsmen tight with alarm and continually glancing to the temple gate and the sounds of moaning beyond it; the troubled eyes of the lictors who stood to either side of the curule seat like living props, and of the jurors, who sat on their benches as the eyes and ears of Rome's upper castes. As the woman walked slowly across that open space, the other two who stood there before the praetor's seat had their eyes fixed on her as well. Julia looked bewildered, seeing who approached. Polycarp looked stricken.

"Regina," he breathed. Caius had summoned *Regina* as a witness? How could this be? For a moment the father faltered. If Regina would not stand the test, then he had surely failed utterly, and the Romans were proven right after all: take the head, and the body of the gathering would stumble. Polycarp's legs failed him, and he found himself kneeling in the dust, his vision blurred with hot tears. Inside the heavy silence of his heart, he cried to his God. *Truth flits from our hands, and there is no faith in us.*

Despair crouched behind him; he could feel the heat of its breath, he could smell the cold-creek clearness of its body. Its paws rested heavy on his shoulders; its maw gaped for him. Hungrier and emptier than the craving dead.

"Regina," he whispered. Doubts tore through him, driven on a high wind that made his thoughts leap and spin inside him.

Regina stopped when she reached him and took her place to stand a few strides from where he knelt, between him and the other witness.

"Dora Syriacae." That was the stern, cold voice of the praetor. "You stand before a jury of Roman citizens, charged with judging a man who may stand under penalty of death. You stand also under penalty if any false word escapes your mouth, for you speak within the grounds of the temple of Justitia, most sacred among goddesses. Will you speak verity and truth, Dora Syriacae?"

"I refuse that name," she said quietly. "I will bear witness to what I have seen, praetor urbanus, but I will not answer to that name."

Polycarp heard the steel in her voice. Heat built within him, blunting the sharp edge of grief and sending wild energy coursing through his body, as though he were translated from a man to a lion. With a growl he sent the beast that crouched behind him slinking away and forced himself back to his feet. He had no time left; therefore, he had no time for despair. He blinked the moisture from his eyes and saw in a blur Regina standing straight as a pillar near him, her eyes dark and her face dry of tears. She wore the same nightdress she'd worn the night the dead came to the insula, but now it was filthied and dirtied, and torn and tattered at the back. Yet she stood very straight, and he caught his breath at the loveliness of her.

Caius stared at her from his curule chair, frowning. He looked taken aback by her manner. "Tell us what you've seen, then," he said.

For a long moment she stood silent. The jurors were silent too, gazing at the witness. The moaning in the city outside the walls of justice was the only sound. A hot gust of wind rushed into the courtyard, lifting dust and driving it across the compound in gray clouds; Polycarp felt the dust coat his legs, dry and gritty.

She lifted her head, looked across the courtyard at Polycarp. Their eyes met. The wind lifted Regina's hair and tugged at the torn strips of her nightdress. In her eyes, Polycarp saw pain and desperation; then, though he was not touching her shoulder or her face with his hand, her eyes *opened* to him, and he gazed inside the rooms of her heart, as he so often had gazed into the eyes of the walking dead. He saw rooms that were locked and chained; he could almost hear the screams behind those shut doors. He saw other rooms that were vast and wide as oceans; in one, her love and faith in him, a faith so profound and unshakable that it shook him to see it. In another room, the many moments when she'd held others in her arms and given them refuge, and the love, deep and maternal and fierce, that she bore now toward each of those she'd sheltered. He saw her loss at having borne no children, and her joy at having found children in the men and women who lived in the insula under Polycarp's care. He saw her determination to preserve them—and him—a resolve that was like a hard, cold wall of rock in her heart.

She turned back to Caius.

"I cannot say what you wish me to say," she said hoarsely. Quivering with the intensity of her emotion. "The dead are eating the city, and you want me to malign *Polycarp*—Rome's one *good* man—and the man who is trying to help you—even while the dead moan outside that wall. I cannot. Not even if you offered every other believer in Rome amnesty could I playact this farce."

She turned to face the jurors, and her voice rose, her eyes shining with rage. "I will *tell* you what I've witnessed. The ancient families close themselves within windowless walls as though stepping early into their tombs; and Roman men and Roman women scream in hunger and illness outside, while those within choose to hear nothing. I've witnessed a woman sell the lives of those nearest to her so that she can wear a finer garment. I've seen men who buy women for less price than you would buy a toga, and beat them until they can neither stand nor sit. I've seen men buy children too." Her voice rose louder and higher, carrying with sharp clarity across the courtyard. "I've seen a woman beat her slave for taking a bite of her bread without permission, while at home that slave's children are but skin stretched thin across their ribs and can't sleep for hunger. You hurl your filth and your sewage and your shit down on us, and then you look across the hills with your self-satisfied faces and don't even glance down at the people whose faces you've smeared with your stinking offal. You accuse us of the desecration of your dead, but day upon day, you *desecrate* the living!"

"Have a care, Dora," Caius growled, his eyes filled with shock.

"*You* have a care. You think I am the only witness to stand here?" Rage had translated her; her face shone, and every line of her body was tense with the violence within her. Her voice rose nearly to a shriek; she gestured at the gate and the groaning beyond it, which sounded nearer than it had before. "Your fathers witness it. They witness everything. They see what you do, and what you don't. They were never so callous as you are; they are ashamed of you. They are ashamed of how you've defiled their memory. How you leave your neighbors dying and uncared for. You deserve to have them lurching out of their tombs to devour you!"

"Be still!" Caius rose from his seat, his face white.

"I will *not* be still! Lash me, Caius Lucius Justus, if you wish! Here before all these men. Show them how a Roman praetor administers justice! But I will not say what you wish to hear. You are contemptible, a small and shrunken man presiding over a small and shrunken city that was once great."

She paused. Her eyes burned; her face was dark with fury. The groans outside were indeed nearer, and loud, as though the dead had come to witness as well, to confirm Regina's words and give their own wordless but vocal condemnation. A few of the jurors cast uneasy glances at the temple gate; the rest couldn't look away from Caius's witness.

Polycarp gazed at Regina with astonishment and pride. He hadn't known what strength she kept locked in her heart. How could he have doubted her?

Julia's eyes were round with shock. She drew in a breath to speak, but before she could say a word, Regina rounded on her fiercely. "*You* have had your say. We've heard you already. We know your quality now, Julia. You chose to serve something small. I've chosen to serve something great. I've been a slave; I will never again serve anything so small that it can fit in my heart without filling me so full that I can serve only with tears of joy."

Julia visibly withered under Regina's eyes. She swayed on her feet, as though she might faint. Her eyes looked to the jurors, then the silent lictors in their line by Caius's curule seat—so many witnesses as she was berated by a former slave. Her face went dark with shame, and she said nothing. She appeared on the verge of tears.

The jury, too, were silent, watching Regina with startled faces. It was possible that they—and most Romans—had never heard a woman speak this way, in public, in open and unconcealed anger. Certainly none of them had ever heard such a declaration from a slave. Such was the force of Regina's voice that they could not think of her as a slave, one who should be lashed for temerity; such words could only be spoken by one who was free, terribly free, more free than most women they knew, more free than most men. A few looked stricken, as though her words had stung them and called them to account; in Regina's face, streaked with dirt and sweat yet hard and intent, some saw the very face of Justitia, her blindfold removed, her eyes hot with wrath and demanding their response. Others shifted in their seats, unsettled, trying to grope for that rage they'd held clutched so tightly only a few moments ago. Their rage had been stolen from them; this woman had walked into the courtyard with an anger more just and more articulate, and in the face of it, the jurors found themselves fumbling. The moans of the dead surged suddenly loud in their ears, and a few began to sweat.

Marcus's eyes were shining. The dampened coals that all day had sat heavy in his chest had now blazed into new fire. Whatever happened this day, the jurors would remember it. They would never forget Polycarp or Regina, or the obligation of hearing and action that their testimony had placed on each of them. His shoulders firmed with that certainty and with the determination to persist in the work these two had begun.

Caius's face was pale, and his voice had lost much of its volume. "Citizens on the jury, pardon my idiocy in summoning as a witness this—this slave and whore. I think it's time we—"

Abrupt and loud, a new sound swept into the courtyard, interrupting him: the cries of geese on the wing. The jurors, Polycarp, the praetor, the witnesses, the guardsmen—for a moment all their faces tilted back and gazed at the sky. Against the glare of the sun and the cloudless heat of the heavens, a dark *V* was flapping swiftly overhead, moving south out of the city. For many heartbeats, they all watched the geese departing. The day was hot; it was too early for a winter flight. It was as though the sacred geese were fleeing a city they could no longer live in, a city no longer worthy of their warning. Or perhaps the flight itself was their last warning.

When the *V* had disappeared behind the roof of the temple, with Justitia's blind face staring sightlessly after them, all was quiet in the courtyard, though the dead still moaned in the street without. Caius's hands shook. "We are done," he said after a moment, even his voice hushed and dismayed. "Give your verdict."

THE APOSTLE'S GIFT

As the dead wailed just outside the temple walls, the first juror stood. It was the young man, the one who'd screamed at Polycarp when he entered. Polycarp met his eyes, and the youth glanced down. "*Condemno*," he said quietly.

The second stood, his voice louder. "*Condemno!*"

"*Condemno!*"

"*Condemno!*"

One after the other, the jurors gave their sentences, some in urgent shouts, a few in quiet, almost ashamed voices. The unanimity was neither a surprise nor a disappointment to Polycarp. He let out his breath slowly; he had known, walking in through that wooden gate, that he entered a temple not to Justitia but to Timor. Fear alone was fed and worshipped here. For a few brief moments he couldn't hear the groaning in the street; the jurors' cries overwhelmed it.

But then they were silent, and the moaning seemed even louder, as though it was right outside the walls.

One juror remained. A youth, a patrician—his aquiline nose proclaimed it. Slowly he rose to his feet to add his sentence. His eyes looked past the curule seat.

"*Absolvo*," Marcus said softly.

Polycarp sucked in a breath. Pride welled up fierce and hot in his chest and, following it, a wave of sorrow that made him close his eyes. *Marcus, Marcus.* That small act of enormous bravery would be unlikely to go unpunished.

The groaning of the dead seemed to rise from the very earth.

"Light the pyre." Cold resolve in Caius's voice.

Regina stiffened, and her face became very white. Polycarp simply watched as a lone guardsman strode to the pit to the right of the curule chair. For the first time, Polycarp saw that this one man held a torch; he'd held it, slow burning, all through the trial, but in the wild heat and brightness of this day, the Ides of Augustus, Polycarp had not noticed it. Now the guardsman bowed his head once to the statue of Justitia and tossed the torch in.

Flames leapt up from the pit, and the air above it shimmered; the temple wall glimpsed through that shimmer became like a painting of a temple wall left in the rain. Polycarp gave the flames a good look. To his own shock, he found in his heart no fear of the fire. He was too distracted, perhaps, by the moaning in the street. And though he felt the fire's warmth on his arms and face even from here, it was a small pit. Barely would a man fit within it; it was smaller than the baptismal pit Polycarp had once seen carved into the floor of a believer's cellar in Smyrna. "Do you light so small a fire to scorch a human life from the earth?" he asked. "Such an undertaking should require a furnace large as the sun."

"It is hot enough, desecrator," Caius said. "By the votes of the jury, you are condemned to—"

He was interrupted by the sound of something heavy thrown against wood; the noise echoed across the courtyard. The groans beyond the wall were terribly loud, making the hairs along Polycarp's arms rise.

Then a great thudding and slamming of flesh against wood, and all eyes swung to the gate to the temple grounds. The wooden door that barred it was rattling hard in its hinges. Even as the door had in Polycarp's dream. He froze, staring at it.

Caius, too, was staring. It was as though the praetor was not seeing the gate but was gazing at some personal horror private to his soul and his soul only—as if that personal horror had lurched now out of his heart and grown to a size monstrous and terrible. The guardsmen looked to him, but Caius gave no direction, only stood there with his face bled of all color. Two of the guardsmen glanced at each other. One of them nodded, and then they both sprinted for the gate. Even as they did, a wooden slat in the gate came loose, then broke; several pale hands reached through the gap, clawing. Fingers caught at the other boards, tearing and pulling, ripping pieces from the gate. The familiar, sickly stench of death came through the opening.

Outside, more groans erupted from what might have been a thousand throats. Polycarp's mouth went dry; it was all a man could do to listen to that sound without emptying his urine down his leg. The sight of the wooden gate leaping and bucking in its place as the dead tore it apart made his heart race.

Perhaps all the dead in Rome were outside that door.

There are too many hurts to heal, Despair hissed to him from where it perched now beside the curule chair.

Maybe, but a man can make a start. Polycarp took a step toward the failing gate. Even as he did, one of the guardsmen swept at the breach with his blade, and severed hands fell to the earth, but there were no cries of pain from without the door: only that low, anguished moaning. The dead tore away more of the wood, and the weakened frame buckled as their bodies slammed against it. Polycarp could see the empty eyes of the dead through the gaps.

In a voice almost more shriek than articulate words, Caius cried out: "Fire! Fire! Get him to the fire! Let his burning be an atonement to our dead!"

Polycarp's guardsman seized his arm—and the one remaining guardsman who hadn't sprinted for the gate, the one who'd held the torch, joined them also.

At that moment the gate crumpled, scraps of wood falling to the ground. The dead lurched through, arms upraised, their mouths open in the wordless wailing of their need. Their clothes were tattered; some wore nothing, their naked bodies mutilated with the terrible wounds made by gouging fingers or teeth. One of the guardsmen at the gate was dragged into the mass of the dead, his screaming cut quickly short. The other fought a retreat, sword out and flashing, but the dead seized him with many hands. As he struggled in their grasp, the corpse of a young woman missing the left side of her face tore into his throat with her teeth. Another of the dead bit away the guardsman's ear.

Julia and Regina's escorts left them and moved toward the gate, though what they might do against the tide of dead pouring through was unclear.

Polycarp's guardsmen stood very still, and Polycarp did also, unable to take his gaze from the bodies that were moving through the door and stumbling into the courtyard like a slow flood; behind those entering, the street was overwhelmed with dead: they were packed like sacks of grain in a merchant's hold. They swarmed to the door, arms lifted, beating on the ones before them, groaning in their need to get at the living.

A few of the jurors began to scream.

At the screams, Caius's body jolted. Every nerve in him came awake, every sinew went taut. His glanced at the jurors, Roman citizens for whom he was ultimately responsible. He had failed to protect and provide for his family, but in this moment, with the Emperor away, the Senate ineffective at best, and the dead coming through that door, he as senior justice stood in the role of *paterfamilias* for the vast family of Rome. The realization of this ran cold through his veins. For half a year he had been playing the role of the failed father to a failed son; but in this moment the screaming jurors, the lictors standing helpless, the guardsmen dying at the gate, and the guardsmen standing by Polycarp were all sons of Rome, all sons in need of their father.

Caius's snarl was feral. Shouting for the guardsmen to hold the gate, he snatched the bound rods from one of his lictors and tore loose the binding cloth. The narrow staves clattered to his feet, discarded symbols of office, but he retained two, one in either hand—thin, stout rods the length of a man's arm, with ends whittled to points. "Lictors, jurors, all of you—into the temple!" He could delay the dead while the others got inside and barred the temple door. His face livid, he strode toward the gate, even as the jurors darted past him, hurrying for the refuge of the temple. Moments before, Caius had stunk with fear; now that there was something visible and embodied to fight, his eyes burned with that cold violence that must once have kindled in the eyes of Caesar or Marius or Cato the Elder.

Caius spoke aloud to his ancestors as his steps carried him to that mass of swarming, hungering bodies. The stench of those bodies was overwhelming. "*Di parentes*," he said under his breath, "I am the last. The last *paterfamilias* of my house. Accept this sacrifice, this atonement. I will recover our honor. Fight with me. All you ancient Lucii, fight with me. I beseech you." With a cry, Caius broke into a run. He threw himself against the lurching crowd with a speed and ferocity that showed his military past; in his hands, the rods of office were both shield and thrusting weapons. With the length of a rod pressed to a corpse's throat, he held back the snapping teeth. A jerk of his hand shot the other rod's point into another corpse's skull. Even as the corpse's face slackened, Caius slid the stake free and leapt back, then stabbed again with both; two more dead slid to the ground. Hands grasped and clutched at his toga, and Caius spun, unraveling it from his body. The toga crumpled to the ground, to hinder the feet of the shambling dead; the Roman officer stood in his loincloth, brown gore dripping from the rods he held onto the trampled, sandy soil of the courtyard, his chest heaving, his face flushed, his short Roman hair damp with sweat.

The dead were closing about him, so many, their arms lifted to grab at him; in their midst he spun and stabbed, screaming hoarsely; two guardsmen, knives out, fought behind him. Caius called out the names of his ancestors, one after the other, as he spun and jabbed with the pointed rods. The names of his ancient and patrician house became battle cries as he cut into the dead. He felt their hands on him, then the sharp burn of teeth biting into his arm. Screaming, he turned and speared his rod into the creature's face. Then the others were dragging him down—such weight! He was pulled from his feet; almost he was on his back in the dust. He surged to his knees with a howl of panic and rage, one hand held immobile, the other striking, driving through one corpse's eye and into its skull, where the rod caught. He pulled at it wildly. At the weight of the corpse, the rod slid from his grip. Fingernails scraped at the back of his scalp, but his hair was too short to be gripped. Other hands caught his shoulders, his arms. Screaming, he was tugged down, their faces blocking out the sun above them—gashed and decaying faces, with ravenous, open mouths, Roman faces, old men and young men, daughters and matrons, patrician noses and the flatter noses of the Roman poor, all hissing and snarling, all ducking toward him to feed, all the Roman dead. Hands clawing at his body, fingernails digging sharply into his skin, gouging and tearing. A shriek of pain. He twisted, struggling to wrench his arms free of them, horror seizing him: the last of his house, devoured by these unclean dead; would his body rise from the earth to walk eating through the streets, unremembered and unrevered? "*Di parentes!*" he shrieked. Agony in the right side of his face, one of the dead biting into his cheek. "*Livius!*"

———

The guardsman's grip on Polycarp's arm tightened, and the father was pulled a step nearer the fire; it was very near now. The other guardsman was gazing at the disaster at the gate, and he was pale as a Celt, his eyes showing their whites. Caius's shouts could be heard above the groans of the dead.

In a quiet, cold voice, Polycarp said, "Do you really mean to burn me while your temple is overrun?"

The guardsman who held his arm didn't look at him. His voice, too, was carefully controlled. "I am a Roman. I do my duty."

"So do I," Polycarp said grimly.

The heat of the fire on his face was like a second noon sun. Fear and anger and shame rushed through him like some dark alcohol, muddying his mind. He would burn then, as the dream had warned. And he had achieved nothing. The dead had come and would devour everyone here. What did it matter then, that his words and Regina's had shaken the jurors, or that seeds had been planted in unready hearts? Those seeds would not last the day.

Cursing, the guardsman gripped both of the old man's arms and began to move him across the dust—only to draw up short. A long knife was pressed sharply to his throat, the blade glinting in the sunlight.

"No more." The other guardsman's words were hardly louder than a whisper. "Keys. Now."

The guardsman who held Polycarp didn't move, didn't release his prisoner's arms. His eyes just flicked from one side to the other. His adam's apple twitched slightly, just above the knife. "Cassius had them."

The other man's gaze shot back to the gate, and he cursed. "All right, let him go."

Polycarp felt the grip on his arms release, and he stepped to the side, unsteady on his feet. The cracking voice of the fire and the heat of its hunger on his face made him feel faint. He stepped back, saw the two guardsmen, the younger one now removing his knife from the other's throat. Beyond them, the dead were milling about the other end of the courtyard; they had dragged Caius beneath them and were feeding. But already a couple of them, unable to get at the meat that was twisting and shrieking on the dry ground, were turning and stumbling toward Polycarp and the guards. And others appeared to have some of the jurors trapped in a corner. Polycarp couldn't see Regina or Marcus or Julia. He began to pray softly under his breath.

The younger guardsman stepped to him, took the prisoner's right wrist, began picking the lock on the manacle. Polycarp could feel the rattle of it all the way up his arm. He stood with the fire at his back, begrudging every second that kept him from moving to face that crowd of dead, from moving to help his people.

"Brutus—" The other guardsman stood by, his face aghast.

"Shut up." Brutus wrenched the manacle free of Polycarp's wrist and dropped it; it dangled at the end of the chain from his other wrist. His eyes met Polycarp's; they were wide with fear and there was a plea in them. "We need you, father," he said softly.

In the next instant two of the dead were upon them, hissing; Brutus leaped back, and the other guardsman plunged his own knife into one's chest; the thing seized his arm, and the guardsman let out a screech of fear that would have shamed him in any place or any moment other than this one.

"Not yet time to rest," Polycarp murmured. Taking up the chain in his left hand, he lifted his right and stepped between the hired guardsman and the dead.

Even as Caius threw himself into the dead, Julia froze, her face white, staring at the approaching corpses. "Come on!" Regina cried to her. The deaconess glanced wildly about the courtyard, taking in the temple door, the jurors rushing past the blind statue and through it, and Polycarp standing between the guardsmen near the fire. Some of the dead were very close, lurching and stumbling, and they came between Polycarp and the witnesses. Several turned toward Julia and Regina, closing on them, hands reaching, clutching—it was like that night fleeing the Subura, except here in the bold sun the dead looked more terrible, because they looked more human. Not silhouetted shapes looming in the dark, but bodies horribly torn and broken, jaws slack in their moaning hunger.

Julia voiced a long whine of fear, still unmoving, and Regina grabbed her arm, her heart pounding. "Wake *up!*"

"They're inside," Julia whispered.

"It's what the man you betrayed wanted to *prevent*," Regina cried, wanting to scream in exasperation and fear, every nerve in her body sharp with the need for flight. She had to get Julia moving inside where she'd be safe, and she had to get to Polycarp.

The dead closed in, and Regina yanked Julia with her, scrambling back across the dust and grit. Julia came with her, shaking, and for a moment Regina felt pity pierce through her. Everything Julia had taken refuge in had shattered with that splintering of the temple gate.

"Come *on*, run!" Regina pulled Julia with her, stumbling toward the temple steps. One of the dead lurched to their side, and Regina sprang away, her heart pounding, not loosing her grip on Julia's arm, but the corpse reached in and seized Julia's hair. Regina heard Julia's shriek and kept pulling her, but the corpse held her, and then there were other corpses on them, hands grasping. Desperate, Regina drove her foot into one's shin, a panicked kick, but it didn't buckle or even wince, just hissed at her, its blind eyes fixed on her. Then the dead were fastened on Julia, strong hands pulling her back, tearing her from Regina's grasp; with a cry Regina fell back, other hands reaching for her.

"*Regina!*" Julia's shriek. "Caius—Regina—help me!" She had fallen, was on her belly; Regina caught a glimpse of the dead covering her, one dragging her back by her ankle, several crouching over her, one on top of her—she disappeared beneath them. Regina stumbled back, one of the dead pursuing her, then turning at Julia's shriek. One raw shriek, then nothing but the cracking and sucking sounds of the dead feeding. The corpse that had taken a step toward Regina hissed, then stumbled back to join the pack crouching over the other woman. Regina shook with horror, her hands trembling as though she were naked on the ice on a winter night.

She was gone. Julia was gone.

Just like that.

Gone—all of her regrets and her fears and her rage and her self-loathing and her bitterness, and any moment that had ever made her laugh or ever made her smile. Her husband, wherever he sheltered, was severed from her. She was gone. The suddenness of it was a spear of ice. There had been no moment to hold her as she died, or remonstrate with her, or curse her, or forgive her, or absolve her. She was simply gone, without farewell. Everything broken and unfinished. With a clarity as violent as lightning on a hill, Regina grasped the import of Polycarp's Gift as she never had before. To finish what had festered unfinished, to say good-night, with grace, to those who had lain terribly awake. She stood stunned, gazing at the feasting dead where they hunched over that unseen body on the earth.

A hard hand grasped her arm, and she jumped. A voice at her ear. Marcus. "Come on! We have to hide!"

"No," she whispered. "We have to stand." Something in her hardened. "Where is he?" She ignored Marcus's pulling at her arm, his pale face; she scanned the courtyard. There. Her breath caught.

Father Polycarp was walking *toward* them. He was maybe twenty feet away, across the courtyard. He was walking in the midst of the dead, like Moses parting the sea. A haze of gold about his hair. His hands touched their shoulders or their faces, and with his gaze into their eyes, emptied bodies slid to the earth.

Yet there were so many. Even as Polycarp came near, several of the dead grasped the loop of chain that hung from one of his hands, pulling him toward their jaws; others grasped his shoulders. One bit deep where Polycarp's neck met the shoulder. A scream tore its way up Regina's throat, and she tried to leap toward him, but Marcus held her. "No!" the youth yelled in her ear.

"Let me go! He'll *die*!"

"It's too late!" he cried.

In panic, Regina slammed her elbow into his gut, then tore free. But even as she ran, she felt herself shoved to the side; then the guardsman, Brutus, was before her, swinging a great torch in his hand; she felt the warmth of it on her face. Grim, he lunged in, stabbing with the torch at the faces of the dead, who hissed and snarled and gave way before the heat. One's hair went alight, a woman whose eyes had been torn from her but whose mouth still gaped open, the gums drawn back from the teeth. The creature fell backward, its face wreathed in flames.

"Grab him!" Brutus yelled, reaching out himself, seizing Polycarp's shoulder and pulling him free of the dead, fending off their groping hands with the flames. They still tried to press forward, so many corpses with their mouths open and hungering, their hands grasping for a garment or anything to clutch. Regina took Polycarp's other arm and then they were dragging the father with them, falling back, the dead closing in from either side. Brutus danced from the left to the right and back, flailing the torch, stabbing with it when one of those things came too close. The smoke from the torch brought no tears to the corpses' eyes.

Marcus got beneath Polycarp's chest and heaved the old father up onto his shoulder, his face red with strain. Turning, he ran for the temple door, the dead grasping at his sleeve but not catching it as he passed. Regina hurried after, a glance over her shoulder to see Brutus with the dead half-closed about him. Waving that torch he must've plucked from the execution pit. "Go on!" he roared. "I'll follow! Go!"

Regina ran.

Her breath sobbed; a stitch burned in her side. There were snarling faces, grasping arms everywhere, to either side, a few dead now between her and Marcus and the door; but Marcus ducked and wove through them, staying free of their hands, shouting wordlessly in his fear and desperation. Then he was through and heaving his way up the marble steps, past the blind and unwatching Justitia.

The doors were ahead in their shadowed recess behind great pillars, and they were closing.

"Stop!" Regina screamed, but her voice was hoarse and small. Something grasped at a strip of her nightdress, but the strip tore free and then she was dashing up the steps, barefoot and disheveled, something inside her screaming at the sight of the blood running down Marcus's back from Polycarp's body.

Marcus reached the door and thrust his hand into the crack as it closed; a howl of pain, and then he got his other hand in the crack, Polycarp precariously balanced on his shoulder, and he was pulling the door open with a roar. Regina reached him and dug her own small hands into the space, gripping the cool cypress wood and pulling. There were frantic shouts within—jurors and lictors, some hysterical with fear. "No! You can't bring him in here! You can't bring him in here!" one of them was shrieking. "He brings the dead! You can't! You can't!"

Regina didn't dare glance over her shoulder; her heart might give out if she saw the moaning dead lurching up the steps behind them, hands outstretched. She put all of her small weight into wrenching open the door. Then a man's voice at her side growled, "*Get back!*" and a hand thrust her head down. There was a great shove of the torch past her head and through the half-open door, and screams inside. The resistance against the door fell away and it swung open, and then a great hand on her back shoved her through. Regina tumbled inside into the dimness, crumpling to her knees, her breath rasping. Then Marcus was beside her, laying Polycarp on his back on the cool marble. She heard footsteps as the others inside fled farther back into the temple, away from the door. Brutus was shouting at the door, and there were snarls of the dead, the hiss and crackle of flame through the air, the snap of the door closing. Then a drumming of hands, a beating of dead hands on wood.

Regina was tearing a great strip from her dress, leaving what was left of it in tatters. Polycarp's life was pulsing out through the great gash at his shoulder—so much blood and life, spilling over the cold marble and then over her hand as she fought to press the cloth into the wound. His eyes, which had been open and gray and barely seeing, now squeezed shut, and the father groaned at the touch on his wound, a sound that terrified Regina with its weakness. She sobbed and pressed the cloth harder. "Help him," she cried to the others. "God, help him!"

———

Pain wild and hot at his throat and shoulder—Polycarp spun dizzily in the dark, panting softly. Eyes tightly closed, teeth clenched against the sharpness of the wound. A bit of cloth pressed there by someone's hand. Nearby there was pounding, relentless pounding, a drumming Polycarp not only heard but felt as a tremor in his body. Thick scents of incense and blood.

Others were crying out, voices moving about.

"Those doors won't hold!" Marcus's voice. That was Marcus.

"Quick!" A deeper voice. The guardsman who had grabbed him out there as he stood among the dead. "See if there are torches in the alcoves—we need more fire!"

"Wait! Barricade the doors first! Brutus! They're coming through!" Marcus's voice shrill with fear.

A cracking of wood, the guardsman cursing, then frantic slamming of objects against each other.

He was needed. He had to stand up. His master had told him to stand, and now the others needed him on his feet. But the pain beat in his throat and side, and he spun again into the dark.

A touch of gentle fingertips on Polycarp's cheek; for a moment he thought of his mother, now buried in a hillside plot far away in Thessaly above the fragrant sea. *It will take you to the one thing you need today, the one thing you need to do. Trust it.*

He coughed, his breath wheezing. Over his mother's voice he heard another woman's. He opened his eyes, saw through a haze of pain Regina's face near his, and above her a low, marble roof. An alcove along the side of the temple's interior, perhaps. It was dim in here.

He drew in breath raggedly.

"No. Don't you leave us! Please. Father. Polycarp." Her voice thick with tears. Regina's hand pressed cloth firmly into the wound at his throat; swallowing back the pain, he looked at her, saw her disheveled hair, her face shining with sweat, and her left shoulder naked and lovely. She had torn away a great strip of her already ruined nightdress, a wad of linen she now held pressed to Polycarp's throat; a flap of ragged fabric hung back over her breast, baring the top of it. Her skin shone softly in the faint sunlight coming in from somewhere above and to the right. He gazed at her in wonder, as though at a messenger in a dream. Her beauty and the vulnerability in her eyes had always called to him, had always been a temptation, but he had never known she was this lovely.

Polycarp drew in another breath, hissed at a flare of pain.

"Don't leave me," Regina whispered.

"I have done my work in the world," he rasped. Lifting his hand to her face, he felt the softness of her skin, held her eyes with his. A moment's regret and yearning swept through him, stronger than the pain, swift and fierce as a fire through wheat, and he almost cried out with the force of it. If he had walked other paths, met her in other circumstances, been other than who he was, she might have been his, and he hers.

But he had no time for regret.

He could feel the last strength leaking from him. He turned his eyes, glimpsed her hand red with his blood. He wet his lips enough to speak again. He could not stand any longer. He was too weak now to carry the Gift. He had to pass it on.

He struggled to speak clearly and to find the lines he must say; the world was still blurred, and that pounding he heard threatened to shake him right out of the world and into the empty dark. "The Apostle's Gift to me, I pass to you." He forced the words out, raised his voice loud enough to hear. "It is yours now to face the living and the dead, and bring them peace. I bless you and anoint you, Regina Romae, mother of the gathering in Rome, in the name of the Father, the Anointed One, and the Comforter of Our Souls."

Her eyes were round and moist. Her lips parted, her face translated in wonder: for the briefest instant Polycarp glimpsed a nimbus of soft light about her and saw a few strands of her hair rise from her head about his hand. His body felt suddenly lighter.

The Gift had been passed.

Regina drew a shuddering breath; the enormity of it filled her eyes.

"Tell Marcus—the others—to hope," Polycarp rasped. "Hope."

"I can't," she cried, taking his hand in hers, taking it from her cheek and pressing her lips to his fingers. Tears pooled in her eyes. "We *need* you," she whispered.

"What do you believe—Regina? What do you know to be true?"

The tears rolled down her face, leaving streaks in the sweat and dirt. "Nothing is broken that cannot be remade," she whispered after a moment, her clasp on his hand tight.

"Yes," he breathed. He was dizzy; Regina above him blurred. He closed his eyes a moment, opened them. Everything was faint. That pounding. And splintering—and hoarse shouts.

"Nothing is ill that cannot be healed." Regina's voice trembled. "Nothing captive that cannot be freed. Polycarp—" Her eyes pleaded with him, with God, with death. "Don't go—don't go— don't go."

"It's all right," he whispered. "If my body wakes, you will give me rest. I do not fear. Now you are needed—at the door. Do not need you here. Regina." His breathing came in short gasps. The temple had become very cold, both the stone beneath him and the inside of his body, everything cold.

He tasted blood in his mouth. Regina and Marcus grew dim, but he could see, beyond their heads, flitting in the shadows about the edge of the chamber, that red beetle, bright, a beacon. Everything else grew dark. He smiled and got slowly to his feet, cold and light as though he were no more than a head of wheat. That beetle darted along the wall, red as fresh blood, inviting him.

Once, in Thessaly, he'd followed a red beetle through a field of wheat and across a mighty stream. He had done so with no sound of wings in his ears and no sight of any beetle red against the sky. He'd had only the faith that he would find it. Across the stream, in a stand of poplars as old as the world, he'd found the little creature again. He'd been shaking from the cold of his swim, and his skin was scratched and torn from his climb up the bank through that hostile brush whose roots cling to the edges of rivers with the same tenacity one sees in barnacles latched to a galley's hull. Yet as he stood panting, there was the beetle, quivering on a bit of twig in the thatched roof of a small cottage above the bank. A cottage with a little garden for turnips and beans behind it, and the poplars to break the wind. The tiny beetle was violently red against the gray of the roof, like a shout.

He stood there looking at the beetle for some time. Then his eyes dropped and he noticed the door was open. A short, stout man with a gray beard—an Easterner—stood there, leaning against the jamb, his ears very large, his thumbs hooked into the sash he wore about his drab, foreign clothes. A few kindly wrinkles had taken residence around his eyes to keep them company.

The boy cleared his throat. "I am Polycarp."

The man nodded. "I am Peter." The boy heard rolling gravel in the man's voice, like the rough song of a fishing boat's keel against the shingle. Peter jerked his head as though to indicate the dark interior of the cottage. "This is the house of Cornelius, and I am a guest in it. But I don't think he will mind if I invite you in."

The boy didn't cast one glance back at the stream he'd forded at peril or at the wheat field behind it; he just glanced up at the beautiful red beetle, whose wings were flicking in and out, in and

out, as though it wanted to take flight again but was only waiting on the boy. His heart beat fast, but his body was tired, and
his steps were slow as he moved up to the door. The fisherman
turned without speaking, and Polycarp the boy followed him into
the cottage.

Thinking of that boy, Polycarp the old man laughed once, a
dry sound like the clack of two sticks of kindling struck together.
Then, having followed his master forty years and six, he stepped
off this broken stage of the world into the dark.

FINIS

ACKNOWLEDGMENTS

A PROJECT *like* The Zombie Bible *is a fearful undertaking and requires the aid, goodwill, encouragement, and advice of many people. I offer my deepest gratitude...*

To Andrew Hallam, for his diligent and enthusiastic reading of my work; to Jeff VanderMeer, my editor, for his insight; to all those who generously gave feedback on excerpts; to my pastor, for his encouragement and prayer; to Alex Carr and the remarkable team at 47North; and to Danielle Tunstall, for graciously permitting me the use of her art.

To the cast and crew of the good ship Qdoba, *who during one critical summer were quick to offer me a quiet corner in which to write during many lunch breaks;*

To the many writers who have moved my heart or inspired my mind, not least among them C. J. Cherryh, for Merchanter's Luck; *Gene Wolfe, for* Soldier in the Mist; *Max Brooks, for* World War

Z; *Kim Paffenroth, for* Valley of the Dead; *Orson Scott Card, for* Seventh Son; *and to the many writers, known and unknown, who have labored across so many centuries of time to deliver to us here, this day, that magnificent and often bewildering record and love letter we call the Bible;*

To my wife, Jessica, whose thoughts about the early Church formed the seeds for this story, and to my daughters, River and Inara—it can't always be easy living with a husband or father whose mind wanders with such frequency into daydreams of the hungry undead, or who leaps often from his chair to scribble a note; if it were not for their patience, their laughter, and their love, you would not now be holding this work in your hands;

And to all of you, my readers—it is you who make these stories breathe.

ABOUT THE AUTHOR

Stant Litore doesn't consider his writing a vocation; he considers it an act of survival. As a youth, he witnessed the 1992 outbreak in the rural Pacific Northwest firsthand, as he glanced up from the feeding bins one dawn to see four dead staggering toward him across the pasture, dark shapes in the morning fog. With little time to think or react, he took a machete from the barn wall and hurried to defend his father's livestock; the experience left him shaken. After that, community was never an easy thing for him. The country people he grew up with looked askance at his later choice of college degree and his eventual graduate research on the history of humanity's encounters with the undead, and the citizens of his college community were sometimes uneasy at the machete and rosary he carried with him at all times, and at his grim look. He did not laugh much, though on those occasions when he did, the laughter came from him in wild guffaws that seemed likely to break him apart. As he became book-learned, to his own surprise he found an intense love of ancient languages, a fierce admiration for his ancestors, and a deepening religious bent. On weekends, he went rock climbing in the cliffs without rope or harness, his fingers clinging to the mountain, in a furious need to accustom himself to the nearness of death and teach his body to meet it. A rainstorm took him once on the cliffs, and he slid thirty-five feet and hit a ledge without breaking a single bone, and concluded that he was either blessed or reserved in particular for a fate far worse. Finding women beautiful and worth the trouble, he married a girl his parents considered a heathen woman, but whose eyes made him smile. She persuaded him to come down from the cliffs, and he persuaded her to wear a small covenant ring on her hand, spending what coin he had to make it one that would shine in starlight and whisper to her heart how much he prized her. Desiring to live in a place with fewer trees (though he misses the forested slopes of his youth), a place where you can scan the horizon for miles and see what is coming for you while it is still well away, he settled in Colorado with his wife and two daughters, and they live there now. The mountains nearby call to him with promises of refuge. Driven again and again to history with an intensity that burns his mind, he corresponds in his thick script for several hours each evening with scholars and archaeologists and even a few national leaders or thugs wearing national leaders' clothes who hoard bits of forgotten past in far countries. He tells stories of his spiritual ancestors to any who will come by to listen, and he labors to set those stories to paper. Sometimes he lies awake beside his sleeping wife and listens in the night for any moan in the hills, but there is only her breathing soft and full and a mystery of beauty beside him. He keeps his machete sharp but hopes not to use it.

zombiebible@gmail.com
@thezombiebible
http://zombiebible.blogspot.com

Made in the USA
Charleston, SC
22 December 2012